THE LOVE CHILD's MOTHER

Suzanne Wright

Published in 2009 by YouWriteOn.com

Copyright © Text Suzanne Wright

First Edition

The author asserts the moral right under the Copyright, Designs and Patents Act 1988 to be identified as the author of this work.

All Rights reserved. No part of this publication may be reproduced, stored in a retrieval system or transmitted, in any form or by any means without the prior consent of the author, nor be otherwise circulated in any form of binding or cover other than that which it is published and without a similar condition being imposed on the subsequent purchaser.

Published by YouWriteOn.com

Chapter 1

September 1984

Dear Sirs,

Susan Stone, dob 6th April 1964

My daughter Susan Stone was born in Nottingham at The Warren Mother and Baby Home and was adopted six weeks later.

I realise that I have no legal rights of any sort, and I do not wish to intrude into her life. However, I would like this letter, with my address, to be placed on her file so that, should she ever decide to look for me, she will know where to find me.

Yours sincerely,

Carol Rose

Social Services, Family Placement Department,
Darwell House
Wigford Wharf West
Nottingham

May 1994

Saturday morning. Carol sat at the kitchen table and gazed, unseeing, through the window up the drive, waiting for the effects of the coffee she held to reach her brain and kick-start the day. Tiredness, bone-deep, beckoned her back to bed, to sleep.

Daggers of sunlight slanted into the room, drawing out the heavy perfume of the hyacinth on the windowsill which, today, failed to evoke the usual lifting of the spirits. Coffee and sunshine she thought sourly, I expect the migraine comes next.

Thursday's late night at the Town Hall, waiting for votes to be counted, was too much on top of the frantic week at school. She was too old for late nights and early mornings. Fifty next – another decade creeping past. She didn't mind losing, even though more successful candidates included an alcoholic, an embezzler, a semi-moron – well, several semi-morons – and at least one victim of senile dementia.

'Look at him,' Paul had said as old James, a fellow candidate, shuffled past, teeth clamped on an unlit pipe, expression benevolent but unfocussed. His age could have been anything from sixty to ninety. In fact he was 82. A blue hand-knitted pullover peeped out from beneath a creased tweed jacket and the lace of one brown shoe was undone. 'He shouldn't be out without a carer, never mind deciding how the Council Tax millions are spent.'

And James had been successful!

All that on top of the extra work involved in applying for a promotion at school! Hours of painstaking detail filling in an application form the size of a small novel, a raid on the shops after work for an interview suit, the mounting tension and adrenaline rush preparing for the interview, culminating in a gruelling session facing a panel of nine interviewers. And then, not only failing, but realising that Gordon Finley, ten years younger and less experienced, was to be the new Head of York House. Ah, well! If she'd been successful the increase in salary, minus the extra tax, would only have been worth about the cost of two new pairs of tights a week.

It was probably a blessing in disguise, since school nowadays reflected the world outside which, for most of their pupils, included crime, racism, drugs, sex and violence rather than the more traditional academic achievements, sport, music and family values.

Truthfully, Carol knew that elections and promotions were not the real issue. They were simply events which came and went, part of the existence she had constructed for herself. They were the rocks in the current and flow of her life, upon which the waters foamed and splashed, giving interest to the landscape, increasing the pace, imparting energy and a sense of purpose.

The real issue, the worm in the bud, eating away the heart of her life, was the growing realisation that it was time to abandon her most cherished dream, the optimism which had always given her existence a shape and focus. The baby, born and adopted so long ago, was never far from her thoughts. She had always hoped that one day she would be given a chance to put right the mistakes made when she had been too young to resist the forces which had pushed her life out of balance. It had always been a thinly-nurtured hope, barely articulated, but hardy and persistent, ready to flourish if opportunity arose, like the seeds in the desert which bloom with instant abundance when rain falls after decades of searing drought.

The failed promotion attempt and election result she could accept easily. The other - well, maybe she'd stopped hoping to meet a real person, her daughter. She had another daughter, upstairs in bed, and she was all anyone could ask - bright and beautiful and with a highly individual sense of self, and Carol loved her dearly. Carol knew her best side - lively, friendly, with tremendous talent - and her worst, when she was unbearable every four weeks, sometimes lacked confidence, and the way the world stopped when she had a problem and they all had to step off until it was solved. But above all she was known - intimately.

Her half-sister, her predecessor in the womb, who had the same pre-birth sharing of a heart-beat, a blood supply, the life-rhythms of eating and sleeping, was a fantasy. She had lost – no, that was too kind a word - given away her baby. Memories of her face, her cries, were thirty years faded. The person she had become was less real than a character in a soap opera.

Over the years Carol had invented endless scenarios in which they met. The tiny girl on the beach, chubby in her pink swimsuit and sunhat, left her yearning to hold the firm little body in her arms. This could so easily have been her own child. She was, possibly, for a few heart-stopping moments, the new girl in Carol's class, a dark-eyed, happy creature, until common sense asserted itself. The new teacher at school, pale and shy, nineteen years her junior, received motherly care and support, because she was living alone and starting her new job, and could so easily have been her child. The nurse in the hospital, who swung down the ward with the same carefree stride as Rob, and had the same dark curly hair, could have been her, and Carole's heart skipped a beat, but her subtle probing revealed that Nurse Lewis was born in Scotland, had three brothers, and was suspicious of the nosy questions. Carol paid close attention to anyone approximately nineteen years younger than herself. But a six-week old baby bears little resemblance to the adult of eighteen, or twenty-eight. The fantasy lacked substance. Even a dream needs nurturing and this one had a meagre supply of information on which to feed.

Susan - or Jessica as she had been since the age of six weeks - had the legal right to find her birth mother. The fact that she had not done so meant she was happy and had no need to. Or she was dead - a childhood illness, or a train crash, or a car accident. Lying in bed at night, Carol lived the horror of her child, injured, dying. She visualised the funeral, the flowers, as her heart wept. Or she'd emigrated, her parents had taken her to New Zealand, or Australia, she lived in the sunshine, spending hours on the beach, happy and tanned. Or she regarded a mother who would allow her child to be given away as no mother at all, just another human being who happened to have this close biological link.

Carol sipped her coffee. The dogs, Eric and Molly, whined and scratched at the garden door and she let them in. The postman dropped some letters into the hall and crunched off up the gravel drive. Galvanised into life Carol reached the letters a split second before Eric, flung them on the table and, lacking a better idea, sat down again. The dogs bustled about, drank, and flopped at her feet, happy as long as they could be within touch. Eric stank like a compost heap and had dead leaves in his fur. He lay, all six stone of him, with head on paws, his nose touching her foot, a sign of possession. Molly, his mother, slimmer and slightly smaller, sat beside Carol's chair, head in her lap, eyelids drooping in ecstasy, nudging whenever Carol stopped stroking her silky domed head. The dogs were oversized for this small cottage, much more suited to the previous house, the one they'd had to leave when they could no longer afford the mortgage.

Alongside the dreams of reunion, the butterfly sunshine flickerings beyond the veil which divided reality and imagination, was a practical thread which tied the fantasies to earth.

Her letter to the Children's Department of the Local Authority of the town where Jessica had been born was carefully written, undemanding, giving her address. She could be found easily by anyone who was looking.

If Jessica requested her birth records, as she had the right to do, she would find the letter. Carol had written again when they moved house two years before and this time they, the faceless unknown workers who were trained to stand in for God, eventually sent a photocopy of a leaflet from the Office of Population Census and Surveys. As a result Carol had contacted other organisations. Only recently The Adoption Contact Register, a potential link, had replied, 'If/when your relative…registers his/her details in Part 1 the information recorded below will be forwarded to him/her.'

Doors were slamming all over the place. School, politics, life. If you don't try you can't fail. Ask for nothing, no-one can refuse you. Seek no acceptance, you will not be rejected. Rubbish, she thought, who needs it?

There were other avenues to try, but if Jessica wasn't looking for her, it was wrong to impose, blunder into her life. The blind faith that they would meet again could withstand anything except the truth. The fact of Jessica's existence might have shaped her life since her daughter's birth, but she meant nothing to Jessica.

'Hire a detective. Find her. Put yourself out of your misery, for better or worse,' said Paul. For better or worse he was still around, though on increasingly hostile terms.

'No,' she said, 'I can't barge into her life. If she's looking she'll find me. If not, I don't have the right.'

'Suit yourself,' he said. He was intimately aware of the pool of misery which lay at the centre of her existence - from time to time he almost drowned in it.

Well, perhaps it was time to shut the door on this one, say goodbye to the past and move on. A little late, to be sure, but so what? Better late than never. Self-pity, expressed in familiar clichés, spread its clawed tentacles tighter round her soul.

Idly she fanned out the letters on the table. A special offer of make-up, a begging letter from a charity, must be the tenth this week, a bank statement. A letter post-marked Yorkshire, some northern part. She knew no-one up there, her family were in Yorkshire but much further south. She opened it.

One sheet of paper. Headed.

Did she remember to breathe? How many times did she read it before the meaning sank in? The words danced on the page. 'Social Services Department', 'your daughter', 'communication'.

At that moment a pure ice-cold breeze stirred and began to move through the dark, sealed-off corners of her life, began to loosen the wisps and threads of sadness, the fuzzy clouds of uncertainty. The dark shadows of unknowing began to yield to a spark, a candle flame, of comforting light.

She was rooted to the chair. She shouted, 'Paul, Paul. Look at this.' Urgently, 'Paul, come quick, Paul!'

Eric leapt to his feet and with his characteristic sharp canine intelligence assessed the situation and began barking and howling, running from kitchen to hall to lounge looking for the intruder he assumed was the cause of the commotion. Molly joined in. She knew damn well there was no burglar but she was enjoying the mayhem. Carol's face, beyond her control, was pulled into a smile of joy, tears of disbelief. She couldn't move. She had to tell someone.

'Paul, Paul, look, Paul,' she wailed.

Heavy footsteps pounded on the stairs.

'Whasamarrer?' he looked round for the cause of the commotion, peering through thick glasses, groping for his dressing gown belt, surprised to see she was sitting at the table apparently unharmed. Her voice had suggested a serious accident, with gallons of blood, and white bones sticking out of red flesh. Or, at the very least, a burglar. Carol held out the letter.

'I can't read it in these. What's the matter?' His extreme short-sightedness demanded a range of lenses, reading glasses, distance glasses and bifocals. He pulled off his specs, held the letter about two inches from his nose and peered intently. 'I'll read it when I've got my lenses in. What does it say? What's wrong?' He was upset, verging on annoyance at being dragged from sleep for anything less than a major disaster.

'I've had a letter,' she explained unsteadily. 'It's from a social worker in Yorkshire. Susan - Jessica has been to see her. She found my letter on her file.'

'Christ! Well, that's good news,' he said slowly. His tone lacked its customary sharpness. 'That's very good. It's what you want - isn't it?' He looked closely at her face, puzzled.

She looked as if she'd suffered a calamity. She was overjoyed - she was standing on a shining mountain top looking at the world spread at her feet - and she was afraid - of the immense voids and chasms which opened below. At one tick of the clock the speculation of three decades became certainty.

Paul found his reading glasses and read the letter out loud, and as she heard the words spoken they fell into place, became real. Jessica was 'pleased and excited' the letter was 'a first step in opening up a possible line of communication.' Furthermore, 'Please contact me at the above address if you would like to take things further.' If - IF! Could there be any doubt? It was what she'd dreamed of for thirty years.

Vanessa wandered in, blonde hair snarled round her head, yesterday's mascara smeared below her eyes, shrugging herself into her dressing-gown.

'Whassup?' she asked sleepily. Eric stalking about like a hero, still on guard in case the burglar came back, Molly lying under the table sniggering at him, her mother sitting at the kitchen table, letter in hand, her father with his arm round her mother. He was being kind and supportive – how unusual, how odd, how uncharacteristic. Had someone died?

'What's the matter mom? What's going on? What's all the noise for?' She looked from one face to another in growing alarm. 'Are you crying? she asked, ready to join in if that was the case.

'I've had a letter. I've found Jessica,' she croaked and held out the letter.

Vanessa was suddenly wide awake. 'No!' Incredulous. 'Mom, that's brilliant.' She read the letter. ''Please contact me if you'd like to take things further.' That's fabulous. Just think she's been in Yorkshire all this time.' She put her arms round Carol's shoulders and kissed her cheek. 'It's amazing - isn't it?' she said kindly. Her mother had longed for this moment for years, and now she seemed stunned rather than overjoyed, as Vanessa would have expected.

Carol's mind raced to turn over all the implications and possibilities, the questions which were about to receive answers. She was bewildered, disbelieving such good fortune, half expecting someone to come along and snatch it all back, insist it was a mistake.

A key scraped and fumbled at the front door.

'Here's Matthew,' said Paul. 'Wonder where he spent the night.'

Matthew, Vanessa's older brother, next born to Susan, looked surprised to see them all in the kitchen.

'Hi..... coffee,' he mumbled, heading for the kettle. He filled the kettle and switched it on then turned to lean on the kitchen sink as he rolled a matchstick thin cigarette. He inhaled, coughed, and then he became aware of the atmosphere. He glanced from face to face - mum had been crying, dad and Van looked kind of excited – no apparent argument. What had he done wrong now?

'What's wrong?'

'You'll never believe this…..' Vanessa began.

'Let your mum tell him,' Paul interrupted.

Matthew's guarded surliness evaporated instantly when he heard the news and read the letter for himself. Excitement bubbled up afresh. His face, closed and bleary with a hangover, opened into a wide smile.

'Just think, mom,' he said, 'you could be a grandmother.' The laughter was hearty, with an edge of thoughtfulness. 'Phone them now – they might be open.'

'What shall I say?'

'You'll think of something,' said Paul. 'Go on, you do that and we'll make some more tea.'

She sat by the phone in the hall. The murmur of conversation drifted through the closed door. She brushed a damp palm over her dressing gown, reached for the phone, and felt the blood pounding in her throat.

In the quietness of the hall she heard the ring, ring of the phone and imagined it echoing in some social services office in Yorkshire. Click.

'The office is now closed. It will be open again on Monday at 8..45. In case of emergency call….'

'Never mind. It was worth a try,' said Paul, and went to get the road map. They spread it out on the kitchen table and located the area where the letter came from – deepest Yorkshire, north of Leeds.

'I wonder what she looks like,' said Van. 'We're both fair with blue eyes like dad. You're dark with blue eyes. What,' she glanced at Paul, assessing if her question would antagonise him, and decided to risk it, 'did you say her dad was like?'

Paul lit a cigarette and listened. He had heard this before, they all had, but he waited to hear how Carol would express it to Vanessa and Matthew today. The dogs shuffled under the table, and the distant chime of church bells floated through the air. Must be a Saturday wedding.

'Dark hair, brown eyes, tall, well-made – he played rugby,' said Carol. Paul was the opposite – fair, blue eyes, slim, very intelligent, totally un-sporty and of late definitely difficult. Rob was, had been, affectionate, good-humoured, but she didn't mention that.

'How old is she now?' asked Matthew.

'Thirty. I was eighteen when I became pregnant, nineteen when she was born. She could be married, and have children.'

'Wonder what she does for a living. Might be a teacher, like you,' said Paul.

'Wonder how she did at school. Maybe she'll like gardening, like you. Or be musical, or a good cook – not like you.' Matthew laughed. 'Sorry mum – joking.'

'Bet she likes reading,' said Vanessa. 'That's a family trait.' Carol noticed the inclusive word 'family.'

She could, Carol realised, be anything. Impossible to guess.

'Main thing is, how does she feel about me. She might be angry. She'd have every right to be.'

'No mum – she wouldn't have tried to get in touch. She was the one who made the first move.' Vanessa was quick with her reassurance.

'No, it was me. I left the letter on her file. And, you know, maybe her adoption wasn't a success. She might have left home, be a single mother – or a homeless drug addict,' said Carol with dawning alarm. 'Maybe she needs help.'

'Well that's typical. Look on the dark side, as usual,' Paul snapped. 'Maybe she's okay. Don't anticipate problems. She's got in touch with you. What more do you want?' he asked as if she'd demanded too much.

The weekend passed - eventually. Carol woke in the early hours of Sunday morning to the sound of rain lashing the windows. Paul lay, his back to her, on the extreme edge of the king-size bed, as he often did these days. It was like sleeping alone. Time stretched out, filled with racing thoughts and anxieties. Long-forgotten words and actions were replayed, reassessed, until finally she fell into a shallow sleep, permeated with dreams of rushing water, dangerous and threatening, which roared and raged and filled her with fear.

'Why don't you stay at home on Monday to make your phone call?' suggested Paul on Sunday evening. 'They can do without you for one morning. You're not indispensable you know,' he said, as if she'd claimed she was.

***

She rang school early and said she'd be in after lunch. No problem – Year 11 were on exam leave, no cover required.

Fingers trembling, she phoned the number on the letterhead. Paul pushed a pad and pencil into her hands. 'You might want these,' then he disappeared into the kitchen.

The social worker was good – calm, kind and professional with, of course, a Yorkshire accent. She was used to dealing with sobbing, inarticulate people and extreme emotions and she had information. Lots of it.

The fantasy began to dissolve and out of the mists a real person became discernable.

'She has dark hair, green eyes, 5'6", married with three children – two boys and a girl. Their names are James and Ben...'

'No – those are the names I was thinking of if Vanessa had been a boy,' Carol interrupted in amazement.

'....and the little girl is Emma.'

'That's Vanessa's middle name.'

'She has five O levels. English Language, English Literature, Art, Domestic Science and History.'

'Mine are exactly the same. What a coincidence.' It was uncanny.

'She's a teacher...'

'So am I.'

'...and her husband is a headmaster,' the voice continued patiently. 'He is seven months older. His birthday is September 10th.' Unlike Paul then, who was best described as an aspiring anarchist, although he was a control freak, and they were both Virgoes. They had both married Virgoes!

'Her parents are still alive and she has an adopted younger sister. She worked in Leeds...'

'I was working there when I met my husband,' this was incredible.

'She's quiet and shy and very reserved. The family is very close.'

Carol scribbled notes, trying to capture the fragments of information before they escaped the whirl of confusion in her brain.

'Almost three quarters of a million children have been adopted since 1926,' said the voice.

That was a million and a half mothers and children, all hiding the truth from family, neighbours and each other.

She was not alone. She was part of a gigantic pattern, a flaw in the fabric of what was once society, an example of its way of dealing with the rule-breakers, the sex-before-marriage sinners, the gamblers and losers, before throwing away the rule-book and declaring universal forgiveness, acceptance and support for single mothers, and a preference for living together before taking on the commitment of marriage.

Some powerful force had separated mother and child over and over again, year upon year, decade after decade, through wars and peace, hardship and plenty, from one generation to another. Shame. And where did it come from? Who imposed it? Why was it now losing its power?

As she listened to the words which confirmed her daughter's separate existence a comforting certainty replaced the void around which her thoughts had picked and pecked for so long. A hard compacted nugget of ice and misery somewhere inside was melting. Secrets, wrapped in misery and shut away in the dark, clamoured to be let out, to join the party. A tiny plant, when the season is right, can grow through a heavy concrete slab. Sunshine, warmth and rain draw the green shoot from its dark cramped space and once the tip shows it is unstoppable. The concrete cracks and gives way, leaves spread, soak up the sun and rain, and grow. So it was with Carol.

From the very beginning she had accepted her parents' insistence on secrecy. No-one must know – aunties, grannies, cousins, sisters, neighbours – no-one. And it had been achieved so successfully.

Secrecy and shame, hand in hand, had moulded her life for so long they were almost a part of her. The secret had been protected, defended with great care. Her father had died with it unmentioned between them. She and her mother never discussed it, and Carol had never confessed that she'd told Matt and Van.

Suddenly the habit of secrecy seemed tired and irrelevant, an unnecessary burden, like a winter coat when spring arrives. Who cared who knew? Anyone who cared anything about her could only be glad.

Her mother would, she knew, prefer to take the secret with her to the grave. She was ashamed, and other people's opinions were important in a small village. The anger which Carol had felt for her for many years, which prevented any closeness between them, was still strong. She would not pick up the phone and share the news. Her mother would take over, become the central focus, and Carol wanted to find her own way through before it was taken away from her. She would decide for herself what she wanted to do. In fact, the decision was already made. She did not need permission, or approval. It was time to put herself first. She wondered why it had taken her so long.

Over yet another cup of tea she related the details to Paul, who listened, occasionally correcting her choice of words, since he couldn't correct the content.

'What comes next?'

'Susan...'

'Jessica,' he interrupted.

'Jessica writes a letter to me and the social worker forwards it on. No addresses exchanged yet. Then I reply.'

'Seems sensible. Then what? You arrange to meet?'

'I guess so. God, I can't believe it – after all this time I'm going to meet her again. She was six weeks old last time I saw her.' She was crying.

'It's what you wanted. It'll be good. You'll see,' Paul insisted with an air of closing the conversation, distancing himself from any discussion which might involve details of feelings or, God forbid, her emotions.

'I know. I'm so thrilled I can't tell you.' For the first time since that awful day she experienced a sense of deeply rooted satisfaction and peace which was almost physical. 'Pity I have to spoil it by going to school.'

Paul was no longer listening, he was reading the newspaper.

** *

At the end of lunch-time, she parked her car on the back drive near the mobiles and checked her face in the driving mirror. Eyes a bit red – not too bad. Through the rain-spattered window of the first scruffy mobile, furthest from the main school building, she saw the dark head and slight figure of Mandy, a friend and colleague, surrounded by a sea of Year 11 GCSE Literature folders which she was moderating whilst eating lunch – a sure recipe for indigestion. The mobile looked out over litter-strewn beaten-up grass and young trees. A magpie sat on a low branch, smart and lively, and fresh spring leaves fluttered in the sunshine. On impulse Carol went in.

'Hi. How are you?' Mandy threw down her pencil, stretched her arms widely, and yawned.

'I'm fine.' Carol sat down in the front row of desks, running her hand over the engrained graffiti of biro, felt tip ink and compass gouges.

'Are you okay? Malc told me you rang in to say you'd be late.' Malc was the Head of English.

'Yes, I'm fine. In fact, I'm great. Tremendous. Couldn't be better.' The secret bubbled inside, shouting, 'Let me out.' Carol grinned.

Mandy, sensing the bursting excitement, looked closely at Carol.

'You look - different.'

'I am different. Something brilliant has happened.' She was almost laughing.

'What? Tell me,' Mandy leaned forward, intrigued. 'Go on, I need some good news. What's happened? You got a new job?'

'I can't believe it myself. No, it's not a new job - it's much better than that. You see,' she paused…breaking a thirty year silence was not easy…maybe she should say nothing….once you've told people you can't take it back...no, no, get it out…. She was suddenly lost for words, decided unadorned simplicity was best. She took a deep breath, 'when I was 18 I became pregnant and the baby was adopted,' Mandy's jaw dropped - literally, 'and two days ago, on Saturday, I had a letter, from a social worker. She, Jessica, has found her birth records and found my letters, which I wrote and left on the file in the hope that she would one day try to find me and want to get in touch with me. I just phoned her this morning - the social worker I mean. She told me all about her.' The words tumbled out.

Carol found she could say all this without crying – another indication of how much things had changed.

'Well….wow,' Mandy's face showed a succession of reactions; surprise, delight, a touch of pity. Pity, as Carol knew, is very difficult to accept - probably it was that which her mother guarded so carefully against. It diminishes your dignity, undermines your self-worth. On this occasion her dignity was doing fine so she could take it. 'How marvellous for you.' Mandy's eyes were full of tears. 'I had no idea. How old is she?'

'Well, she's thirty now,' saying the words made it seem longer. 'It's been a long time. But apparently most people trace their parents when they have children of their own. And - guess what - she has three. Two boys and a little girl, only a few weeks old. The social worker says people often leave it until they're in their late twenties or early thirties before looking for birth parents,' she replied.

'Yes, you'd want to know things like your medical history.'

'Like, is this baby I'm expecting likely to be twins.'

'Or have red hair.'

'So - you're a granny,' she laughed, changing the subject.

'Yes - three times - isn't it brilliant?'

'Granny Carol. You don't look like one.'

'I don't feel like one.'

'What does Paul think? Does he know?' This was a loaded question, with many layers of implication beneath it.

'Of course. He's s known since the kids were babies.'

'My God, what did he say?'

'He was absolutely brilliant. I told Matt and Van when they were younger. They're thrilled - really pleased for me. Hardly anyone else knows outside my family. Actually, you're the first person I've told about this.'

'Well, I'm chuffed you chose me first.' She seemed to mean it. 'I'm so pleased for you.

Allowing Mandy to share her news was like giving away presents, handing out happiness to be shared. To talk openly about Jessica after all these years of silence was deeply satisfying.

A strident, ear-splitting clamour from the bell in the foyer of the classroom signalled the end of lunch-time and Carol hurried off to take the register in her form room. The afternoon session lumbered into motion.

The last lesson of the afternoon, tired and scarcely able to concentrate, Carol took her Year 7's to the library for a reading lesson. Once the kids were settled with a book to read, a longer process than anyone might imagine, she wandered into the Library office. The Teacher-Librarian, June, peered over her glasses.

'You look rather pleased with yourself today, she said with her usual vinegar expression.

'I am. Oh I am,' Carol replied, grinning, 'never better.' She decided to tell June too. If she didn't Mandy would, and it would be nice to see her smile. She repeated the story, watching with interest to see the look on June's face. The distracted Monday-afternoon cloak of half-attention was tweaked aside, and the blue eyes showed delight and concern. June hesitated, then,

'I have a younger brother who is adopted,' she said, cautiously.

'Really! Are you adopted too?' Stupid question.

'No, I have a real sister and an adopted brother. He was very difficult actually. He caused havoc in the family,' the words were measured and considered, she spoke almost unwillingly.

'Did he settle down?' Carol prompted.

'I don't know. He's in his late twenties now. He left home years ago and we don't know where he is. He was alright when he was younger then, when he was a teenager, he was out of control. Such a temper. Intimidating, he was'

Carol listened with dread and fear – her worst nightmares were realised in June's orderly, middle-class, liberal family.

'How sad! I'm sorry to hear that.'

'He ruined my teenage years,' she said. There was resentment, and Carole was left feeling that her joy and happiness were slightly tarnished by association.

Later, after the last bell, after the corridors had filled to jamming point with sixteen hundred yelling teenagers whose sole aim in life was to get out of the building as fast as possible, the school was quiet and empty and Carol began to tidy her classroom, looking forward to going home. The last few days had been exhausting, and now she felt a point had been reached when she could relax, take stock. The door opened and Marie, slim, trim and smart as paint, popped her head in.

'Hi – how are you?,' she trilled. 'Heard you were out this morning. Pity its Parents Evening tonight.'

'Oh no. I'd completely forgotten about that.' Carol's face fell.

'Sandwiches and tea in the Staff Room. Are you feeling up to it? You look very pleased with yourself,' Marie commented in her usual cheery, brisk manner.

'I am pleased. I had some brilliant news this weekend.'

No-nonsense, ambitious Marie listened, tried hard to smile, but was clearly deeply shocked. She said all the right things, but the tone was wrong. Carol was taken aback. She had convinced herself that the attitudes of the 60's had changed but they were not so far away after all.

Nevertheless, each time she shared the news the burden of secrecy grew lighter. She could be herself, and people could judge as they wished.

At 4.20 Carol gathered her mark books, homework records, list of appointments, and scribbled comments, and made her way to the classroom where she and five other teachers would spend the next three hours. Teachers and cleaners had worked hard and the school looked its best, with colourful wall displays, not yet torn or graffitied, and polished wooden floors, not yet muddied or littered. And without the pupils, it was peaceful, pleasant and quietly academic. Usually Carol enjoyed parents' evenings. Tonight she longed to go home, sit quietly and be alone with her thoughts for a short while. Instead she had an appointment every ten minutes with people who would listen carefully to every word, the most attentive audience in the world, parents at a parents' evening.

* * *

By 7.0pm her head throbbed and she was ready to scream. And then Mr and Mrs. Watson arrived, accompanied by Ralph. In a class of difficult students, most with behaviour problems, Ralph Watson stood out as the most extreme. He read quite well, but he talked constantly, wandered about the classroom, and had an attention span of about 30 seconds, which meant he rarely did enough work to tell how he was getting on, and never did homework. For fifteen minutes, unable to get a word in edgeways, Carol listened to his parents who told her, simultaneously, what she already knew, that his school-work was poor and his behaviour bizarre. Ralph, abjectly embarrassed, made several attempts to interrupt and defend himself.

Carol discovered that, as punishment for one misdemeanour, his dad had smashed Ralph's beloved computer with a hammer! His dad was an educational psychologist! She began to feel sympathy for Ralph on both counts. His mother had, she said, 'three degrees' - subject unspecified, but obviously none of them involved listening skills. She was, apparently, in the habit of taking over Ralph's English homework from time to time, checking every detail, 'suggesting' ideas, even sentences, and bawling him out for every single mistake of spelling, grammar or punctuation. Carol began to see that it was a miracle that the child retained enough confidence to speak let alone write. Unfortunately for him he had two older siblings, both doing well at grammar school. All three, she learned, were adopted.

'If he don't improve, settle down and make some progress at school, he's going to be sent away,' Ralph's father threatened. He didn't say where to. Ralph, sitting to attention on the edge of his chair, slanted a fearful sideways glance at his father. Head drooped, for once he was silent.

***

It was after ten that night when Carol sat in the silent kitchen and tried to write her letter. Thoughts of Ralph and June's brother intruded, hard evidence that adoptions were not always successful, adoptive parents not always perfect. And how ironic that she should become aware of them today. It was impossible to begin to write. What could she say to someone who meant such a lot to her, but she'd never met as an adult? What did Jessica want to hear? The burden of guilt weighed heavily - she was Jessica's mother, but she'd given her away, failed her, given her to strangers. She gave up and went to bed and woke in the early hours of the morning, reliving those few weeks when everything changed. Memories, long buried in her sub-conscious, fought their way back to the surface and refused to be patted back into place.

The next morning she received a letter and photographs from Jessica. Baby photos, school photos, wedding and holiday pictures, thoughtfully chosen, showing that at three she looked like Rob, at twelve like Carol, and at twenty and twenty-nine like herself. Carol sat on the hall chair, coat on, ready to leave for school, and absorbed each photograph with avid curiosity. There was no greeting at the top, no return address, no signature at the bottom, but Carol was too overjoyed to register the possible significance. The letter read a little like a police statement with a great deal of factual information. There were reassurances that she had made the right decision and Jessica had had a very happy life with the love and support of her parents and family. The overall tone was reserved and unemotional - but the letter did express the hope that they could keep in touch 'if that is what you want'. Carol received everything with uncritical joy and read the letter several times.

She crept into the darkened bedroom where Paul, buried in the duvet, slept. She shook his shoulder and told him about the letter. He grunted his approval and fell back into a deep sleep. Carol pushed the letter into her handbag so she could read it again at break, and dashed off to school.

The week progressed slowly, and it was impossible to concentrate

On Wednesday, after the fourth sleepless night, she was bewildered, confused, and so tired. Daily routines for herself, Vanessa, Matt and Paul marched on, school, college, office, Job Club, building a layer of reality over the excitement, burying it, before it was ready to be buried. The reply was still unwritten.

At break on Wednesday morning she passed Steve Godley, a Maths teacher, in the corridor. He was young, and sensitive, more like a Drama teacher, and unlike the majority of the rest of his Department. What was it with male maths teachers?

'Hi Carol. Are you okay? Is everything alright?' he asked his face full of concern. She hadn't spoken to him, but it was obvious that the grapevine had been working overtime. His kindness was the last straw.

'Yes, fine,' she nodded, smiled, then fled into the Ladies and locked herself into a cubicle. The tears were unstoppable, accompanied by great shuddering sobs. The bell went, the noises of school faded as children settled into classrooms. Someone came in, used the loo, washed her hands, and left. Her next lesson was a free period and she had planned to do some marking in the staff room. Instead, she decided to see the Deputy Head, John, tell him she had to go home. She waited in the corridor outside his office, while his voice rose and fell behind the door, bawling out some child. The door opened and a six foot boy emerged, defiant and angry, and strode off up the corridor.

'Come in, come in,' urged John, hyped up, stressed out, almost twitching. 'I've only got a minute. What can I do for you?'

Carol stood in front of his desk and told him the whole story, and kept it as brief as possible because he was pacing the office like a caged bull. Twice she stopped whilst he answered the phone with snapped off monosyllables. She felt like a pupil confessing a misdemeanour. She said she wanted to go home.

'Yes, yes of course,' he agreed immediately. 'Can't have you in the classroom in this state.' His eyes were kind and sympathetic, his words accurate and crass. 'You must be feeling pretty upset - the guilt. Thirty years of guilt.' He nodded sagely.

'Yes, something like that,' she said, wanting to strangle him.

Paul, for once, was out, probably at the Job Club. The economic crisis had developed into a full blown recession and he attended regularly applying unsuccessfully for jobs which attracted thousands of other applications. The whole process was destructive and hopeless.

In the silence of the empty house she picked up pen and paper.

The letter was the most difficult thing she had ever written. The factual bits were easy - married, two children, both temporarily and reluctantly back at home after university. Husband, once super-successful in the computer field, now unemployed. Carol - a teacher. Hobbies, reading, gardening, politics, pets, two ageing dogs the size of small donkeys.

Leave out, of course, the divorce proceedings of three years before, now abandoned, the repeated leaving, over the years, to stay with friends and relations when Paul became unendurable. Also the attempt to rebuild a marriage in a new house, and the feeling that life could be better, if only some magic thing was different. Omit the feeling that she must hold things together because, if ever Jessica came back, she wanted her to find a happy family ready to welcome her. She could not admit another failure in her life; if she tried hard enough, worked hard enough, everything would work out.

She searched for words to explain how important Jessica was and always had been. She tried to show how her conception was not some casual passing event, soon forgotten.

It took days to write this letter and every word was chosen with great care, each sentence written, rewritten, then changed again. After it was posted she waited anxiously for a reply.

It was, when it came, warmer. As yet Jessica's parents knew nothing. Until they knew, she felt she was betraying them. Her mother was a semi-invalid. When Jessica was eighteen her parents gave her all the information they had about her adoption. She was old enough to find her birth mother if she chose. However, her mother had made it clear that though she would not oppose this, she could not bear the hurt of knowing about it, worrying that blood would be thicker than water. Jessica's loyalty to her adoptive mother was admirable and clear – she had never, until now, attempted to contact Carol. Carol found this difficult to understand, feeling that a mother would unquestioningly welcome whatever would make her child happy.

The following weeks were a roller-coaster of elation and despair. Letters and photographs flew between them. Carol spent hours alone in her little cupboard of a study on the landing, writing letters, leaving the others to get on without her, absorbed and happy. She was aware of Paul's resentment, though it seemed more to do with his lack of control of the situation than any animosity about Jessica. Superficially he was supportive, even encouraging. It could, he said spitefully, put an end to her moods, which had blighted his life for so long.

Carol and Jessica arranged to meet in mid-June.

***

Carol travelled north alone, by train, not trusting herself to concentrate well enough on the motorways. 'It's best if your first meeting is between just the two of you,' advised the counsellor from the Adoption Service. 'Your families can meet later.'

She changed at Manchester, took a local train which snaked slowly across the Pennines. Eternal green slopes, sheep grazing so closely she could see the gently rotating jaws and dozy expressions. Sunshine hot on thick woolly coats. The words of 'Jerusalem' 'and did those feet in ancient time walk upon England's mountains green?' jumped into her head and whirled there meaninglessly. These mountains? Whose feet? The train carriage, hot and dusty. Passengers, sealed in little pods of private thoughts, reading, gazing silently at the passing scenery. Was that woman also on the way to one of the most important meetings of her life? Did the old chap with the shopping bag have some war-time romance in his past with a love-child he'd never seen?

Hands hot and clammy in the sunshine. Carol checked her appearance - pale linen jacket, beige longish flowered skirt, plain stone-coloured shoes, black handbag, white blouse. Bobbed brown hair, a little make-up, gold ear-rings. Neutral, inoffensive, acceptable but motherly. Vanessa had helped choose the clothes and had checked her over, adjusting the hairstyle, choosing different ear-rings..

'If I found you were my mum I'd be pleased,' she said, approvingly.

'Well, I am your mum.'

'Yes.' She giggled. 'And I'm pleased. I think you're the best mum I know.'

How would anyone like their mother to look, the originator of half their genes? Not some sad old wreckage, defeated by life, nor a tasteless frump, all perm and crimplene. Carol didn't want her daughter to be ashamed or alienated, she wanted to be what Jessica hoped she would be - but she had no idea what that was

A station came into view. Carol fumbled for her handbag with suddenly nerveless fingers. Her mouth was dry, strength flowed from her legs and she could barely stand to leave the train. The platform, cool and shadowed from the June sunshine, was empty. No-one was waiting. Paving slabs, Victorian York stone, stretched away to infinity. She noted the stone building, iron Victorian arches and hanging baskets, neat and pretty, like a picture on a jigsaw box. The few alighting passengers disappeared down into the dark mouth of the distant subway towards the exit. She was the only person left in the world.

The sound of the departing train faded into the distance and the peace and tranquillity of the sunny hillside beyond the train lines crept back onto the platform.

Carol waited and a feeling of dread began to take hold. She took out the letter from her bag, checked the date and recalled how, significantly it now seemed, the first letter had had no greeting at the top, no return address and no signature at the bottom.

'Well, you're here, find the exit,' she told herself. Maybe she'd got the instructions wrong and Jessica was waiting at the ticket barrier. She walked along the deserted platform, footsteps echoing softly, stepped uncertainly down into the darkness of a broad flight of stone stairs and set off along the subterranean passage. The uneven slabs and dark damp stone walls were strangely wholesome compared to the city counterpart. She faltered, blinded by the glare of sunshine from the far end of the tunnel. A silhouetted figure appeared, footsteps echoing; as she came closer Carol saw a girl, slim, dark bobbed hair, black trousers, white tee-shirt. Closer. Her father's cheekbones, his dark curly hair. She had Carol's smile, uncertain and tremulous, and Carol's eyes, though green, filling with tears.

'Jessica?' She didn't need to ask. The world dissolved under welling tears. She wanted this wonderful, amazing moment to stretch into infinity, never end, to blot out all past problems and all future disappointments. The thinly-clad shoulders were soft and warm in her embrace.

'Hello, Jessica. I've waited such a long time for this.' She kissed the smooth young cheek.

The returning hug held some resistance, a hint of reluctance and reserve. Carol released her daughter, and looked into her face. Jessica was trying not to cry.

'Hello, Carol,' she was nervous, unsure what to say. 'I've wanted to meet you as well.'

Jessica glanced nervously round, perhaps to see if anyone was looking, embarrassed. Carol wanted to keep her daughter in her arms, hug her and never let her go, but some instinct told her not to. Instead she tried to act and sound normal, and took out a handkerchief to mop up the tears. The moment was so fragile and precious she was afraid to say or do the wrong thing. It was a once-only chance, she must not get it wrong. It mattered too much.

They walked together out of the station into the square of the small, stone-built Pennine town, two strangers who hadn't had the practice of walking as a couple, anticipating where the other person would step, who would go first. It was lunch-time and groups of school-uniformed teenagers filled the pavements. Some of them greeted Jessica, 'Hello Mrs. Lucas' and glanced with curiosity at Carol. She realised that, as the Headmaster's wife, Jessica was probably well known and would not want to be part of a public display of emotion.

'Would you like a cup of tea? In here?' Jessica indicated a small tea shop. They chose a table near the back and ordered tea.

Facing each other closely across a small table, conscious of the possible interest of strangers, conversation was stilted. Carol's imagination had never carried her this far. She had visualised meeting her daughter, never dared look beyond that.

'So - do Matthew and Vanessa know you're here today?'

'Yes. They're very excited about it. They want to meet you as well.'

'I'd like to meet them. But it's a bit awkward with my mother and that.' She had a Yorkshire accent. 'My mum doesn't know yet.' Carol knew this, from her letters.

'My brother and sister have only known recently,' she offered. This also had been in her letter. Carol picked up her cup and tea slopped into the saucer.

'What does your sister think?' she asked as she put a paper napkin under the cup to mop up the spill. Why was she so awkward?

'I only told her last week.' She didn't answer the question.

'Does she live locally?'

'Yes, with her boy-friend. Mum and dad don't approve of that. They're a bit straight-laced in some ways.' Carol sipped her tea which went down the wrong way and made her cough. Embarrassingly the cough got worse until she thought she'd never draw breath again. What a fool she was. Eventually, she asked,

'Do they go to church?' Why did she ask that?

'Yes. That was part of the adoption thing, that they should bring us up as Christians.'

'Of course.' She should have remembered - the Church of England Children's Society had arranged the adoption.

'So what does she think? Your sister?'

'She feels that - I hope this doesn't upset you - that her mother gave her away and she doesn't want to know anything about her.'

'I see. I suppose that's fair.' She wanted to ask, 'Do you feel the same way?' but couldn't.

'It was a shock to me when I found your letter on the file. I hadn't expected it.'

'Was it easy to get hold of your file?'

'No. It took nearly two years. I wanted to look at my medical history, actually. Because of the children. Your letters came right out of the blue.' Was she saying that she hadn't wanted to find her mother, but was unable to resist the temptation because the possibility existed? She wanted to ask, but was afraid she wouldn't like the answer. A small silence began, and grew. They both tried to end it together.

'Do you think…'

'Would you like…' Their social skills were equally inept. Was that an inherited trait?

'After you.'

'No you go first.'

'I was going to ask who is looking after the children this afternoon.'

'Ben's at school. Jamie and Lucy are with Ivan. Actually, he's waiting for us in the car park, in the square. He's taken the afternoon off. He'd like to meet you.'

A tall slim man, somehow fatherly despite his relative youth, was leaning on a car boot, arms folded. As they approached he drew upright and welcomed Carol warmly with a hug. He glanced keenly at his wife, protective, gauging her reaction. Carol glimpsed a baby asleep in a car seat, and a little boy was sitting in the drivers' seat, pretending to drive.

The atmosphere lightened with the addition of another person, especially one with the practised warmth and kindliness of Ivan. He released the baby's seatbelts, and lifted her out of the car into the sunshine, where she blinked sleepily. He held her out to Carol and she reached for the child, overwhelmed, and cried, but happily. Jamie saw them and demanded to be let out, turning shy when his daddy picked him up and he came face to face with Carol. They filled Carol's mind with memories, calling forth an easy and automatic response, and seemed more real to her than the quiet girl at her side. Ivan now took over responsibility for the conversation, creating the illusion they were all part of it when really Carol couldn't think of a word to say because her mind was so full of things she couldn't say. Jessica seemed strangely quiet, too.

'Why don't you come back home with us? You can see where we live, and we can talk more easily,' Ivan said.

They drove along a beautiful river valley. June sunshine flickered through tall oaks. The house turned out to be lovely. Ivan poured wine, gave a conducted tour. It was a family home, comfortable and attractive, with colourful bedrooms and a playroom behind the kitchen, full of toys, showing clearly the central role and importance of the children.

Suddenly, as if by arrangement, Ivan left, taking Jamie with him, to pick Ben up from school. The departure of Ivan and his easy-going chatter left a gulf of awkwardness. Carol was alone with her daughter.

They sat on the sofa. Carol held the baby in her lap. She looked exactly like Jessica did on that last day when, as a six-week old baby, she'd been handed over to Sister Dearborn and vanished. The same eyes, the dome of the forehead, the warm heaviness. Beside her on the sofa was the daughter she'd lost - now a young woman, fully adult, mother of her own children. Her senses were confused. The baby became the baby she had lost, now restored. Who was the daughter?

The adoption file lay between them on the sofa. It contained the doctor's report, various official forms, handwritten and dated in their layout and the flimsiness of the paper, and the very letter she had written, to be put in this file, just before Jessica was born.

A question. 'Did you ever consider abortion?' Carol was shocked - no, it was illegal then, she had no knowledge of it and it didn't even enter her mind as a possibility.

'If it happened today, would you?'

'I've no idea. I guess that's what happens today in most cases. I've never thought about it.'

'I have and I'm totally against it.'

Another question. 'Having had three children, I can't understand how anyone could give away their baby. How did it happen?'

This could be a lawyer asking routine questions, but was there anger as wel?. She had every right to be angry.

Carol didn't meet her eyes, which must have seemed like an evasion. She was face to face with the truth, with the one person to whom it mattered most. Ivan had left them alone together so that they could talk, but she needed help. Frozen, numb, her brain slowed down and any social graces she had ever possessed deserted her. She was a middle-aged woman with teenager's gawkiness. The memories swirled like the sculpted pattern on the carpet which filled her eyes. The impossibility of conveying with mere words what had happened, of condensing that great mass of seething confusion into ordinary speech. For three decades she had tried hard to drown the turbulence of those few hectic weeks when decisions were made, words were said, things were done. Now she was trying to dredge them back, re-examine them, be objective, see things as they really were, evaluate with her present maturity the actions of her inexperience and ineptitude. Actions which brought into being this person beside her.

Jessica looked at her, her eyes a mix between her father's brown and her mother's blue. Her hair was like Rob's, not fair like Paul, Matt and Van. Her accent was as Carol's had been, unlike Paul and the kids. Her sentences were short and to the point, not like her family where no-one could get a word in edgeways, everyone had an opinion to express, and they could argue for ages about anything - who should walk the dogs, current politics, the war poets or any other thing. Her manner was reserved and cautious. Sometimes she reminded Carol of Rob's mother, sometimes of herself, sometimes of Rob. She had not seen Rob since five months before Jessica's birth, but now she tried to grasp all the whispy memories to compare them with his daughter.

A picture flashed into her mind. His mother's living room, music, Rob wearing her big yellow jumper, dancing about, teasing, his brown eyes flecked with tawny yellow, happy and full of life, in stark contrast to this awkward and unhappy scene.

Her outward appearance was easy to see. All afternoon Carol had wanted to stare. She had kept looking, long and hard, and sometimes Jessica glanced up and found her staring, trying to take in all the details, to see beyond the dark fringe and un-made-up face and see her as a person. When Jessica found her staring, Carol looked away guiltily. Once she found Jessica staring at her.

She had a few clues about Jessica's upbringing - middle-class and professional with strict standards. Her father was a doctor, her mother a nurse. They disapproved of her sister living with her boy-friend. Her adoption had been kept a secret outside the family, people believed she was their natural daughter. They were still a very close and loving family, visiting each other frequently, taking holidays together. Jessica didn't talk much about herself at all, except to insist she had a happy childhood. Carol had made the right decision in giving her up. That cut both ways - Carol was relieved and contented she had been happy, sad to be reminded that her best contribution to her child's well-being had been to give her to strangers. Their closeness and family completeness emphasised the sense of being an outsider, the skeleton in the cupboard. She had been so used to keeping the secret of her baby's existence it had not occurred to her that her own existence was a matter of shame.

The question hung between them. There was the truth glimmering out from the swirling mists of a distant landscape and consistent efforts to forget. There was the harsh reality of relationships in her family and the question of whether Jessica could or should hear about that. There was how she felt at the time, hardly remembered but for the sharp prickly bits which were more of a physical sensation.

What happened then, happened to another person to the one she had become, a person who had no control of her life, and lived in a world which, unaware, lay poised on the brink of the fastest changes in history. The span of her life had its beginnings in the slow, steady and ignorant world which contained the remnants of the middle ages, its endings reached into the fast, information-ridden uncertainties of a new millennium.

How could she explain what happened? It was a long, complicated story, and anyway it happened to someone else, in a different world, one which she had fought hard to leave, not to her.

Chapter 2

October 1963

Carol pushed the battered swing door of the tiny, red-plush cinema. A mid-afternoon listlessness, emphasised by organ music and faded art deco, filled the air. She breathed in the damp kennel smell compounded of cigarette ash and old overcoats, overlaid with a hint of chocolate and orange peel, and checked out the sparsely scattered audience.

No-one she knew, as far as it was possible to tell by looking at the backs of their heads. This was a relief, even though it had been unlikely, this far from the village. Choosing a seat as far as possible from anyone else, she sat in the middle of an empty row. She took out a book from her bag and began to read 'Lady Chatterley's Lover'; the book cover read, 'Children of the New Forest'. Brown hair swung forward and hid her face.

'Don't let anyone know where you are. It's none of their business. No-one will recognise you there,' her mother had said. So she had to be careful.

A few more people came in out of the October rain, the lights began to dim and sweet wrappings rustled in the row behind. In that moment of utter darkness before the film began a man in a mackintosh came and sat next to her. Carol glanced at him without interest, mildly surprised he should choose to sit next to her when there were so many empty seats, but then the programme began and she forgot he was there.

The main film was a fairy tale story about several children on a journey, separated from the adults, in danger, struggling to survive. A very young Michael Crawford, blonde and blue-eyed, a caring hero, charming and articulate, was the eldest and was falling in love in an innocent, adolescent way with Hayley Mills, adorable and helpless with trusting blue eyes and perfect vowels.

The man in the next seat was restless. He had the whole of their shared armrest, and his left knee was almost touching Carol's right one. There was no excuse for it, he wasn't even particularly fat, though it was hard to tell in that great floppy mac.

Michael Crawford found Hayley Mills a safe place to rest on a rocky outcrop in the forest. She was tired, and had a tiny smudge on her pretty cheek. Admiration flowed from her blue eyes and gentle smile.

Carol felt the man's knee against hers and absently moved hers away.

Michael Crawford began to outline his plan.

Again her knee was nudged. She glanced down, peering through the darkness, her mind still on the screen. By its flickering light she could see that the man was sitting with his knees widely spaced out, fidgeting about in his raincoat pockets. If he spreads out any further, she thought, he'll be in my seat. She hunched even further away from him.

On the screen Michael was beginning to tell Hayley how he felt about her.

That knee again! Nudge, nudge. What was wrong with him? She could move away, tell him to stop it, or even complain to the manager. His knee pushed against hers again, rhythmically. Without thinking too much, Carol drew her right foot back as far as possible and without taking her eyes off the screen kicked him sharply on the ankle. There was a surprised grunt. The fumbling ceased. The knee was withdrawn. He was still for a few seconds, then he stood up and made his way rapidly along the row, muttering to himself.

Michael gathered the children and, like the hero he was, led them out of danger. Hayley, confident of his power to take care of them, held his hand. The man and his raincoat were forgotten as Carol succumbed to the protective charm, posh accent and exquisite manners of the youthful Michael, and fell yearningly and tenderly, once in a lifetime, in love with him, or at least with the idea of him. At this stage of her relationships with men, it was all academic anyway.

The baby stirred and Carol rested her palms on what used to be her waist and felt the faint flutter. The credits rolled and the lights went up. There was no sign of the man in the mac. Whatever he had been doing had been somehow furtive.

Hopefully anonymous in her disguise of flat shoes, glasses and huge coat, Carol stood at the bus stop. It was early evening, damp and chilly and already nearly dark. A small middle-aged woman joined her, forming the beginning of a queue.

Rain pattered down out of a tumbling black and grey sky, lamplight gleamed on uneven paving slabs and broken kerbs. The gutters gurgled and trams clattered and sparked. Early evening crowds bustled about, in and out of shops, on and off buses, along pavements, taking no notice whatsoever of anyone else, including her. She might have been invisible.

This was a pleasant contrast to the first eighteen years of her life. She had grown up in a small Yorkshire mining village where everyone knew everyone else, their family and family history back two generations, when a mineshaft had been sunk in open green fields and a village quickly built around it. Miners and their families had moved there from other coalfields throughout the United Kingdom, forming a new community which blended into the native Yorkshire culture - stubborn, proud and outspoken - or rude and bigoted if you looked at it from another point of view. Carol's first attempt to break free from the claustrophobic village was short-lived – she joined the WRAF, and found herself in a remote little camp in Lancashire, surrounded by fields, miles from anywhere. The homesickness came as a surprise. Not so much homesickness as missing Rob. Warm, cuddly Rob. She had then made the disastrous and unforgivable mistake .

At first she had ignored the evidence - she had never been good at working out when her period was due – but had eventually made an appointment with the Medical Officer. His office was quiet and peaceful, his voice reassuringly calm and businesslike as his fingers pressed, prodded and invaded. Afterwards he had sat her down in the chair next to his desk and offered her a cigarette, which she had accepted but didn't really want, before telling her that she was pregnant. With trembling hand she tapped the cigarette ash into the ash-tray, trying to look and sound adult and in control. The smell of the smoke was nauseating and she wanted to cry.

'What do you think you'd like to do now?' He was young, and sympathetic.

'I'll get married. My boyfriend is in the army, he's only joined recently. We'll get married and have married quarters.' She spoke, she hoped, with confidence.

'Fine. Well, obviously your parents will have to know. Presumably your boyfriend knows, or has some idea already.'

'No, no he hasn't.'

'Humm...okay,' he paused, thinking. 'Ma'am Clark is in charge of all female staff. She will have to be informed so she can arrange your discharge.'

Ma'am Clark was young, fat and unattractive, with a shiny face and an earnest, Christian manner, probably at home on a hockey-field but out of her depth when it came to people. Carol groaned inwardly.

'Do I have to tell her?'

'I'm afraid so. All the women on the station are her responsibility.'

The M.O. insisted: it was unavoidable. An appointment was made.

Ma'am Clark was not too pleased that a girl in her care had become pregnant. She took it personally.

'Do you know who the father is?'

'Yes. Oh yes. He's been my boyfriend since I was 16.'

'There is no-one else on camp involved? None of the male staff?'

'No. I've never had any other boy-friend.'

'How did it happen?' How did she think it had happened? Had no-one told her the facts of life?

'I missed him a lot when I was here. The last time I went on leave, it must have been then it happened. At the end of July.'

'Does he know?'

'No. Not yet.'

She told Carol that she should have controlled herself. She herself had a boyfriend in London, she missed him very much and saw him when she was on leave, like Carol and Rob. However, Carol was given to understand, despite their passion for each other, they controlled their emotions. Ma'am Clark's brown eyes shone with virtue, her vast bosom straining the little white buttons on the front of her shirt as she leaned forward across the polished desk. Her face, innocent of make-up, was a little flushed and sweaty. Brown hair was pushed untidily behind her ears, and bits of it stuck out around her face. Shaggy black eyebrows moved up and down with sincerity. Carol tried to imagine the man who would be carried away by his passion for Ma'am Clark. A picture popped into her mind of a mousy little man in RAF uniform, standing in Charlie Chaplin pose, feet splayed, clasping his hat to his tiny chest.

'Obviously you will need to go home this weekend and talk to your parents and your boyfriend.'

Thoughts of home pulled Carol out of the daydream. Home –it was only thirty or forty miles from this very bus stop – but it might as well have been in another country. Carol shifted her weight and looked for the bus – no sign of it. The rain was soaking through her coat into her shoulders.

She couldn't even remember telling Rob the following Friday evening. She did remember that they both assumed they'd be getting married. The event was completely eclipsed by the dread of telling her mother.

She chose a time later that evening, when her father was out. They were sitting together quietly in the kitchen, her mother knitting, she reading, the telly talking to itself in the corner. Carol had opened her mouth to speak several times, but words would not come. The coal fire crackled, the clock ticked. Twice Carol began the sentence, 'Mum…' then changed it to something else. Finally she'd given up and decided to go to bed, then turned back and blurted it all out.

'Mum...'

'What?' distracted, counting stitches.

'I...I have to tell you something.'

Sharply. 'What? What is it? Tell me,' she put the knitting down.

'I....I....I'm pregnant.'

Her mother was on her feet. 'I knew it,' her hands grasped tightly together in anguish. 'I knew there was something wrong.' She looked closely into Carol's face, her eyes searching, 'are you sure?'

'Yes,' her voice was low, 'the Medical Officer says so.'

Her mother's sigh was deep and full of sorrow.

'I don't know!' Another sigh, then a contradiction. 'I knew it. You'll have to tell your dad. You and him.' She seized the situation, turned it into a problem and made it her own. Angrily, 'Does his mother know?' Rob's mother was a widow with three children. Her mother did not know her well, but didn't like what she did know. She smoked, and drank, and had a boyfriend. And smiled a lot.

'No.'

'Well, don't tell her. I don't want her knowing our business. God knows what your dad'll say. Does Rob know?'

'Yes. I told him earlier tonight.'

'You can tell your dad tomorrow. The two of you. I'm not telling him.'

Her dad had, as usual for a Saturday afternoon, been out in the back in his pigeon shed. On race days no-one was allowed in the back garden in case they caused the returning birds to delay entering the loft, where they could be caught and the leg ring stamped in the pigeon clock, thus registering their time of arrival. Rob had opened the back window and called to him awkwardly, 'Can I have a word?' Instead of coming inside he'd come to the window, impatient at the interruption, still carrying the can of pigeon-corn which he had been shaking to attract returning racers.

Deeply suspicious, he'd asked sharply, 'What do you want?' He pushed up the brim of his flat cap, drew on his Woodbine and blew the smoke into the room. Carol felt sick with apprehension and the smell of the smoke.

Rob tried to inject some dignity and maturity into his voice, but his youth and inexperience robbed him of his effect and he looked and sounded gauche.

'Carol's having a baby and we want to get married.'

Carol didn't know what she'd expected, but he sounded pathetic, even to her.

'You what?' bellowed her father then, without further thought, 'Well, you're not bloody well getting married, so you needn't think you are.' He drew deeply on his cigarette and threw it to the ground, grinding his boot furiously in the glowing speck. He glared into the room again, then turned abruptly, dismissing them both, and returned to the more urgent matter of his birds. The race was important and he didn't want to miss the chance of clocking in a possible winner.

Thirty years later Carol still felt a shiver of fear at the memory of the searing anger in his icy blue eyes.

The subject was never again raised between Carol and her father. Her mother became the intermediary.

The following weeks became a kaleidoscope of weekdays of worry in camp, with no-one to confide in, and fragmented weekends at home, full of angry silence, blame and weeping, always furtive and suppressed so Carol's younger brother and sisters would not hear. Rob was not there – he was banished from the house. Fleeting discussion took place, always terminated by the need to be back at camp. No-one asked what she wanted.

Mr. Stone changed his mind and ordered Carol, through her mother, to get married, then changed it again.

Ma'am Clark and Rob's officer exchanged letters. There were to be no married quarters. They were both eighteen and needed permission to marry, from parents and from Commanding Officers, and it was not forthcoming.

Control of the situation slipped away from Carol and Rob as her mother and father assumed the dominant role. Rob had to return to his camp in Yorkshire, couldn't get leave, and wasn't a good letter writer. There were no telephones. Carol realised, with growing agitation, that it was no use counting on him.

As soon as she entered the house on weekend visits her father, if he was not at work, would disappear into the garden and begin cleaning his pigeon shed, or constructing some mysterious addition to 'Pigeon Palace'. Sounds of furious hammering rang out on the late summer air. Her mother, pushed into the role of organiser and go-between, was far too anxious to do either very well

'I've been to see the Church of England Children's Society,' she told Carol one night when they were alone together.

'Did my dad go with you?'

'No,' emphatically, 'you know him, he won't talk to anybody.'
The word 'adoption' entered the discussion, though Carol could never remember how. Her mother gathered information, passed it on to her father, and he, perhaps, made the decision which was then relayed to Carol via her mother.

Rob had been excluded from this process early on. Her father had always treated him with amused contempt, and Rob was too young to stand up to him, and perhaps did not want to.

'You can tell Rob that you made a mistake, you're not pregnant,' her mother instructed. 'There's no need for his family to know.' Uneasily and in confusion she had agreed, and wrote to him. In the gap of time and distance which had developed between them they had grown out of touch with each other's feelings. He had not replied to her letter.

Everyone believed she was still in the WRAF at the other side of the country. No-one, except her parents, knew she was here, only thirty miles from home, in this teeming city, alone among strangers.

It all happened so quickly. Suddenly here she was, in a home for wayward women, the sort of place she would never have imagined existed outside a Charles Dickens novel

'Don't let on to nobody.' Her mother was quite fierce about this - Granny, younger brother and sisters, Aunties Joan, Iris and Glad, cousins, no-one. They were not going to be given the opportunity to take the moral high ground, make judgements, have opinions. If anyone asked her about her background she must lie. If anyone asked her later when it was all over about this period of her life, she must lie.

'Have you been here long love?'

Startled, Carol noticed for the first time the little lady standing next to her waiting for the bus. Lie. Lie.

'About four weeks.' The truth slipped out. She needed more practice.

The woman's face reflected her incomprehension. Then she smiled.

'Oh. Aye. You mean it seems like four weeks. The 51 is due at 20 past. It's late again. Rush hour in't it? Have you been here long - at the bus stop?'

'Ah - the bus stop! Oh - um - yes. About ten minutes I think.'

'There'll be three here in a minute. Should have been a 23 at quarter past. So you've only been here four weeks?' The woman looked with interest at Carol's bulging coat.

What could she say? 'Yes.'

'Where you from then, love?'

The famous Yorkshire friendliness, easily confused at times with nosiness, filled the woman's voice with warmth, inviting a candid response.

'Well, I am from Yorkshire.' Panic. How did you avoid telling people the truth? What did you say instead? The woman smiled and nodded.

'Well, if the bus is much longer,' she said with a smile, 'you'll be having your baby at the bus stop.' Oh God, she'd noticed. 'Is your husband from Yorkshire as well?'

Carol looked at the Woolworths 'gold' wedding ring on her third finger. Did it look convincing?

'Yes. Yes he is. Well, he's not here at the moment, he's in the army.' Shut up. Don't tell her that.

'When's your baby due?'

'My baby? MY baby?' she thought. 'End of March.' That was true anyway, no need to lie about that.

'Is it your first?'

'Yes. Yes it is.'

'Have you decided on a name?' The mention of a name suddenly gave the baby a reality which it never had before. It was going to be a real person, and in real life people chose names for their babies. This woman's assumption that she could choose a name herself, that as the mother she had the right to do that, was odd. She stood lost in thought.

'No, no, I haven't chosen a name.'

'Oh look, here's the bus,' said the woman with relief.

Five minutes later Carol got off the bus at the top of Bedale Road and set off down the street of large Victorian terraces which sloped away down the hill. She lifted the latch on the garden gate of the third house on the left. No-one had referred to the baby in a normal conversational context so far, it seemed odd to discuss it easily without anger or guilt. Discussions with her mother were worried and anxious and concerned with secrecy; the brief conversations with officers and social workers were detached and problem-solving and on her part tearful. She had had to go and see some woman who sat at the far side of a vast shiny desk and asked questions to which Carol had no answers. Carol had cried and the woman sat there looking at her with cold snaky eyes, waiting until the tears stopped and the questions could continue. Carol was still not sure who the woman was or the purpose of the interview. She couldn't think straight, or make decisions. Her feelings and emotions and any implication that the baby was hers to plan for and keep were not part of this. Well, the old woman on the bus would never guess the truth.

As she turned into the gate Carol glimpsed the face of the woman on the bus, watching her, and realised that she knew all about the house in Bedale Road. There must be a constant stream of girls and they only stayed a short while, then moved on. It must be well known in the neighbourhood.

* * *

At the sound of the outside door opening Mrs. Thomas levered her bulky frame out of the armchair and lumbered to the door of her little sitting-room. Opening the door a crack she peered round it into the gloom to see who had come in. A faint ashy cigarette smell escaped into the hall.

'Is that you Carol?' she asked, a natural authority in her rasping middle-class voice.

Yes, it's me.'

'You've been a long time.' Mrs. Thomas's's door opened a fraction more and she spoke through the gap, as though she didn't want the interior of her room to be seen.

'Yes. I went to see a film. I finished the vegetables before I went. I'm not late am I?'

'No. Dinner's in an hour at six. Is it your turn to set the table? I believe it is. Don't forget you've left some laundry on the line. Yvonne put it in the scullery.' She might be infirm but she didn't miss a thing.

'OK. Thanks Mrs.Thomas.' The door closed. Resisting the impulse to stand to attention and salute before dismissing, Carol hung her coat on the hall pegs and walked down the dark narrow passage to the kitchen at the back of the old house. The smell of boiling cabbage drifted from the scullery to meet her.

The kitchen was dominated by an enormous polished table with fifteen chairs of assorted styles around it. Beyond that the scullery gave access to the small back garden with a tiny lawn and some straggling late-summer perennials. A huge elm in the garden next door filtered out most of the natural light and night had already descended there. A long, golden autumn of blue skies and crisp leaves underfoot was slipping into the chill and damp of early winter.

Mrs. D, the cook, was orchestrating the final stages of dinner and danced about, whipping off lids and poking into cauldrons of steam, whisking lethal pans of bubbling fat from the oven and basting the string-bound roll of breast of lamb and rows of potatoes.

'Hello, love - mind your back,' she called over her shoulder, chewing furiously on a piece of gum.

Carol hung her laundry on the maiden above the boiler and slowly mounted the steep narrow stairs.

The large but crowded first floor bedroom looked out onto the street. It contained eight single beds with lockers beside them, set out like a dormitory. Shiny mauve bedspreads, dark wallpaper and the dim light gave the room a funeral parlour aspect, enhanced by the autumn chill which seeped in from outside. Six of the eight girls who slept here were pregnant, and they lolled about the room imparting a hint of a harem atmosphere, a harem devoid of warmth or luxury, but all-pervadingly female.

A skinny untidy girl with hunched shoulders and features like Jacqueline Kennedy was stretched out on the end bed reading a magazine. 'Hi there,' she drawled in a Canadian accent. Kay was one of the unpregnant ones, though before Carol left she had joined the club.

'Hello,' Carol replied, glad that someone recognised she existed.

'Where have you been then?' This was Maddy, small, blonde and plump with pouting lips and slightly squinty eyes. She was seventeen and nearly six months pregnant and would soon move on to the Mother and Baby home in the city. Her maternity clothes were smart and new. Maddy had been born to a mother who was only sixteen, and adopted by a wealthy and childless couple. The father of her baby was married and her parents were giving her their full support whilst the divorce went through. When the baby was born she would marry the father and return to live near her parents, wherever that was, and they'd have another baby in their lives.

'I went to see a film.'

'Well, it's alright for some. I've been at work all morning. Why don't you get a job? What do you do?' she demanded.

'I am, or was, a secretary - well, shorthand typist. How do you get a job?'

'If you want a shitty job like mine you walk right into some little store and ask for one,' drawled Kay. Kay said she was one quarter Red Indian. She wore her clothes as if they belonged to someone else. Carol imagined her in fringed buckskins and turquoise blue beadwork, astride a pinto pony in the Rockies. She knew Kay would have died laughing if she'd known.

'I don't want one anyway,' chimed in Jeanette. She was next after Maddy at five and a half months. 'My damned mother can support me.' Jeanette was also seventeen. Even being pregnant hadn't dented her confidence.

'Well, when I've paid my rent I've got 7s. 6d. a week, so I can manage,' Carol said.

Little hard-faced red-haired Ruth who had only arrived that week looked up with interest. Although pregnant she still looked slim. 'So how do you get a job? I worked in an office.'

'How do you think? Newspaper adverts - that's how I got mine. Or the agency,' snapped Maddy as if Ruth should have known and was an idiot for asking.

'What's an agency?' asked Carol.

'Where have you been? Don't you know anything? It's like, well like a shop for jobs. You register your name and address and they send you for interviews. But don't tell them you're pregnant. If they think you'll be leaving, they won't give you anything.' Maddy savoured her role as expert. As she talked she changed out of her working clothes, revealing a strangely shaped skirt waist with odd fastenings and underwear which accommodated her shape. Carol wanted to look closer and ask questions. She was already having trouble with suspender belts and knickers which kept slipping down under her bump. However, Maddy was a snappy individual, and anyway the clothes looked expensive and she knew without asking that she couldn't afford them.

'But they'll soon know. They might think you're a bit overweight to begin with but you can soon tell it's a baby,' said Ruth sharply.

'It's too late by then. They won't sack you. And even if they do, you haven't lost anything,' said Yvonne. 'I did it. I'm leaving in another two weeks.'

'Do you have to give your real name?' asked Carol. 'What if someone recognises you?'

There was a moment's quiet. All six pregnant girls were aware that this was the main reason they were here - to avoid recognition.

Alice's placid broad Yorkshire voice butted in - if she could ever be said to do anything so assertive as to butt in - 'I'm not bothering.' She adjusted the pillow under her head, wobbling the piled up auburn beehive hairdo. Her black eyes, heavily outlined in black eye-liner, looked drowsy. 'It's not worth it. It's only a few weeks, then you can't work anyway.'

The door banged open and little Sandy breezed in from school. 'Hello ladies,' she mocked, emphasising the second word, and flashed them a wicked grin. At thirteen she was provocative and out of control. She had run away from her home in Essex and somehow wound up here. Her Essex accent stood out from the flat Yorkshire vowels. If she could be believed, she was working hard on joining the ranks of the unmarried mothers despite all the efforts of her social workers to settle her in a foster home.

'I just met that old geezer again in the park, you know the one I told you about.'

'You should be more careful,' warned Yvonne. 'It's not safe.'

'Nah, I can look after myself. She laughed. 'I tell you he can't hardly walk now, after what I done to him.' Her stories were all about 'geezers' she'd met, what they tried to do to her, and how she took wicked revenge.

'Well, I need the money,' resumed Ruth. 'I'm getting married next year. Me and Dave have got a house to furnish.' Ruth carried on folding her underwear into a drawer, and looked up as she became aware that an awkward hush had descended.

'If you're getting married to the baby's father what are you doing here?' Trust Maddy to ask. Silence. Everyone pretended they weren't listening.

'We're not ready for a baby yet. We can't afford it. We're having it adopted then we're having a white wedding and a new house next year. It's all planned. We don't want kids for at least five years, until we've got what we want, seen life a bit. We don't want to be tied down with a kid.'

'Well,' said Maddy primly, 'I don't know how you can. You've got no excuse not to marry the father and keep the baby.'

'Who asked you?' Ruth snapped.

'There's no need to speak like that. I only said....'

'Yes well, mind your own bloody business.'

Maddy clucked and flapped like a wet hen, bustling about folding clothes and muttering, but backed off.

Yvonne spoke up for the first time. 'Hey up, keep it quiet or we'll have Ma Thomas up here.' Yvonne was sensible and older, possibly in her early twenties, but still not smart enough to have grasped the idea of contraception.

'Nah, come on girls, slog it out, lets have a bit of excitement,' laughed Sandy, jumping on her bed. 'I'll be referee.' She pranced about, long blonde hair flying, stabbing punches at thin air. 'Yeah, man, yeah.' When she had everyone's attention she bounced giggling onto her back in the middle of the bed. The springs twanged.

The dinner bell rang and since it was not possible to argue in front of Mrs. Thomas the bickering stopped.

* * *

There were thirteen at the dinner table. They included Elsie and Florrie, two ladies who had lived with MrsThomas in the home almost twenty years. All three were now approaching sixty. Elsie, sharp and defensive, worked in the umbrella factory nearby. Florrie, with the innocently clear face of a fifteen year old, was a cleaner. Both had immense respect and affection for Mrs. Thomas. Widowed, childless, crippled with arthritis and a vicious smoker's cough, she seemed as sad a figure as the residents, though you'd as soon feel sorry for a grizzly bear. Florrie and Elsie spoiled her, as much as they could, with constant attention, cups of tea and any little errands they could do. Mrs. Thomas in turn was like a mother to them. She praised their kind actions, took an interest in their lives, imparted a sense of home and belonging in this shifting population of girls all immersed in their own troubles. The younger residents hardly noticed the two old ladies. Carol looked at Florrie and Elsie and wondered, will I be like them?

Josie arrived late and flew in to take her place at the table, patting her hair and apologising prettily to Mrs. Thomas. Josie was thirty four, a slim, dark-haired once-beautiful woman, tense to the point of neurosis. She had two exquisite children, both half African, in care. They had different fathers, both students now returned to Africa. She visited the children often, and took them out on little excursions but she was too unstable and too poor to make a home for them. When she wasn't with her children she was with her current African boyfriend. As she got older her fading beauty balanced less favourably with her neurotic temperament and she was having a hard time holding his attention. Josie seemed convinced that her life was glamorous and full of promise and never viewed her situation as the tragedy it surely was. Carol wondered what the future held for this little family, and hoped her baby would have a better life than Josie's children.

Two chairs at the table remained empty. They were for visitors.

Carol's mother had occupied one of them a few Saturdays before when she had delivered Carol to the home. The two women had taken the short bus ride from the city centre together, tension dissolving the further they travelled away from the central bus station and possible recognition. They found the road, and counted the houses until they found the right one, opposite a small grocers. Down the path, knock on the door, an anxious wait to get inside, away from prying eyes. Mrs. Thomas opened the door.

'Don't I know you? It's Nurse Clark isn't it?'

'Sister Thomas?' Carol's mother looked as if she hoped the floor would open and swallow her up.

Mrs. Thomas had been that semi-deity, a ward sister, at the hospital where Mrs. Stone had done her nursing training. After all the lengths she'd gone to to preserve secrecy, shut out calamity, here she was face to face with the last person she could have expected. The fragile shell of self-respect crumbled, and she wept.

Mrs. Thomas invited her to stay for lunch.

As the slices of cold belly pork, dishes of bubble and squeak and jars of pickle were passed round the tears flowed and she dabbed at her eyes with her hanky. By the time rice pudding was handed round, the hanky was sodden, reduced to a rag from being twisted in her mother's anguished fingers, and the sobbing was becoming demented. Carol tried to eat but couldn't swallow.

The twelve girls at the table, all strangers, were polite and tried not to show they'd noticed the crying. They carefully avoided staring and spoke very little, and then in hushed voices. In the end it had been a relief to see her mother leave to catch the train back to the village, leaving her to find out for herself how to fit into this strange new community.

Now, after grace, and the serving of a plain but substantial meal, Mrs. Thomas presided over the dinner-table talk. Everyone was included, recently departed residents enquired after, new babies of ex-residents mentioned, each separate and isolated person was drawn into the circle. New girls discovered the routines for ante-natal visits, finding jobs, registering with doctors, registering unemployed, moving on to mother and baby homes. The depressed were cheered up, the transgressors rebuked, and the business of the home forwarded another day.

* * *

It was early evening, after dinner, and dark outside. Mrs. T. was safely in her bed-sitting room. Jeanette was upstairs, taking her turn on the bath rota. With one bathroom and fourteen residents everyone was allowed fifteen minutes three times a week. Florrie and Elsie were upstairs at the top of the house in their one-room two-person household. Josie was out, probably working on her next baby. The rest of the girls settled like a flock of plump pigeons round the small kitchen coal fire, reading, sewing, doing their nails or each other's hair, knitting baby clothes, anything to avoid going up to the chilly bedroom. Carol sat with them, lying back in the deep comfortable armchair which she'd bagged, reading a book, 'Little Women', which rested comfortably on top of the steadily growing bump, part of the group but detached from it. She was wearing the new maternity pinafore dress she had made herself. There were some in C & A but they were six guineas. The pattern hadn't been difficult to follow. With a pinafore dress you could wear it every day with different blouses and jumpers underneath.

There was an unspoken agreement not to pry into other people's background, especially where they came from, but otherwise the conversation was easy and relaxed. It was a temporary refuge from all the worries of family, babies, uncertainty, decisions, and the knowledge that they were part of a process in which they had no choice.

The kitchen was dark and warm. Two low-watt lamps and the firelight cast soft shadows. Despite the battered furniture and worn rugs it was cosy too. The rain lashed down outside, beating on the window panes, making the kitchen seem safer and warmer. There was no television just a radio, and men were never seen here.

The conversation meandered but returned inevitably to babies, birth, stitches, stretch marks and the comparative effectiveness of pethidine or gas and air. Old wives tales were mixed up with information from the booklet which they'd all received from the ante-natal clinic. Adoption was at the centre of everyone's mind but it was a vague event in the future, and no-one had any concrete information beyond the obvious. Though they were all pregnant, none of them had personal experience of babies. At six months girls moved on, the baby was born, and six weeks later the new parents took it away. There was much discussion about how girls who were known to Yvonne and Maddy, but not to more recent arrivals, had reacted to this. Many of them, having had their babies, did not want to give them up for adoption, but there was little choice in the matter. Mothers rarely brought their babies back to visit in Bedale Road.

Jeanette returned with a towel round her wet hair trailing cloying clouds of Coty L'aimant. The belt of her dressing gown was tied round the widest point of her bump, and she resembled a gigantic pink Easter Egg. She embarked on a long story about her baby's father, who was a policeman, her mother, who thought he wasn't good enough, and a party at which Jeanette had flirted with another bloke so much it had started a fight. She had no regard for peace and quiet and luxuriated in her position at the centre of strife, preferably of her own making so that she was in control.

Alice told them a true ghost story. Voices were lowered and they all huddled nearer the fire.

'Do you believe in ghosts?' asked Ruth of no-one in particular.

'No - I would if I saw one,' Yvonne replied.

'Has anyone ever seen one?' Carol asked. Mostly she sat and listened.

'Yes - my Aunty Mary,' offered Alice, referring to her story.

'No, I mean yourself.'

'I think I could believe in them - I know people who think they've seen one,' Jeanette replied.

'If there were any, there would be one in this house,' said Carol.

They all nodded agreement, and one or two glanced nervously into the darker corners of the room. Dark, old, spooky, with lots of unhappy people, even tragedies, this house would surely have a ghost if they existed at all.

'No, you never see them, they're not here,' said Maddy firmly, wanting it to be true, but reluctant to go to bed first and be alone.

'What's that then, moving under that chair?' Sandy was always teasing, but she looked serious enough now. She pointed to a dark corner, rising from her stool and moving away. 'There, under Yvonne's chair.'

'Ooh, you bugger!' Yvonne jumped up, agile despite her advanced state of pregnancy, and moved quickly to the other side of the table. Alice and Jeanette clambered on their chairs squealing.

'It's a ghost.'

'It must be a little one if it's under a chair.'

'It's running towards the fireplace.'

'Bloody hell, look at the speed of it.'

'Ghosts don't move as fast as that.'

'It's not a ghost. Don't be daft,' Ruth yelled, standing on her chair and pointing. 'It's a spider.' She was laughing, but still didn't get down.

'Do spiders have ghosts?' asked Alice, worried and confused.

'Oh God, oh God I hate spiders. How big is it?' moaned Kay the quarter Red Indian.

'I don't know. But it's eating a mouse,' replied Ruth, almost peeing herself laughing.

None of them were really scared, but it was a diversion.

Mrs. Thomas wheezed in. Silence descended, and a certain sheepishness.

'What's going on? Why are you all standing on chairs? Get down at once. What's the matter? A spider? Silly girls. Give me a broom.' She walloped the spider and swept its carcass into a dustpan then threw it into the fire where it crackled and burst into green flames. 'Kay, put the milk on. Such silliness. Ruth - get the biscuits out please. And you should know better than to stand on chairs in your state Yvonne. Cocoa everyone? No, Alice you can't have tea, cocoa is better for your baby. Ghost stories - really. No, we don't have ghosts here. Nonsense.'

In bed later, in the silent room with seven sleepers, Carol thought about the people in her new life which had replaced so completely the old one. Thin columns of pale street light shone in between the curtains at the tall windows, falling onto the beds opposite. The baby fluttered gently, a soft butterfly wing. Her days fitted a crowded pattern full of people from waking to sleeping, but no one person was close, or a real friend, no-one and nothing touched her inside where she was numb, her feelings shut off to protect them. She didn't cry much now, but she didn't feel much at all. It was like living in a cotton-wool ball, and reality was somewhere else.

Where would they all end up? Where would Rob be now? Did he think of her? Carol's thoughts wheeled back to the weekend before she'd left home. It was after dark, an early autumn fog mixed with coal smoke hung about the streets. She had felt a sudden need for some fresh air, and had thrown on her old school blazer and set off to walk down the village to visit Auntie Joan. The privet shadows round the corner from the house were dark. A piece of shadow detached itself and became a huge figure in soldier's uniform. Steel-shod boots clicked on the paving as he stepped towards her and called her name. The dark curly hair had been shorn to bristles, throwing his features into alien prominence. The severe line of a black beret dissected the forehead and increased the strangeness. It was some stranger pretending to be Rob. Carol's heart lurched, and she avoided his touch.

'I want to talk to you,' he muttered hoarsely.

'Okay,' she agreed, unsure whether or not it was a good idea. He fumbled for a cigarette packet and matches, then sucked deeply on the smoke. They walked quietly for a while and she told him the truth about the baby, the adoption and the plans to keep it all secret. No matter what her parents thought, he deserved to know. He said he loved her, and they would get married, but he knew they couldn't, they were only words. He had nothing practical to offer. He had no more idea of how to deal with this than she had. They had nowhere to live, no money, needed consent to marry, and neither of them had the confidence to face her father, his rage and withering scorn. They cried and argued and the hopelessness of the situation pushed them further apart. The physical hunger and excitement which had first drawn them together died in the face of adult responsibility, and there was nothing to carry them any further, except empty romantic words. They parted, and Carol closed her mind to his memory, but her body was not so easy to control. For a few moments she remembered vividly her baby's father - not just his physical appearance, but the warmth of his arms round her, the laugh in his flecked brown eyes , his affection and his kisses - and the way he'd failed completely to stand up to her Dad.

Now if that had been the boy in the film, with his lovely smile, his assurance and charm, he'd have handled it differently. He wouldn't have been put off so easily. But then, in a film, she wouldn't be pregnant.

The baby's gentle movements settled down. In waves of loneliness and longing for something vague but not obtainable, Carol drifted off to sleep, curled into a ball. The tears soon dried, but it was all still there the following day.

* * *

'Why do you want the job?' the woman at the other side of the desk in the dark wood and glass office asked. Beyond the fluted glass partition a typewriter clattered into the drowsy mid-afternoon silence.

'I need the money.'

'What did you do since leaving the WRAF?' Crisp white blouse, boring perm, hands folded neatly under upholstered ample bosom - women like her didn't have breasts - red lipstick. No warmth.

'I spent some time at home with my mother.'

'You know it's a permanent job? We don't want someone who will leave in four months.'

'Yes.'

'Would you be able to stay?' She looked directly into Carol's eyes, her expression carefully neutral, watchful.

Lie. Lie. Eyes averted, blushing deeply, squirming inside, Carol replied, 'Well, yes, er yes.'

'There's no reason you'd leave?'

'No.' The woman looked at the papers on her desk, checking the letter of application.

'You live in Bedale Road I see.' She knew.

'Yes.'

'Okay, we'll get in touch. We have to interview another four girls this afternoon.'

Humiliated, Carol held her stomach in as much as possible as she left the office, but even she had to admit the woman could probably tell. Not many would miss it now

* * *

'How are you? Are you alright?'

'I'm fine, considering.'

'Did you have a good journey?'

'Yes, it were alright. How are you getting on? Mrs. Stone nodded at Carol's middle. 'You're putting some weight on. How much do you weigh now?'

Carol eased herself more comfortably into the ancient leather armchair. She felt her mother's eyes piercing the loose dress to voraciously gobble up every detail of her shape, and shrank from the possessively depersonalising hunger.

'Eleven stone eight. I was weighed at the ante-natal clinic at the hospital last week.'

'Were there many there?'

Carol correctly interpreted this question and gave the information her mother was seeking. 'No, only about six, and no-one I knew.' She tried to change the subject.

'How is everyone at home?'

Mrs. Stone's face clouded over with bitterness. 'They're all alright. I ran into your Auntie Joan at the market last Friday. She was asking if you'd be home for Christmas. Nosy bugger - I'm not telling her anything. Her and your Grandma. It's none of their business. Your Grandma was asking our Linda about you, trying to find out where you were. But our Linda doesn't know anything. I've told her you're on duty over Christmas. I'm not having them know anything about it - my kids are as good as theirs any day, if not better. Your Auntie Joan she can't even cook a proper Sunday dinner and your Grandma has no idea how to keep house. They're not looking down on us. Bloody Margaret has had everything, she's never wanted for anything, they treat her like a little queen. They're not looking down on my family. We're as good as they are any day.'

The guilt of causing all this bitterness sat in a hard miserable ball in the middle of Carol's chest. Life had been so unfair to her mother, giving her a husband who was more interested in his pigeons than his wife or children. She had always wanted to protect her mother from unhappiness and from her father, now she herself was the cause of grief.

Silence fell on the overcrowded little room and the radio could be heard faintly from the kitchen next door. It was Matt Munroe singing 'Softly, softly'. Rob had requested it for her on the camp radio when she was doing basic training. The words were loving and romantic. The gas fire spluttered and rain pelted gently on the window behind the lace curtain. The oddments of furniture, solid Victorian pieces donated by the benefactors and highly polished every week by the succession of girls on the cleaning rota, gleamed in the gloom. The little sitting-room was only ever used for visitors, and was stifled with the weight of years of visits by parents and close family friends to the girls who found a home here for a few weeks of their lives. Sometimes the visitors were kind and loving, trying to bring cheerfulness and friendliness from the outside world, like bedside visitors to a hospital. Often they were quiet, creeping in and out anonymously, singly or in pairs.

Carol's only visitor was her mother. No-one else knew she was here except her father, and he never came. She didn't want him to anyway.

'Has my dad said anything?.

'No.'

'Did he know you were coming?'

'Yes.' Nothing more. 'So you're, what did you say? Eleven stone eight?'

'Yes.'

'Well last time I was here you said you had trouble with your brassiere not fitting. Have your breasts got bigger?' Her eyes raked Carol's body as she reached for a large shopping bag. 'So I got you this.' She pulled out a paper bag and from it extracted a huge garment of white cotton with lots of seams, hooks and eyes, flaps, peepholes and straps.

Carol cringed inside, repulsed by the semi-medical old-ladyishness of the thing.

'What is it?' She didn't reach for it.

'It's a nursing bra. You'll need it after the baby's born but you can wear it before like an ordinary bra. Is your milk coming in yet?' Mrs. Stone placed the contraption on Carol's lap.

'What?' Picking the garment up gingerly, she hardly heard the question.

'Have you got milk in your breasts?' Mrs. Stone demanded in her best nurse's voice.

'No. I don't know, I haven't looked,' Carol whispered.

'Well, you will. You'll have to wash your flesh well when it does, keep yourself clean. These pads need washing every day an' all.' Each cup of the bra had a detachable cotton towelling pad, and there was a spare pair.

'Right.'

'Have your spots cleared up?'

'A bit. I've still got a few.'

'Well drink a lot of water. Flush your kidneys. Do you drink your milk allowance?'

'We give the tokens to Mrs. Thomas. The milk's used for cooking and drinks.'

'Right. I've brought you some cakes as well. Here you are.' She handed over a big biscuit tin. Carol opened it - an iced chocolate sponge with buttercream filling, half a fruit cake, some scones and a slab of iced Bakewell tart.

'Thanks. That's nice.'

'And I got you these.' Two huge pairs of white aertex bloomers.

'Thank you.' Carol was nearly in tears for some reason she didn't understand to do with the hideousness of the bra and pants.

'What are you looking like that for? You'll have to have these things. I don't know, I wish to God this had never happened. I'm at my wits end. I come off nights, and I've got your Grandma and your Auntie Joan and their nosy questions, and the worry of it all. I think I'm going mad. I saw Rob's mother last week giving me a funny look.'

Carol looked up.

'They say he's got a new girl-friend. A lass in the army. Good luck to him I say. If he's got somebody else he won't be trying to find you. The less anybody knows the better. Anyway, how are you love?'

Carol burst into tears.

Mrs.Thomas, hearing the sobs, popped her head round the door and offered tea, which Yvonne brought in shortly on a tray. Yvonne glanced up at Carol's face as she put the tray down, noticing the red eyes, and went back to report to the other girls in the kitchen next door. Mrs. Stone had closed the shutters again, raising her impenetrable, impersonal don't-come-close-to-me shield against pity or judgement. No-one was going to feel sorry for her.

* * *

Raj was a student at the university, the son of a good friend of Mrs. Thomas's, the substitute for the child she never had. Mrs. Thomas lavished a mother's affection on Raj who was quiet, intelligent and unfailingly courteous.

Just before Christmas the household moved to new, more spacious premises, a reflection of the increased prosperity of the husbands of the committee. There was a big Christmas tree and traditional Christmas food.

Raj spent much of Christmas with Mrs. Thomas and the girls. He was the only man present when they all sat down to Christmas dinner. Mrs. Thomas, old and wrinkly, became charming and youthful, wreathed in gracious smiles.

After dinner phone calls were received from Delhi and from some of the parents. Thoughts turned to home and family. Maddy's parents visited briefly with piles of gifts for their darling daughter. Yvonne and Alice became tearful. Carol wondered what they were all doing at home. Mrs Thomas quickly began the party games and no-one was allowed to bow out, or be alone. Raj produced a little heap of wrapped parcels each containing a tiny gift from India. He must have asked his mother to send them. The winner of each game received a prize from him. Mrs. Thomas's was a lovely silver filigree butterfly brooch.

Carol, after a good bit of manoeuvring on the part of Mrs. Thomas, won 'Pass the Parcel' and received a small heavy object, inexpertly wrapped. Inside she found a small terracotta elephant standing on its back legs, trunk curled over its head, painted in a white pattern on black background, an incongruous touch of the exotic, speaking of hot sun and bright colours, far away from this place. It contrasted with the cold darkness in her head, surrounded by people but lonely and isolated. Here was the spacious sitting room, the enormous Christmas tree, the flock of shabby girls in their cheap cotton maternity smocks, and the sense of being displaced from life, going through the actions of normal people but not feeling real, like a machine with faulty mechanism. The little elephant would be a direct link to the time when her baby was a part of her, safe inside her, hers alone, to stay with her and share her life.

On New Year's Eve it snowed. At midnight Carol stood by the front door with Alice, holding a piece of bread, a piece of coal, and a shilling, waiting to be let in. The frost nipped sharply and twinkled like diamonds on the fresh snow. She looked up at the cold brilliant stars and wondered where she'd be next year. The baby stirred. She or he would be eight months old, and with the new family.

Carol never doubted that the new family would be much better at giving her baby a loving home than she could ever be. Her child would not be like Josie's children. She had no idea what would happen to her, where she would go, what she would do, when it was all over, whether she'd end up like Florrie and Elsie, or even Mrs. Thomas, but it wouldn't be back home to the village and her family. She couldn't face them. Shame and anger were building a barrier which grew stronger. Somewhere inside a rock-hard decision was being made, never to depend on them again. Never let anyone control your life. Never trust anyone. Never be dependent. If she had any control now, this would not be happening.

She thought of her dad's rage, her mother's hurt pride, Rob and his new girl-friend. The adoptive parents were a protected haven in which to place her baby, a place of love, and a way of life which was civilised and caring, not full of argument and bitterness, threats and bullying. The baby would have nice things, be treated with consideration, have a lovely home, never lack for anything, and would be happy. She - or he - would have a good life, two parents and a loving family. Carol had complete faith in the adoption society who would choose these two perfect human beings for her baby.

On January 14th, after her 19th birthday Carol packed her bags. After many goodbyes - not too sad, because there was one in this household every few weeks, and they were used to it - her mother collected her. Carol buttoned the winter coat tightly round her huge bump and picked up her handbag and two carrier bags, whilst her mother took the suitcase which still had her RAF number on the side and they made their way through the snow to the station. There was a moment of panic when Carol saw, on the platform, someone she thought she recognised, a girl she had once worked with briefly. She quickly hid round the corner of the booking office and told herself that she was hardly recognisable now to someone who knew her a year before.

Together Carol and Mrs. Stone took the train to the unknown city where, some time in the next ten weeks, her baby would be born.

Chapter 3

1963

The spirit and influence of successive centuries came storming up the hill from the medieval cathedral, made a sharp left towards Wragby and, sometime in Victoria's reign, left behind it the time-warp world that was The Warren. While 'Dr. Who' conquered time travel on telly every Saturday night the sisters of the Church of England Mother and Baby Home put in a twenty four hour day and seven day week and kept the calendar fixed somewhere around the 1940's.

'This can't be it,' said Carol's mother as they passed through the wrought-iron gates in the high stone wall which surrounded the grounds. With every step Carol and her mother took up the gravel drive towards the sheer grey-stone walls, the sights and sounds of the 1960's became more muted and distant. Carol heard the bird-song which echoed in the towering bare branches of elms and melancholy thickets of rhododendrons. High narrow windows overlooked a snow-filled sunken garden. Like a prison, Carol thought, or a castle.

By the time they were admitted through the vast oaken front door into the bare, gracefully proportioned hall, with their array of carrier bags and tatty suitcase, it was easy to imagine a Bertie Wooster descending the broad and imposing staircase, sherry in one hand, monocle in another, braying, 'Hello, old chap,' while a neat little maid in white cap and apron struck the huge bronze gong to announce dinner.

Instead the door was opened to Carol and her mother by a young girl who appeared to be at least ten months pregnant. The only visible uniform was the traditional navy dress, white cap and cuffs worn by the woman who sped lightly down the final bend of the stairs to greet them, smiling with the sweetness of a wingless angel gliding down from heaven.

It was Matron. She whisked them into her office and took down details. Mrs. Stone was given tea and despatched home, and Carol was shown to the little bedroom she was to share with five other girls.

Once again she was with strangers, all links with previous existences severed.

Well at least she wouldn't waste time trying to make friends with girls who turned out to have a special interest in other girls, as she had done once in the WRAF. Chances were none of these would be lesbians.

* * *

Two days later Carol sat with Matron in the Sisters' sitting room overlooking the sunken garden. Dust motes danced silently in the sunshine. The furnishings, classical and shabby, had probably been there since the house was built. A bowl of blue hyacinths on a low polished table filled the air with heady perfume, which reminded Carol of childhood walks in bluebell woods, when everything was so much simpler. Matron had on her lap an open folder containing forms and sheets of paper.

She began with the easy stuff, full name, date of birth, address. Then the questions became more personal, about 'the father'.

'How long have you known him?'

'Since I was sixteen,' Scribble.

'Have you had a relationship with any other men?' asked Matron softly.

'No, have you?' thought Carol. 'I had one or two boyfriends before but not like Rob. He's the only serious one,' she said. Scribble scribble.

'Have you had intercourse with any other men?' she continued, her tone conversational and pleasant.

'No.'

'Did you have intercourse with him once, or more often?' so pleasant and civilised ...and bloody nosy.

Why did she want to know that? Was this a 'moral examination' and the choice of parents would depend on the answer? If you give the wrong answer your baby gets dissolute parents? No, no, all the parents would be C of E, all good people, all morally sound.

'More than once.' Scribble.

A lot more than once. The first time, significantly it now seemed, on Mother's Day. Carol looked down to avoid Matron's watchful, probing gaze.

Other questions followed. Did you think of getting married? Why didn't you? Do you have brothers and sisters? Is your health good? Where were you educated? What were your exam results?

'If you wish you may write a note which will be put into your records, about why you have chosen to have your baby adopted. Would you like to do that?'

'Will my baby see it? One day?'

'Possibly. It's hard to say. These are official, legal documents, but it is possible.'

Left alone with pen and paper, after deep thought and lots of false starts, Carol wrote:

'It is unfair to my baby to try and bring her up my self as I can't afford to keep her and give her a normal upbringing, either financially or otherwise. She would have no father as would her friends, and I think that a fath (crossed out) father is an important person in a child's life. When I compare what I have to offer her with what adoptive parents would, such as a proper home, the love of two parents, and a happy family life, I realise it is much better for her.' She wondered if this message represented her true thoughts, or what she'd been told. The baby should be born in ten weeks, but it might be twenty years before he or she read this. If ever.

* * *

Carol lay back in a faded chintz armchair by the chipped marble fireplace. Quiet conversations in other parts of the large room lapped the edges of her consciousness. A coal fire flickered and glowed behind the latticed mesh of the fireguard. Beyond the tall mullioned windows at the end of the room black branches waved in the steady breeze, their roots one floor below at the back of the house. The sky was a perfect dazzling blue. Sunlight bounced off the snow and reflected onto the high ceiling revealing the previously unnoticed network of cracks and delicate swags of cobwebs. After so many weeks the snow seemed permanent. The radio murmured a familiar signature tune, an introduction to 'Down Your Way' which had followed on from 'Housewives Choice'.

A peaceful blankness filled Carol's mind, induced by the hypnotic flickering of sunlight through branches, flames through lattice, the comfort and pervading warmth of the armchair and the fire. Her body, full and heavy, boneless, was soothed into blissful relaxation, and her mind floated free in the transcendental haze, detached from sensation and the worries of the future.

Nothing mattered - she wanted nothing, needed nothing, had nothing. There was no past, no future, and the present was held in a warm, slow-moving daze. Only the next moment had any significance.

The baby was ten days overdue, the head so far down that walking was reduced to a wide waddle, the pressure in her pelvis constant. She was tired, too, of living inside her heavy body, lugging it around, up and down stairs, in and out of the bath, in and out of clothes, on and off chairs.

Across the wide expanse of threadbare carpet the door burst open. A large wooden trolley clattered in laden with the unvarying burden of battered aluminium jugs of cocoa, stacks of thick white cups and saucers and plates of malted shortbread biscuits.

Two mums, Tatty Liz and Jan, steered it to the middle of the room. Tatty Liz called out cheerfully, 'Come on ladies, cocoa is served.' Cliff Richard came on the radio singing 'Lucky Lips' and they joined in the chorus, 'With lucky lips you'll always have a baby in your arms,' then disappeared, laughing, back to the kitchen.

'Thanks, Cliff, just what I want,' called Tatty Liz. The trolley was surrounded by a crowd of jostling very heavily-pregnant girls reaching like starving orphans for cocoa and biscuits.

Matron entered and clapped her hands for attention. The sunlight played on her saintly white marble face, free of any trace of make-up. With her white cap, which caught the sun like a halo, and nursing uniform of dark Madonna-blue she could have been a figure in one of the stained glass windows in the cathedral nearby. Turned sideways and laid flat she would suitably adorn a medieval tomb without any change whatsoever. Her posture was stiffly upright and perfect - a reflection of her mind, no doubt, thought Carol.

She wondered what could have happened to make a woman who was still fairly young and reasonably attractive choose to renounce the outside world and live here in nun-like seclusion. Someone had mentioned a fiance killed in the war, someone else said she was from a rich Quaker family, another said she'd had a baby herself, and was working out her guilt, but no-one knew. She had nice hair and eyes. If she wore make-up and feminine clothes and loosened up a bit, met some men, learned to smile more convincingly - but at the idea of Matron flirting the imagination closed down. She carried a surface brittle brightness and cheeriness, like a shell protecting the human being inside.

Matron announced the relaxation classes for the afternoon. She reminded them all to bring a pillow, spoke a few words to selected individuals, and marched briskly off to other duties.

Over in the corner by the window-seat a group of girls who had been sitting with heads close together suddenly broke apart with loud sniggering laughs at something Maureen had been telling them. Maureen had been a taxi-driver. She had a repertoire of dirty stories and jokes and an appropriate vocabulary for delivering them. She was really funny, but crude.

Carol felt her stomach tightening in the familiar uncomfortable spasm which would eventually become labour. 'Is this it?' she thought in panic. 'I'm not ready, I can't do it.' The tightness ebbed away. Not a pain, not at all. Just tightness. She slowly edged her way out of the armchair.

Carol poured three cups of cocoa and, balancing one on top of another, took them through the hall into the Green Room. Dora waddled after her with another three cups. The Green Room was much smaller than the big sitting-room, its walls distempered a depressing doctor's-waiting-room green, the floor covered in dark shiny lino, the furniture darker and shinier old leather sofa and chairs. Jill and Jean stood in front of a tiny spluttering gas fire, less cheerful than the coal fire in the larger sitting-room, which gave just enough heat to take the chill off the room. A small conservatory opened off, Matron's private domain, full of cold and browning plants which were fighting a losing battle against the prolonged winter.

Most of the girls had morning cocoa in the big sitting-room. These few chose the lesser comforts of the Green Room as the price of the luxury of choosing their companions. Membership was informal and unenforceable, but to be made welcome in the Green Room you had to be invited. The tarty, loud-mouthed girls were not invited. The quieter, more sensible, middle-class girls were the self-selected green room occupants, Jean their snob-in-chief. Carol had been invited in soon after she arrived and joined them without realising the significance of the invitation. She still felt she was here under false pretences, but the smaller circle seemed less intimidating, more secure than the larger group, so she stayed.

There was no choice in any other aspect of life in The Warren. Beds were in crowded dormitories of six to eight for pregnant girls, and Matron decided who slept where. Companions in the sunlit first floor lying-in-room were those who gave birth at the same time. Mothers all slept together in the huge downstairs dormitory which opened onto the sunken garden, next to the nursery. Dining-room places were allocated by the Sisters, household duties assigned for morning and evening, bath-times controlled by a strict rota, relaxation classes arranged for weekly afternoons, visitors allowed at set times. Nurseries were out of bounds except to mothers at feeding time and bath-times. For two hours in the afternoons girls could choose to go for a walk, go shopping in town or, later, push their babies out in one of the ramshackle donated prams. Except that the snow had been so deep for so long that it was impossible to get a pram out of the door.

Brigit burst in carrying her two-week-old daughter. The baby was tightly wrapped, practically mummified, a neat little parcel with a tiny sleeping face peeping out at one end. Brigit's short dark hair was brushed severely back from her face, and she carried a faintly antiseptic smell as a result of her personal war on germs. She prowled round the room restlessly. She wasn't allowed up here with the baby and should have been downstairs with the other mums in the bottom nursery. However, her Irish temper was well known and respected, and no-one was likely to start telling her what she should be doing.

'How's the baby this morning?' enquired Jean.

'Sure, she's fine. Sleeping like a little angel.'

'Can she breathe in that shawl? She's wrapped up so tightly she can't move,' Jean asked.

'Oh indeed she can. We wrapped the babies up like this on the maternity ward where I nursed. It makes them feel secure, like they're back in the womb, and they don't cry so much. See.' Her baby remained sound asleep despite being suddenly whisked upright. 'Any sign of yours yet?'

Jean looked down at herself; she hadn't an ounce of fat on her tall thin frame and her bump was low and compactly rounded, like a football stuck under her jumper.

'No, not a murmur. He's decided to stay put where it's nice and warm.'

'Have you heard from his daddy yet?'

Jean's baby's father was an army officer. He'd decided he wanted nothing to do with the baby, and didn't really believe it was his. Brigit's was a doctor who, she claimed, had got her drunk at a party and had his wicked way. He, of course, said this was untrue. She was very bitter about him. She'd been dismissed, and he'd been promoted.

Jean did a lady-like pretend spit to one side.

'No - the swine. What about you Carol? You can't be much longer. How do you feel?'

'Big. I can hardly get up the stairs. Ten days overdue.'

'I heard Joanne went into labour last night,' said Angela from the depths of the armchair. Her half-empty cup and saucer stood on top of her bump while she rested her arms by her side. 'She's in the Labour Room now. The lying-in room is full. Pam Robins had hers yesterday. A little boy. She screamed the place down.'

Brigit prowled round and round the sofa holding her sleeping daughter firmly in the crook of her arm.

'Yes, she would,' said Jean, who thought Pam was the type of person who made the Green Room necessary.

'Hey look at that. Would you believe it? The little rascal's just kicked my cocoa off,' said Angela, mopping her smock under which the baby did a few back-flips and hand-stands.

Matron strode in, saintly expression serene as ever, her smile calm and remote.

'Good morning ladies. Now Brigit, what are you doing up here? Come on now, off you go back to the nursery.' Brigit said nothing, smiled charmingly at Matron and then ignored her. 'Ah, Carol, still here? How are you dear? Any contractions yet?'

'No, not really. It keeps tightening up now and then but nothing serious.'

'Well, we'll give it a few more days, then we'll have to try paraffin oil and orange juice. That always works.'

Carol looked dubious. 'What do you do with that then?'

'First thing in the morning, a small glass, you drink it down and hey presto - works like a dream.'

'Sounds foul,' Carol murmured to herself, feeling queasy at the thought of it.

'Oh by the way, your mother phoned again last night to see how you were. Ten days late now, tut tut.' She shook her head in mock reproof. 'Oh,' Carol hadn't seen her mother for nearly three weeks. Probably the heavy snow had something to do with it.

'Yes. She phoned at the weekend as well. Dora, how long do you have to go? I think you must have two in there.' She smiled sweetly at her own joke, head tipped slightly to one side like a little bird.

'Two weeks Matron. I was twelve pounds at birth, and ten of my eleven brothers and sisters were too. I think mine will be a big baby.' Where did Dora learn to be so humble, Carol thought. Her bump really was gigantic.

'Good gracious. Your poor mother. I think you're right, it will be big. It will probably come out walking and talking.' Another joke, with accompanying smile. 'Now girls, we have parents coming in at 11.00 so no-one in the Hall please, use the back stairs. Alright? Fine. Also, prayers in the Chapel at 7.0 to which you are more than welcome.' She directed a beaming smile reassuringly at no-one in particular. 'Two more minutes, Brigit, then back to the nursery please.' She left, having cleverly asserted her authority without losing face by staying to see it ignored.

'Who's leaving today, then?' asked Angela.

'Jane. Sure didn't you see her last night at dinner? She was crying all day yesterday,' said Brigit. She laid the baby on the sideboard, lit a cigarette, which was strictly forbidden, and picked up her baby again.

'Is anyone with her?' asked Jean.

'Yes, Sister Dearborn's down in the bottom nursery with her, and two of the girls,' Brigit replied. She drew deeply on the cigarette and plumes of smoke curled menacingly from her nostrils.

'She's knitted her baby a lovely matinee coat and bought her a really pretty dress,' said Dora softly.

'It makes no difference,' snapped Brigit as if it didn't matter to her at all. 'They undress the baby and give it to the mother wrapped up in a shawl, like it's new-born. She brings her own baby clothes to dress it in.' She crossed her arms across her baby and hugged the little girl to herself tightly.

'Yes, well, even so, you can't let your baby go wearing Warren clothes, can you?' Dora said sadly.

'What happens if you buy your baby, say, a locket, or a bracelet? Do they let them keep them?' asked Carol.

'No, nothing. Not even a nappy,' Brigit's reply was fierce, as if she had made the rules herself. ' Sister takes the baby up to the Sisters' sitting room next to the Hall. The baby is undressed and taken through the door into Matron's office' her voice took on a mocking tone, 'where the happy parents are waiting. Their prayers are answered.' She paused. 'The door to that is near the front door, in the lobby - they go out tru dat,' she said quietly.

'So they don't walk back through the main hall with the baby?' asked Carol.

'No.'

Brigit seemed to know all the details. She was a mother now and the mothers were closer to all those things. It seemed that Carol would not see the parents who had been selected for her baby.

Carol thought she could ask Gwen. She'd shared cleaning tasks with her, and she was the nearest thing to a friend Carol had in this place, until Gwen had had her baby six days before, and moved to the mothers' dormitory. Now Carol only saw her briefly at meal-times across the room on the mothers' table, and there was no chance to talk.

Carol had compared notes with Gwen about the interview with Matron. When Gwen had been asked the question about her bonking habits she had replied, 'Well, it didn't feature regularly in the week's entertainment.'

It was a bit lonely without her. They had discussed plans to go to Australia when it was all over.

At lunch-time in the crowded little dining room Carol sat, as usual, facing big, dim, slack-jawed Brenda. As Brenda shovelled marmalade sponge pudding and custard into her mouth a big blob fell, trickled down her jumper and came to a stop upon her ample boobs. Squinting down through her thick glasses, she ran her finger up the trail and scooped the pudding into her mouth, already bearing traces of food, then rubbed the remaining snail-trail on her jumper with a flattened palm. Her loose breasts wobbled wildly under this assault. Brenda's tongue gathered most of the remaining food smeared round her mouth and she smacked her lips and burped. Carol showed her disgust in her face, then caught the disapproving glance of Sister Dearborn sitting opposite on the staff table, and looked away, ashamed. It was cruel to be unkind to Brenda - she couldn't help it.

The plates were cleared away, all the left-overs scraped onto one dish. Sister Scott supervised, crooning, 'Sheer waste, sheer waste,' at the sight of the horrid pile of rejected food. Her cold fishy eyes blinked slowly, bloodless dry lips parted in a humourless smile. 'Sheer Waste' was her nick name.

After lunch the pregnant girls collected in the main lounge each carrying a pillow from their own bed. Lying in rows across the cleared space of the floor, they spent an hour doing breathing exercises, being taught how to give birth without pain, a trick they somehow all failed to acquire. After relaxation class Carol climbed the grand main staircase to the first floor landing. On impulse she crept to the door of the nursery next to the lying-in room. The room was quiet and dimly lit, empty except for a little row of cots, eight cotton shapes slung on wheeled metal frames, each containing a tiny baby. Gwen's baby must be one of them. Curiosity impelled her to tip-toe in and look more closely. As she approached the first cot, Sister Scott came bustling in.

'What are you doing here? No-one is allowed in the nursery except mothers, and then only at feeding times. Come on, we can't have everyone bringing their germs in. We must think of the babies.' She clapped her hands together, smiled the cold fishy smile and made shooing gestures with opened palms.

Carol was ushered out, feeling guilty and disappointed. She hadn't held a baby since she was thirteen, when her cousin was born. Brigit wouldn't let anyone hold hers.

There was little opportunity for privacy at The Warren. The crowded, unheated room where Carol slept contained six metal-framed hospital beds, each of different design, and one ancient dressing-table. The lino floor was freezing in the cold winter weather. It took ages to get warm in bed at night. Most people slept in nighties with cardigans and bedsocks as well, and wandered about at bed-time carrying hot water bottles and looking like Ken Dodd's Diddy Men. This was the room she had been taken to when she first arrived. A quick, anxious check had revealed that there were no familiar faces, no-one from home. Gradually they had become individuals, superficially differentiated from each other. Roz was tall, curly-haired and lisped, and seemed to be constantly puzzled about how to deal with new situations. The youngest, Ann, was just sixteen and was herself adopted. Rosemary wrote often to her baby's father, a Spanish waiter she'd met very briefly on holiday. He spoke no English and her letters were returned unanswered. Rachel told stories about how rich and important her family were when they lived in Africa. She spoke with a very refined accent, her suitcase was old and battered, and she had no visitors.

Another was young and spoiled, the darling of her doting elderly parents who visited her frequently. Carol had only just got to know the girls in the last place, and didn't much want to know this lot. She had slipped quietly into their midst, listened to the chatter, read a lot, P.G. Wodehouse and Agatha Christie whose settings seemed like a distant opulent echo of The Warren, and gradually began to feel some sense of being one of them.

It was a particularly long winter. Snow fell freshly almost every day. The sense of isolation from the rest of the world was complete. Beyond the perimeter wall the traffic swished between slushy ruts, barely visible through snow-laden trees. Inside the business of the home continued its relentless course. Babies were born, fed, washed, meals eaten, prayers said, laundry and ironing done and put away. Visitors came and went, more snow fell.

Carol's mother visited once a fortnight. They would go out and walk down the hill and round the shops, returning in time for Carol to have tea and Mrs. Stone to catch the train home. There was no opportunity, as they stumbled over ice-glazed snow, in freezing winter winds, for a conversation beyond the superficialities, no habit of intimacy or closeness or communication.

The Warren was a Church of England home. Before each meal there was grace, and evening prayer meetings in the chapel twice a week for those who wished to attend, as well as the mandatory service on Sunday accompanied by embarrassingly unenthusiastic hymn-singing. Carol occasionally turned up to evening prayers to oblige Jean who liked to keep the Sisters' regard for the Green Room people.
Carol was never sure how many girls stayed at The Warren. It was a shifting population. Almost every week a baby was adopted and the mother returned to the outside world to pick up the threads, and every week new girls arrived, nervous and weepy, and were left to find their feet in the little community. There was no common denominator, beyond youth, pregnancy, and the absence of a father for the baby.

Some of the girls were more noticeable than others. Tatty Liz, for example, was pretty, not very bright, and dead common. Her hair was a smooth construction of beehive with French pleat, and was never taken apart. Unkindly, some people said she had mice in it. Others said that was a mean thing to say, they were only nits. Her big blue eyes were ringed in black lines, her eyelashes coated in thick layers of mascara which, to save wasting time and money, she rarely washed off. She had an uncontrolled temper and limited though powerful vocabulary. She made no secret of the fact that she'd had so many men she didn't know who was the father, or even what colour the baby would be. Julie was sweet, pretty, well-brought up by rich parents. Sophie was half Korean, with very feminine and graceful mannerisms. Angela was middle-class and had two very supportive friends who came to visit her. Judy was a Geordie and smoked addictively, despite being pregnant. Paula had huge blue eyes and dark hair and a wealthy father. Amy's baby's father was a black American airman. Hetty was a nurse, and was planning to pick up her career again afterwards, like Brigit. There was another Carol, a Meg, a Beth, a Wendy and others on the outer fringes of Carol's awareness whose names she never learned, each defined by superficial details.

Mothers and babies, new life, reproduction, nature triumphing over social convention and the teaching of the church. Carol wondered how the babies would grow up? Which would dominate, the characteristics of the natural father and mother or the upbringing and influence of new parents? What about intelligence, sense of humour, sensitivity, happiness, kindness, physical fitness, artistic ability? Behind the superficial chatter about whether a child looked like its mother - and it was surprising how often they did - were other deeper thoughts.
Jean and Angela, well spoken and civilised, maintained the confidence and good manners which were the direct result of their upbringing. Jean was a snob, but that wasn't an inherited trait. Tatty Liz's volatile temper and swearing were due to her inability to cope with stress; under normal circumstances she was amiable, just a bit insensitive and prickly. Her gross personal habits must be caused by her upbringing. If her baby looked like her it would be blue-eyed, fair and handsome. If

the parents brought the child up well, he could be happy and confident. Rob was handsome, though not Brain of Britain material. She had five 'O' levels, and knew enough to know she knew practically nothing. Brenda, on the other hand, was unintelligent, shambling and slow. If her baby boy developed into a teenage male Brenda, how disappointed the loving parents would be. Or maybe Brenda was like that because of the way she was treated as a little girl.

If that was true, how should children be treated to help them develop into the best they could be? Carol had seen young mothers in the city streets on Saturdays, walloping their whinging toddlers. Everyone was brought up in one family, with one experience, which they would then use on their children. Everyone thought their way was right, because they didn't know any other way.

Please God, give my child kind, loving and happy parents, thought Carol, and this was the only genuine prayer she ever prayed.

* * *

The bedroom was dark and silent except when the moon, shining fitfully from behind dark clouds, glittered on the frost flowers on the inside of the window-pane. Carol knew she had to get out of bed to go to the loo yet again. She'd been twice already and it was bloody cold out there. Her slippers would be like ice, the floor would be freezing, the air was cold, but she knew she'd have to get out of the warm cocoon before long. She pulled her dressing gown under the blankets to warm it up.

A glance at the clock showed that it was 4.30 am. Everyone was asleep. Matron was going to administer the dreaded paraffin and orange juice this morning, before breakfast.

No use putting it off. She had to go. Reluctantly she pushed back the blankets and with great difficulty put her legs over the side of the high bed and rolled upright. Her warm breath exhaled in silver clouds in the monochrome moonlight, and her skin shivered into goose-bumps. She struggled into her dressing-gown; her warm feet flinched from the icy floor as she groped for her slippers. The bump was so low she could hardly stand, and the cold made all her muscles clench tightly. She shuffled quietly towards the door and paused as the tightness increased, then carried on towards the bathroom when it relaxed again. Leaving the bathroom, her brain still fogged with sleep, the tightness gripped her again, leaving her breathless, and she stood leaning on the door-post waiting until it passed. She longed to get back into the warm bed. It wasn't until another fierce spasm began as she pulled back the blankets that it occurred to her that this might be it! The pain was more intense and had a forcefulness which previous tightnesses lacked. There was no doubt in her mind. Panic mingled with determination - no-one was going to do this for her, she was on her own.

She couldn't wake anyone up, it was too early. She decided to go round to the main landing and find the Sister on duty. Plenty of time. Could still be a false alarm.

The blue-shaded night-light glowed dimly on the landing. The door to the Delivery Room was closed, with a light showing underneath. Someone was in labour. They'd be busy, better not interrupt them. Perhaps there would be someone in the other place, what was it, the Labour Room. Yes. Go there. She shuffled across to the far end of the landing, pausing to let the next wave of pain ripple away. Shit, no-one in there. What now? The Delivery Room, that's where they all were. She'd have to knock and interrupt them. Slowly she began to lumber back. In the middle of the landing a fierce pain gripped her back, and she leaned heavily on the banister, gasping with shock, waiting for it to pass. She hadn't had an enema, or been shaved, or anything. In the middle of the pain, something warm began to trickle down her legs. The trickle increased to a steady unstoppable flow, which gathered on the lino into a puddle.

At that moment the Delivery Room door flew open. Sister Ryland, immaculate in green delivery gown and mask, sailed out and saw

Carol crouched over the banister in a puddle of broken waters. The good Christian sister exclaimed in annoyance, 'Oh, really, look at the mess. Couldn't you have made it to the bathroom?' She pulled the mask down under her chin and stood, pale lips compressed, hands on hips, looking at the puddle. The edges grew steadily and began to trickle between the banister rail, down, down into the darkened hall below.

'You stupid woman. Do you think I did it on purpose?' she wanted to shout, and heard her own voice murmuring, 'Sorry, sorry, I couldn't help it. Sorry.' Despite her best efforts her face crumpled, a huge lump formed in her throat and tears began to flow.

Sister Ryland either didn't notice or chose to ignore the tears, and Carol quickly wiped them away.

'Go back to your bedroom and pack your suitcase. Put your overnight things into your bag, and bring it to the Labour Room. You have plenty of time yet.' Sister Ryland vanished into the bathroom and reappeared with a mop and bucket. She sloshed the mop in the bucket and began to spread dirty water and amniotic fluid in wide sweeps across the lino. 'How long between contractions?'

'I don't know. I haven't timed it. Not that long.'

The suitcase was virtually packed already. Someone – Rosemary - woke up as she fumbled about for her toilet bag, helped her back to the Labour Room, and installed her on the narrow padded bed.
Girls, well-meaning but insignificant strangers, popped in before and after breakfast with offers of cups of tea, and to rub her back. Mothers gave expert reassurance born of recent experience. The pains increased and she noticed them less and less as she retreated into herself and became familiar with the nature of the sensation. When they became serious, the pregnant girls were shooed out so that they should not become alarmed by previewing their own fate. Various Sisters appeared to check progress and vanished again.

The birth in the Delivery Room was completed, the mother and her new baby moved into the lying-in room, and Carol was transferred across the landing to take her place. Her nightie was removed and replaced with a surgical gown, her legs hoisted into stirrups.

The sky was still dark in contrast to the pool of bright light beneath the green shade over the bottom of the delivery bed. A large uncurtained window at the far end bothered Carol for a while, but Matron assured her that there were only trees outside, no-one could see in. She soon ceased to notice details of her surroundings as her world shrank to encompass only the shocking unrelenting pain. She wouldn't have noticed if the entire top deck of the distantly passing bus stood up and waved.

Carol was aware of Matron and her instructions to pant, to hold back, to relax. There was a white-coated lady doctor somewhere down by her feet, a stranger who spoke only to the Sisters. Sister Scott tut tutted when Carol swore. 'Bloody hell, oh my God.' The immodest posture enforced by the stirrups ceased to matter and her mind became crystal clear and focussed on the immediate necessity of paying full attention to the pain.

When her body was seized with the almighty urge to push, nothing else existed. It didn't matter that she was surrounded by strangers, they were only shadows on the edge of the real world. All doubts about the future, keeping secrets, shame, vanished, blotted out by massive swamping shuddering pains, her body deciding quite independently how to respond, how to expel. It was savage and unbelievable, and it went on and on. Instruments clinked in metal dishes somewhere far away. She heard Matron say, 'The head is crowned,' and didn't know what she meant. She struggled to give birth, the baby struggled to be born. After centuries of grinding agony Matron's voice, disembodied and distant, gave encouragement, 'The head is born, one more push, and one more.' Then, a great hot slithering sloosh, sudden blessed cessation and, 'It's a little girl.'

Carol lay spread-eagled and limp whilst the attention of the Sisters was focussed somewhere beyond her knees. She heard an unhappy snuffling little cry.

Suddenly a small white-wrapped bundle was thrust into her arms and there at last was her tiny beautiful baby.

The whole world vanished away and Carol's entire existence was centred in her eyes as she drank in the awesome perfection of the minute little being. The baby nestled in the crook of Carol's right arm. Somewhere between laughing and crying she experienced a feeling of serene completeness and belonging.

The baby's eyes were closed, with long dark eye-lashes. Her skin was a soft warm peach, the head covered in dark fluff. One tiny fist peeped out. The perfection of the detail of nails, ears, nose was entrancing, magical. The warmth of the little baby seeped through the blanket into her arm, the weight made her real. Carol absorbed the curve of the forehead, the sweetly puckered little mouth, the roundness of the cheek. A great surge of joy and contentment filled her, as the months of detachment and disorientation dissolved away.

Every detail was etched forever in her consciousness, but the weight and warmth of the little bundle stayed with her most, left the greatest void by their eventual absence.

Matron took the baby and stood by the delivery bed whilst someone kneaded Carol's stomach to release the placenta. She said, 'Well, mum, what are you going to call her?'

Carol looked past Matron to the window. The sky was stained with pink light. Spring was beginning. She wanted to share the joy with someone else who thought it was important, who was aware of the enormity of the fact that her daughter existed. The Sisters were calm and matter of fact - kind but uninvolved. For them this was just one

more baby. There was none of the excitement, the adoration, the praise, the congratulations of other births. She wanted a name which made up for this. No name seemed good enough.
'Susan. I'll call her Susan.'

'Hello, Susan,' said Matron. 'I'm going to put you into your cot over here while we give your mum some stitches.'

From this moment on, the clock began ticking away the six weeks.

* * *

The lying-in room was spacious and sunny, pastel blue with matching bed-spreads, the best room in the whole house, and all six beds were occupied. Spring sunshine slanted in through the tall windows and a bowl of daffodils caught in the light glowed like molten gold. The nursery smells of milk and baby powder and the antiseptic smell familiar to hospitals mingled with hints of dinner which had just been cleared away. The girls in the beds chatted intermittently about nothing in particular. The quiet noises of the house drifted in through the half-open door as the girls downstairs returned from the dining-room. Feeding time had just finished. The babies were being changed in the nursery next door, and Sister Scott could be heard talking to them. Their cries had the distinctive new baby snuffle and wail, as if they were still practising.

Visiting time was about to begin.

Carol lay back on her pillows, thinking complicated, tortuous thoughts.

What would Rob think of his daughter if he was there? Would he care? He knew where she was. If he tried he could find them.

Was there any way she could keep the baby? Where could they live? Who would support them? How could she buy a pram, and baby clothes, and pay for rent and food, when she hadn't a penny? If she had to work, where could she leave the baby, who with? Would Susan be safe? If she became ill, what would happen to Susan?

What about her dad? Why wasn't he interested? Was he still angry? It was his granddaughter, after all, his first grandchild. Was he really the one who made the decisions or was he manipulated by her mother and her pride? No letter, no phone calls, no message with her mother. Complete silence.

If she took the baby back to the village her parents would be angry. What would Rob's mother say and do? Maybe she could stay with her Granny. But her mother would have a breakdown if her Granny was told about Susan. There would be endless arguments and bitterness, and the baby would be in the middle of it.

People in the village could be narrow-minded and cruel, the kind of place where they mocked if you used a long word. Everyone knew everyone else's business. What sort of life would Susan have if she were brought up with no father?

Maybe she could stay with her Gran, marry Rob, and keep the baby. Rob would be away in the Army for years yet, so she would be virtually on her own. But no, her mother had told her, Rob had a new girl-friend.

If she begged her parents to let her go back to them, where could she stay? There were only three bedrooms, and her brother had one and her sisters shared another. They were always short of money. She would be dependent on her parents again, a burden. Her father, always domineering, would be unbearable. He would be able to dictate everything, and she would have no power to resist. Would he be nasty to the baby? If they had argued before, how much worse would it be then? The baby would be in the middle of it, would grow up to hear the arguments, as she had grown up hearing her mother and father arguing into the night.

Without consciously making a decision, Carol knew what the outcome must be.

Susan is not having that life, she thought with determination. She had managed to get through the pregnancy on her own, had given birth among strangers. Susan deserved a good life, better than the one she could give her.

She had had no chance to talk to anyone. Her mother's fortnightly visits were brief, their conversations about nothing important. She'd telephoned and been told about the birth, that was all. How would she be now the baby was a reality?

Carol eased her weight on the inflated cushion which was supposed to relieve the stitches. Yesterday, following childbirth, she had hardly noticed them. Today it was like sitting on a bed of barbed wire.

Suddenly the door flew wide open and Mrs. Stone entered at a trot, panting slightly. She glanced wildly round, identified Carol's bed and, her voice trembling with emotion called, 'Where is she?'

Carol noted coldly that her mother had decided on 'demented grief' as her role for the day. With a sense of dread and resentment she waited to see where the performance was going.

'In the nursery.'

At that moment Sister Scott entered, pushing Susan in her wheeled cot.

'Good afternoon,' she said politely. 'Mrs. Stone?'

'Is that her?' Mrs. Stone interrupted the pleasantries with an air of desperation. 'Can I hold her?' she pleaded in a little-girl voice.

Sister Scott, a little surprised, assented.

Mrs. Stone began to pull off the blankets like a pig rooting for truffles. The other girls looked on in surprise. She uncovered the baby and snatched her up, holding her up in front of her face, crooning. Susan's tiny shoulders were pushed up round her sleeping face, her arms resting on Mrs. Stone's two hands, her legs dangling free. Her eyes opened and closed. 'Oh, bless her,' she said, then snuggled Susan into her arm as if they would never be parted. 'Eeh, she's gorgeous.' Three of the girls ignored her, one smiled weakly, one looked embarrassed.. Mrs. Stone sat by Carol's bed, clutching the baby. 'What a lovely little face. Eeh, she's lovely.' She looked up at Carol in appeal. 'Don't you think she's beautiful?' she asked as if she was the first person to notice it, and Carol might have missed it if she hadn't had it pointed out to her.

'Yes. She is.'

'Oh, she is. I think she's gorgeous.' The emphasis was on the 'I' as if she was challenging someone who thought the baby wasn't gorgeous. 'Don't you think she is? I can't get over it. Her lovely little face.' She shook the tiny hand gently, shaking her head from side to side, moved almost to tears at the feelings she felt for her first grandchild, the pity she felt for herself at the imminent loss, oblivious to the murderous reaction she was stirring up in her daughter. Then she smiled bravely at Carol, conquering her tears. Carol wanted to slap her face. Cold flames of anger and resentment burned inside.

Why was she doing this?

Carol struggled to control her fury. This parade of emotion was unbearable. She wanted to snatch her baby back.

'If she really feels like this,' thought Carol, 'what the flaming bloody hell am I doing here?'

'I've been up to the phone box every night this week, standing in the cold, trying to get through.' Mrs. Stone spoke to Carol, her eyes locked on Susan. 'People must be wondering what I was doing, but I had to know if you'd had it. Her. I were so worried.'

'Yes, you poor thing, you must have been,' said Carol quietly, eyes narrowed.

'I've been waiting and waiting, not knowing.'

'Yes.' Then, 'Me too.'

Mrs. Stone looked up in surprise, as if she'd just remembered that Carol had some involvement in the birth, too.

'How was it then? How long were you in labour?'

'Well, you know, it hurt, but I suppose it wasn't long, compared to some people.......'

She could hardly wait for Carol to finish the sentence. 'When our Ian were born I were in labour 21 hours. I were exhausted.' The voice changed to baby talk as she concentrated on Susan again, 'But she's worth it, aren't you? Yes you are. She's beautiful.'

'Does my dad know?'

'Know what?' she looked up in surprise.

'That she's born.'

'Yes.' A pause, then, 'He came to the phone box with me.'

So - he was interested enough to walk to the phone box!

As Mrs. Stone developed her role, Carol felt herself pushed to the edge, an onlooker. Her mother had swallowed her up again, taken over her feelings and lived them, elbowing her aside, leaving her standing on the edge, a spectator watching someone else feast off her life. Even now, with her first child, she couldn't be allowed to have her own feelings acknowledged, be treated as a separate human being; she was nothing.

'That's my baby,' she wanted to shout. 'I had her. I love her. I think she's wonderful.' But Mrs. Stone was absorbed and noticed nothing. This woman, whose chief priority in life had been to prevent any knowledge about the baby leaking out to the rest of the family, whose pride demanded that no-one should know, was now the proud grandmother wickedly denied her grandchild and torn to pieces. The about-face, the treachery, was breathtaking.

'Give her to me.'

'What?'

'I want her back.'

'Oh. Alright. Here you are.' Reluctantly she handed the baby back, and Carol immediately felt happier. Mrs. Stoned looked on jealously then began fussing about with flowers, and matinee coats which she had knitted in secret. But Carol didn't care any more. She had her baby safely in her arms.

All the protective love she had felt for her mother since she was a little girl, witnessing the ferocious rows between her parents, was switched to the tiny daughter. She was repulsed by her mother's display. She reacted by retreating into herself, putting up a barrier to prevent this crass performance from reaching inside her, making even more chaos in what was already a boiling mass of anxiety and confusion.

* * *

The other mothers had been born knowing what to do. Carol sat on a low chair, in the upstairs nursery next to the lying-in room, trying to insert her left nipple into Susan's tiny mouth, and watching them all bustle about bathing, dressing, weighing and feeding their babies. Baby baths on stands stood by low chairs, wet towels and heaps of baby clothes beside them on the floor. Piles of freshly laundered nappies, dresses and matinee jackets had just been delivered from the laundry downstairs and Meg was riffling through them looking for something special for her baby. Some of the mothers were fully dressed, ready to be transferred to the downstairs nursery, others were still in nighties, because they were still lying-in.

Susan was slow to feed and kept falling asleep. Carol had weighed her before feeding and the scales now said she'd only had two and a half ounces, but she seemed not to want any more. She had to have enough because they weren't allowed to feed babies except at feeding time. Susan woke up and cried, then began to suck hungrily at her fist. Carol began breast-feeding again. The baby sucked hard for a few seconds then stopped and cried.

'Do you think I'm doing this wrong?' she asked Betsy, sitting next to her. 'Is she ill, do you think?'

'I don't know,' Betsy replied quietly, absorbed in her own infant. 'Ask Sister.'

Sister Scott was busy with three other mums at her elbows.

'Just a minute. Just a minute. Look at this milk powder. Spilt everywhere. Sheer waste. Sheer waste.' Hands on hips she glared at the table in the corner, covered with a litter of electric kettle, tins of milk powder, bottles and sterilizers.

Carol returned to her seat and tried again.

The baby cried again. Sister Scott, shaking her head in disapproval, turned and vanished through the door. The baby sucked her fist and whimpered softly. What was wrong? Had she made a mistake? Did her milk taste bad? Was the baby sick? Everyone else knew what to do, but no-one had time to explain.

Tears ran down her cheeks as she held the crying baby on her lap. Suddenly Sister Dearborn appeared. She was the youngest of the Sisters, a big, jolly untidy person whose natural sympathy and warmth were like sunshine.

'Hello, what have we here?' She knelt in front of them. 'Both crying. Oh, dear me, oh dear,' she smiled and put her arms round them both, hugging them to her. 'Oh, come on then, tell Sister what's the matter?' She sat back on her heels and looked at them both, nodding and smiling as Carol explained the difficulties.

'No problem, no problem at all. You just haven't got enough milk and she's hungry. Let's give her a nice little bottle.

And they did. And everything was alright.

* * *

Carol hurried down the long echoing quarry-tiled corridor, passed the dining-room and turned left into the empty kitchen. Skirting the enormous central table she grabbed a pinafore and turned towards the stove.

The two dominant personalities in the kitchen were the cook, Mrs. Dorrit, and the stove. They were both ill-tempered and unpredictable, both wreaked instant revenge if not handled properly. They understood each other and co-existed in mutual unfriendly respect. Outsiders found them difficult to handle. Together they generated an atmosphere of disgruntlement and uncertainty.

Mrs. Dorrit was in her mid-fifties. As an attractive young woman she'd had an exciting social life centred on the local RAF bases in the war and was not one to make trivial concessions to changing times. She wore heavy Max Factor make-up and a Joan Fontayne war-time hair-do, rolled into a sausage round her head and held in place with a fine hair-net. She worked with whoever was assigned to kitchen duties, and called them all 'girlie'. The kitchen was considered unsuitable for pregnant girls so only mums worked there, and they had a tendency to be tearful and easily upset, traits which evoked no sympathy from Mrs. Dorrit, only exasperation. Meals had to be put on the table promptly three times a day. If her helpers were indulging in tears and tantrums she had to do more herself, an unsatisfactory situation as she had quite enough to do to start with.

The stove, when installed, represented the proudest achievements of Victorian invention and manufacture, and, like Mrs Dorrit, its best days were also in the past. Now, decades later, it crouched cantankerously along the left-hand wall exuding a dusty coke-dried heat and an air of menace. The dull early-morning light gleamed greasily on green-tinged steel surfaces, the lids and hot plates on the top, the many doors, handles, switches and knobs on the front. It was the ancestral Aga, unadorned by namby-pamby coloured enamels, resisting weak-minded innovations in the direction of gas or electricity. In complexity, size and construction it was almost industrial. This matriarch of domestic equipment demanded and received proper attention and respect.

Carol went down on her knees in front of the stove. Head bowed, she reached out and lifted the heavy metal latch on one of the many doors along the front face, near the bottom. A blast of searing heat struck her face, drying the inside of her nostrils. Head turned to protect her eyes, she took a long poker and began raking the dead ash out of the fire, into the ash-pan below. The newly fallen ash glowed red on top of the soft grey heap in the pan.

Carol began to cover the red hot embers with fresh coke, heaving it into the square space from the scuttle so it would fall far back. The temperature subsided as the stove began to devour the fresh fuel. Now there would be enough heat to cook breakfast.

Taking a thick protective cloth she lifted the heavy ash pan in both hands and began to walk carefully towards the door, heading for the dustbin. Pam Robins stood in the doorway.

'Look what you're doing with that. You'll burn somebody.'

'Move, quick, it's heavy. I'll drop it,' gasped Carol.

Insolently, slowly, Pam moved aside. 'Tut,' she said loudly, eyes raised to heaven.

When Carol returned Pam was standing by the window gazing moodily out at the dark morning, chewing and picking her fingernails. Carol swept up the ash and coal-dust from the quarry tiles in front of the stove with a badly singed brush, then washed her hands. She began to haul the heavy blackened baking sheets out of the cupboard under the table. Pam did not move. Carol began rubbing lard across the flat surfaces, took a large packet of streaky bacon from the fridge and began to arrange it on the baking sheets.

She wanted to be downstairs in the nursery with Susan, making sure she was settled, not up here doing this. Maybe if she finished soon she could sneak down before breakfast. She felt impatient, hassled, irritated and angry.

'Are you going to help me?'

'What?' Pam threw the words over her shoulder.

'I've done the fire. Can you help me with this?'

'I did the fire yesterday,' Pam snapped.

'Well, I'm not doing it all.'

'Who asked you to? You think you do everything.'

'No, I don't.'

'Yes you do. Who do you think you are? Snooty cow.'

'Well, I'm not an idle, ignorant…..'

They were shouting and screeching. Pam was standing in front of her, hands on hips, dark-circled eyes bulging, shouting at the top of her voice. Her fury was awesome.

Mrs. Dorrit and Matron came rushing in and Pam was taken away, Matron's arm round her shoulders, sobbing and defeated. Mrs. Dorrit began to clatter about by the sink, muttering and complaining audibly to herself. In silence, feeling guilty, Carol finished her work and crept out of the kitchen.

'Did you hear about Pam?' asked Joan over dinner. 'The Adoption Board turned her baby down. Something to do with a health check.' It was the first time Carol had heard of the existence of such a Board, and imagined a row of dusty elderly people sitting in judgement behind a long table while a naked crying baby lay in the brass pan of an old-fashioned weighing scale. 'Pam's mum and dad won't have her at home with the baby. The father doesn't want to know. She's got nowhere to go. She was crying all last night.'

'I wonder what will happen to her,' Dora said. 'I hear she's going to work in the laundry. But I don't know where she can go when her six weeks are up. She could end up living here for ever.'

* * *

'Well, I think we've finished. You've had a nice supper.'

The silence of night filled the dimly-lit downstairs nursery. Babies slept in a row of cots which loomed at the edge of the pool of light thrown by the one shaded bulb in the middle of the room. The plumbing ceased to gurgle, the chatter in the dorm next door subsided as the mothers settled down for the night after the last feed. Carol sat on with Susan on her lap on one of the long forms which formed a rough circle on the red lino, where the mothers did their feeding and bathing. Susan had finished her bottle, and Carol chatted quietly to the baby, who made little gurgles in response. Her eyes were surely looking at Carol's face.

'I know it's only milk, but there you are. Would you like a chip butty next week?'

The baby was definitely smiling at her. They said it was only wind when little babies seemed to smile, but this wasn't wind.

'Yes? Alright then, I'll see what I can do. Is there any more wind? No? Well, it's time for bed. Yes. You need your beauty sleep and so do I, so we'll have to put you in your cot. I know you don't want to go. But you have to. Where else would you sleep? With me? You want to sleep with me? Well, Matron says we can't do that. No, it's naughty. She says you have to sleep here.' The baby waved her arms. 'Oh you don't want to do that? What did you say? 'Bugger Matron?' Well, let me see. They're all asleep. No-one will know. Now, if you promise to be quiet, you can come in with me just for a little while. Okay? Don't forget now. Shush.'

She kissed the baby, wrapped her up in her shawl and tip-toed into the dorm. Each bed, in rows down the sides of the long room, contained a silent humped figure. Moonlight reflected on snow beyond the French doors at the end of the room, and shone on the bare wooden floor. No-one stirred.

Susan settled quietly, nestled in her mother's arms. Happily, Carol kissed her tiny head and hugged her close.

'If Matron catches you there'll be hell to pay,' a sleepy voice murmured from the darkness. Sleep closed in on them both.

A flashlight flickered on her eyelids, and Carol struggled against the enveloping blackness of sleep. The shadowy figure behind it spoke with Matron's voice, kind but with iron authority.

'Babies are not allowed in bed with mothers. It's dangerous. You could roll on her in your sleep. Give her to me.'

Dragging herself awake, resentfully, reluctantly, Carol handed over her sleeping baby.

'Naughty girl,' said Matron gently. Carol watched as she walked purposefully in the dark towards the door. Then she laid back in the yawning emptiness of the bed and tried to get to sleep.

* * *

Paula decided to organise a night out. She rounded up five girls, including Carol, told Matron they were going to Sunday evensong at St. Mary's and took them all to a busy pub in the town. The bar was crowded and noisy, full of cigarette smoke and awash with the smell of beer. Men and women talked and laughed together with the intense concentration and eye-contact which Carol had not seen for many months. People edged past carrying trays of drinks. Paula lit a fag, smiled with contentment and pushed her way to the bar. Carol felt fat and frumpy and out of place. She sat uneasily with the others sipping her half of shandy until it was time to go back to the safety of The Warren.

* * *

Two weeks after leaving Julie and Sophie came back on a visit wearing make-up, high heels and new fashionable clothes with waistlines. Both had glamorous hair-does. They giggled a lot, cried a bit; they were strangers who belonged to the world outside.

* * *

On May 16th the snow still lay in patches but the sun was stronger; winter was giving way to spring. Daffodils, long caught in suspended animation, came belatedly into full bloom. The birdsong was deafening, the trees were covered in fresh green buds.

Susan was six weeks old.

In the nursery Carol bathed and dressed Susan carefully in her new dress and jacket. She concentrated hard, fumbling over buttons and safety pins.

It was like waiting for an execution. It had to come. This ordinary morning was her last and she tried to wring every memory from it, to store it up in her mind because soon that would be all she had. Here was her baby, living, breathing, solid flesh and blood, being washed, dressed, fed, changed, and soon she would be gone, beyond Carol's knowledge. Susan's life was going to change course forever in the next few hours. Carol felt that hers would end.

Would Susan be happy? Yes, of course she would. Her new parents wanted her very badly, and would love her dearly. She would have her own room, a beautiful cot and pram, new clothes, lots of toys. She would have a family, live in a nice house, have lovely holidays. Her mum and dad would know all about children, how to bring them up, how to make them happy.

Would they ever meet again? Susan would not remember the last six weeks, but Carol would never forget them. It was impossible to believe that after such closeness there would be nothing. Surely, one day, they would meet again.

The other mothers finished feeding, tucked their babies into cots for a sleep and went off to their various duties. Carol sat on, talking to Susan, singing to her, tears falling on the baby's head. Could she refuse?

Time was running out. The decision was made. It was all for the best. There was no alternative. But inside was a leaden pain. Rational thoughts and arguments gave way to a hard weight inside her chest, a physical pervading misery. The tears would not stop and turned into deep ugly sobs.

Dora put her head round the door and went off to get a Sister. Sister Dearborn came in. She murmured soft, clucking, motherly words of comfort and cuddled them both. Then she took the baby gently from Carol's arms.

'Bye mummy,' she said softly. She turned and walked away, shoes squeaking on the expanse of brown linoleum. Carol did not protest or struggle, but sobbed and sobbed. The pain was indescribable.

Sister Dearborn turned at the door and looked back, the little pink bundle in her arms, smiled sadly, then she was gone.

The room boomed and echoed with intolerable silence and emptiness. Carol stood, arms empty but still warm, still feeling the weight of the baby. Dora said many reassuring and comforting words which Carol did not hear. She wrung her hands, her eyes fixed on the door, imagining Sister Dearborn mounting the stairs to the Hall, entering the Sisters' sitting room with Susan. Carol could guess and visualise the next few minutes but then Susan would be in a separate world, unknown and unreachable. Their paths, now divided, would increasingly diverge, perhaps never to cross again. The best she could do for her child was to let her go, unaccompanied, into a world of strangers.

She was powerless, useless, helpless. A heavy emptiness settled into her chest, a dull miserable weight.

Eventually, slowly, Carol and Dora made their way up the back stairs onto the landing and into the now-empty Delivery Room. The window over-looked the front door. A large white car was parked on the gravel.

They waited. A dark-haired man in a suit emerged and held the door open, looking back into the Hall. A woman, small and blonde, dressed very smartly, came out slowly . She carried, with great care, a baby, Susan, wrapped in a lacy shawl. She seemed oblivious to everything, head down, gazing intently at the baby. Through a blur of tears Carol saw the man put his arm round her shoulders as if he would protect them both and guide her over to the car. He opened the door and settled her with infinite tenderness in the front seat, baby on her lap. He leaned over her, gently pulled down the edge of the shawl to see the baby and spoke to his wife, who smiled happily up into his face.

Carol noted greedily all the signs of affection, every detail which said they were close, and would make a happy, loving family. They looked prosperous, grown-up and responsible, the sort of people who knew how to organise their lives, get what they wanted. They would be perfect parents.

He closed the car door, walked round and got in the driver's seat. The car moved off, gliding round the curve of the drive, and disappeared, and they went off to live their ideal, beautiful lives somewhere far away, which had no place for a spare mother, a person who was too stupid, worthless and incompetent to deserve a baby.

I will see her again, Carol vowed fiercely, even if it takes thirty years I'll see her again. She'll find me, when she's ready.

Chapter 4

The steam train hissed and screeched to a halt. Carol hauled the blue RAF kitbag from the luggage rack, adjusted the black tie under the blue shirt collar, fastened the RAF raincoat, crammed the blue beret onto her head, and hitched the regulation black leather bag over her shoulder. Who would know she'd bought them all from the Army and Navy Store the week before? Who would guess she was no longer WRAF Leading Aircraftwoman Stone? Everyone in the family, her mother hoped.

She picked up her old suitcase with her RAF number on the side and lurched down the aisle of the train. Her tongue burned from the unaccustomed five Embassy cigarettes, chain smoked on the journey. The platform heaved with clamouring noise and bustling confusion. Long beams of sunlight slanted down through billows of steam below the echoing roof span. Across the track was the platform where her mother had stood and tearfully waved goodbye sixteen months before, as she'd left to join the WRAF. As usual her dad hadn't been there, and also as usual her mum had turned the occasion into a tragedy. Well - that had been a short career! The smoky sulphurous air caught in her throat as she headed reluctantly for the exit and the bus station.

'Please God, don't let me meet anyone I know,' she thought forty minutes later, as she walked down the familiar road of semis. A woman stood outside No. 40, arms folded across her flowery pinafore, and nodded as she passed. Who was that? A friend of her mother's? She tripped over an uneven paving slab, regained her balance. Gimlet eyes followed right to the gate of No. 53.

The house had shrunk. The tree by the gate carried a pink froth of cherry blossom. The path, a carpet of petals, fluttered in the soft breeze – bridal and celebratory, and totally inappropriate. She did not want to go in; she wanted to hide, far away, somewhere dark and silent.

Was it possible that no-one knew what had happened that very morning? Couldn't they tell just by looking at her?

The house was quiet; a coal fire burned cheerfully, there was a smell of newly baked bread. She didn't want to be there. Her mother came bustling downstairs.

'Hello love. How long have you been here?' She did not respond to her mother's embrace. She didn't want to be hugged, either. What she wanted was to kill someone. They ate lunch together, avoiding the subject which was uppermost in both their minds.

Her dad arrived back from work. 'Hello. You're back then, are you?' he said as if she'd never been away, never had a baby, had not given her child away that very morning, and went to let his pigeons out.

The uniform was a lie and now the lies must begin in earnest.

Granny Stone popped in that afternoon, 'Hello love, I've not seen you for a while. How are you keeping? By you've put a bit of weight on,' she said, and gave her a hug.

Her friend Pauline said, when she saw her at the shops, 'Hey up. Long time no see. How's the RAF? Still enjoying it?'

Lie. Lie. 'Oh yes, you know. It's fine.'

'You've put a few pounds on, haven't you? How long are you home for?' Pauline had her two-year old in a pushchair and she was pregnant.

Carol visited Auntie Jean next day. 'Hello love. Eeh its nice to see you again. How long have you got on leave?'

Lie. 'Just a few days. Going back soon.'

Keep it vague, no details. Can she tell I'm lying?

'Have you put weight on? They must be feeding you well.'

She was waiting for a bus at the shops when she spotted Kip Taylor, Rob's old school friend, sauntering past, hands in pockets. His eyes drifted over the queue. 'Don't let him notice me, let him walk past,' she groaned, averting her face.

'Hey, Carol, is that you?' he said. 'Haven't seen you for ages. You're looking well – a bit plump, like.'

'Sod off,' she thought.

'Hi,' she replied reluctantly.

'Did you know Rob's getting married in two weeks?'

So her mother had been right. He did have another girl friend. He certainly hadn't waited long. She imagined all the wedding preparations, the excitement, the families meeting. She wondered if the new girlfriend was pregnant as well.

'I can get you an invitation if you want. You can come with me.' You'd have to be as stupid as Kip Taylor to ask such a question. Everyone in the bus queue pretended they weren't listening.

'No thanks.' What could be worse than going to Rob's wedding? 'Just remembered, I need to go to the Post Office. Have to go. See you again. Bye.' She had to get away, before she throttled him.

Each time she answered a question Carol felt the word LIAR emblazoned on her forehead, each lie produced an inward squirm. Worse still, the words between lies had to be guarded carefully, checked for errors before being allowed utterance. She learned to disguise the desolation she felt and pretend to be someone she used to be.

On her third morning back Carol slept in, beyond the time when she should have been in the nursery with the others, feeding Susan, and came down to the cold little kitchen in search of coffee. She missed The Warren, the bustle and friendly faces, where she had a place, and a purpose. Her mother was standing by the sink looking tragically out at the back garden, hands in a bowl of washing-up.

'Eeh, I wonder where she is now,' she sighed.

Carol, who had lain awake for the best part of several nights, said nothing.

'It breaks my heart to think I shall never see her again,' Mrs. Stone went on.

No reply. It was like having a wound prodded to see if there was any feeling in it.

'I hope they'll love her a lot. I said to Sister, I said, 'Tell them to love her a lot.''

Carol stood with her head down, fighting the raging feelings which threatened to swamp her. It had taken a lot of effort to get through the past two days. There had seemed no point in getting up this morning, no point in breathing. During the hours on the train and in bed last night she had reviewed every single detail, chewed it all over until she could think no more. She was like a boxer, beaten into submission, lying on the ground, almost counted out, who manages to get back on his feet only to receive the final punch which knocks him down for ever.

'I've worried myself sick, I have,' her mother snivelled. She wanted to take her mother by the shoulders and scream at her.

With one last supreme effort, Carol heaved herself off the canvas and stepped out of the ring.

'Is there any coffee?' she asked in a flat voice.

* * *

Obviously the 'leave' had to end some time and Carol, six days later, became a resident of the YWCA in Leeds.

Fiona Findlay-Campbell, citizen of Nigeria, was a student of Law at the University of Leeds. Fiona was as skinny as a rake, her skin a rich blue-black. She had the bossiness natural to the daughter of a powerful man. On this Saturday she and two friends had arranged a little treat. They had spent the morning shopping for beans, spices and vegetables and were now cooking them up on a portable stove placed on the floor of Fiona's room at the YWCA. Between the two neatly made beds with their primrose bedspreads they knelt or sat on the carpet, wrapped from head to toe in the rich printed fabrics of full African dress, surrounded by unwrapped packets and jars of food. Steam, and the powerful spicy smell from the cooking pot, filled the room and drifted out of the wide-open window.

Mrs. Smith, the Assistant Warden, overweight and moustachioed, escorted Carol through the Hall - cream gloss painted walls and varnished woodwork - and toiled up the flight of red-painted concrete stairs and along the corridor.

'I'm putting you in with Fiona for now,' she panted. 'She hasn't had a room-mate for a few weeks so she's not used to sharing but it is a double room. We don't have many rules, they're mostly for safety. No smoking or cooking in the rooms. The outside door is locked at 11.00 pm. No visitors upstairs, there's a visitors' sitting room downstairs.'

She stopped at the last door at the end of the long corridor, paused to regain her breath, knocked, opened the door and walked in. Carol followed. Her jaw dropped as the unfamiliar sounds of an African language ground to a halt. The rich smell of unfamiliar food billowed out with a cloud of steam into the corridor, and she met three pairs of startled brown eyes.

* * *

Carol got a job in a wholesale chemists typing invoices. It was deadly boring, but required no interaction with other people. All day she pounded the ancient manual typewriter – columns of figures, demanding close attention.

* **

The area between the YWCA and the town centre had been demolished. The land sloped uphill to Scott Road; with eyes half closed it was possible to imagine it had been returned to its original status of farmland, and visualise the hawthorn hedges dividing the fields. The old roads and pavements remained, the slum terraces of the industrial revolution which had once crowded together under the smoke pall to shut out the sunlight were now swept away. Impossible to believe so many people had lived their lives in these cramped acres. All that remained was a scattering of house bricks on the barren earth. This urban desert was fringed with distant factories and the raw ends of deserted terraces still awaiting extinction. At the bottom of the hill on South Street the fumes and smoke from the roaring traffic drifted up from beyond the single remaining row of ancient scruffy buildings and created an air of more active dereliction.

Carol walked home along Scott Road every day from work. There were always a few cars crawling along, not many as the road led nowhere. Frequently a car would pull up and a man - always a man, never a woman - would say, 'Hello, love, d'you want a ride?' It was nice of them to ask, thought Carol, but somehow they were not really friendly. Sometimes they asked something about, 'Are you open for business?' Occasionally they asked for directions then appeared not to listen. In the village if you had a car you'd offer a lift to people, but she didn't know these men. Anyway, the hostel was so near she didn't need a lift.

When the other girls explained, she felt quite offended and wondered if her dress sense was at fault. The heroines in Naomi Jacobs books never got mistaken for a prostitute. Then she thought maybe she should be thinking of John Steinbeck instead - say 'Sweet Thursday' - and felt better.

* * *

In the hostel dining room Carol sat next to June Knight. She was a machinist and sewed men's suits at Burtons, a big girl with black hair and flashing black eyes who ate everyone else's left-overs.

'So, you don't know Leeds, then. You can come wi' me and Sally to t'Mecca on Saturday afternoon.'

The entrance to the Mecca was inside a Victorian arcade. In the wide-open carpeted doorway a black girl with very large lips and teeth came smiling up to June. She was not in African dress, and looked much more friendly than Fiona. June called out, 'Hey, Julie.' Carol wondered if she spoke English.

'Heyup, love, are y' alright?' Julie had the broadest Yorkshire accent Carol had ever heard.

On the dance floor below the glittering, revolving mirrored ball dozens of couples, mostly girls, twirled without enthusiasm to a record. There was a dress code - giant hair rollers covered with a chiffon headscarf, cardigans and flat shoes. June explained that they would all go home for 'us tea', take out the rollers, put on make-up, a dress, stilettos and lots of petticoats and return, transformed, for the evening session.

On the way back to the hostel for 'tea' which was really dinner, June, Sally and Julie linked arms with her and walked along the broad pavements singing. A teenaged pink-faced policeman walked in the opposite direction at the other side of the road.

'Alright, girls,' called June, 'ready.'

They began singing loudly, 'I wanna be - Bobby's girl, da da da, Bobby's girl'.

The policeman blushed scarlet and raised his helmet. They wolf-whistled him and blew kisses.

Carol grinned - an unconvincing, embarrassed little grin. Part of her admired their high spirits and wanted to join in. The other, larger part wanted to sink into the floor, and felt sorry for the policeman. She made an excuse to avoid returning for the evening, thus losing her opportunity of seeing at first hand the young DJ who was to become so famous over the next few decades.

* * *

A social worker called to see Carol soon after she arrived and took her, one Sunday, to church near the University. The congregation was full of mummy's-darling students and the prayers were for exam success. It seemed a little unfair asking God to help you with your exams. Carol wasn't taking any exams, hated hymns, and currently hated her mother, her father, and anything to do with home, so she didn't go again.

* * *

Many nights, long after her room-mate was asleep, Carol lay awake thinking of Susan. There was a constant cloud of misery - uncertainty and doom mixed with a sense of loss - which hovered around her all day, through which she saw the world. Days succeeded days and it became a pattern, a way of life.

After some weeks, or was it months, the social worker made an appointment to pick her up at the hostel to 'sign some papers'. In the hostel sitting room, looking out over the bleak sooty garden, she explained – adoption papers, to be signed in front of a Justice of the Peace. The explanation was adequate enough, but rising panic, a feeling of dread, and a sense that this was it, the final parting, rendered her words into meaninglessness. She didn't answer questions, only gave information. They went in a taxi through the uncaring city. They travelled in funereal silence, as the car threaded through the busy Saturday morning streets of the suburbs. Wide pavements, crowded with shop displays of lettuce, tomatoes and flowers, tin buckets, brooms, mops and deck-chairs, heaved with shoppers. Families with young children weaved their way through or stood in groups gossiping and blocking the flow of traffic. The sun shone on brightly striped shop awnings.

'If...' her voice wavered and refused to be heard. She coughed and began again.

'If anything happens to her parents, will they let me know? If I am able to look after her, can I ...can I ...have her back?'

The reply came after a pause, detached and impersonal, informative and neutral.

'No. Once she is adopted she is legally a member of the family and they will deal with it as a family.'

That made sense. She was not needed, never would be. Other, more capable people, would look after Susan. You've done your bit, she told herself unreasonably, now sign the papers and bugger off and don't bother us again.

The house was large with an imposing front door.

Like a prisoner she was escorted into a big room. A middle-aged woman, a Justice of the Peace, stood behind a desk, silhouetted against a vast sunny window. The sunshine dazzled, and threw the rest of the room into deep contrasting shadow. Carol wanted to argue, ask questions, talk about it, but she didn't know what to ask, and there was no-one to argue with or talk to. Weeping silently she approached the desk and stood to sign the papers. The task completed, she was accompanied back to the taxi and returned to the hostel, back to the void. The rest of the day passed in a stunned blur, which extended to other days, weekends, weeks, months.

She continued to avoid questions, and perfected the art of telling lies. Misery walked by her side like a shadow. By now the habit of secrecy was so deeply ingrained that thumb-screws and the rack would probably not have wrung it out of her. She had ceased to ask herself why. It went beyond question, it was just one of the guiding necessities of her life. No-one must know.

An envelope arrived, forwarded from home. It contained a photograph of Susan at six months. She wore a beautiful dress and sat on a blanket, chubby hands held in front of her. She had put on weight, her features had changed, her expression was serious. The photograph was enclosed in a letter from Matron who quoted extracts from a letter she, in turn, had received from Susan's new mum, about what a wonderful baby she was. Susan was now Jessica.

The letter and the photograph widened the gap created by time and distance. Jessica was not her baby any longer, she had a new family and existed somewhere else in a lovely house with toys and flowers and her own room. Carol knew that all she could do was spoil it. Susan, or Jessica, deserved peace to grow up with her new family.

* * *

Linda Emmis came to live at the hostel. She was seventeen and full of confidence with a broad Yorkshire accent which was undergoing reconstruction. She had lots of lovely clothes and on her dressing table she kept a glass fruit bowl containing water, stones and two terrapins like live green jewels. Marie Baker soon followed - small, dark, pretty, ex-Catholic boarding school and well spoken. Then Jane Long; eighteen, quick-witted and sensible, but longing for 'life' to happen to her, she was a Laboratory Assistant at the hospital. Gillian Nutt arrived; tall and slender, spoiled and regrettably spotty eldest daughter of rich parents and a school mate of Sue's, she was reluctantly allowed by her parents to live and work in the big bad city. Maggie was Scottish, very proper and a Civil Servant, and shared Carol's room when she was moved out of Fiona's.

Gradually a group formed. They borrowed each other's clothes and cigarettes, visited the coffee bars, compared notes on men - mostly theories - shrank their jeans to fit by sitting in a bath of water with them on, gave each other hairdos, helped with dress alterations and laughed at the 'flasher' who appeared now and then at the back of the hostel at weekends. They discussed the new Spanish girl who walked around with her dressing gown open showing her great swinging boobs, Hetty, who was over 40, rather masculine, and invited them into her single room for cigarettes and coffee, and Miss Mack, the relief Warden who talked nonsense and stank of gin.

In the autumn when the students returned to the city they went to a 'rave' together. Carol was wearing Marie's trendy jumper and dancing in the near dark with a hairy, specky student from Norwich. She mentioned the only person she knew from Norwich - Rosemary.

'Oh, didn't she have a baby or something? How do you know her?'

Carol covered her lapse of concentration without missing a step.

'My brother used to go on fishing trips up there. He knows her dad. Isn't the music brilliant?'

The DJ played a new number - 'Love Me Do'. Magic. Bliss. Instant happiness. The wail of the mouth organ, raw guitars, harmonised voices - unlike all the American 'Bobby' singers - Bobby Darin, Bobby Vee, Bobby this and Bobby that. The waves of sound generated an excitement and thrill which suggested that life could be lived in another plane, on another level.

Her next partner was a forceful lad in wire-rimmed specs who spoke with a foreign accent and said his dad was The Minister for War in Venezuela. He was clumsy and wanted to explain the Communist ideal, which didn't interest Carol greatly at the time.

Phil, a student of architecture, took her home in his little car. He kissed her goodnight. She kissed him back. He stuffed his hand up her jumper. She leapt out of the car and bolted into the hostel like a frightened rabbit.

Another night Ben, a bearded art student, brought her back in his dad's station wagon. He opened the tailgate, picked up his guitar and played and sang to her. It was very romantic. He looked like Rolf Harris and didn't try to kiss her. He was Jewish and had given his love to a nice Jewish girl called Magda, who was away visiting friends for the weekend.

She met Jim at a party. He asked her to marry him when they danced. She said yes, but he danced with Marie and asked her to marry him as well.

She met someone at the Majestic Ballroom who gave her a lift home. He wanted a goodnight kiss and because he had horrid teeth and, as she discovered, the charm of a wart-hog, she said no.

'What do you mean, no, I gave you a lift home,' he shouted angrily before jumping into his scruffy van and driving off.

A charming salesman took her out to dinner and made an expert attempt at seduction. She wanted to, but fear prevented it. She moped about him for weeks but he never came back.

There was some evidence of the reported sexual freedom of the Swinging Sixties. Mrs. Smith the Assistant Warden complained that when Eileen came in after kissing her boyfriend goodnight she always went into the downstairs cloakroom, leaving behind a used 'Rubber Johnny' which refused to be flushed away. Mrs. Smith's use of the phrase indicated that she knew something about sex, which seemed shocking. Eileen always laughed and, eyes wide open, hand on heart, asked incredulously, 'Who, me?'

A visiting Scottish Territorial Army group issued a general invitation to the girls of the YWCA for an evening out. Carol played billiards with a nice little scotsman who worked in a knitwear factory, and won. She had never played before, so he must have rigged it. He said he would send her a Scottish jumper as a prize. Surprisingly he did. It was beautiful, pale blue merino wool, but she washed it in the washing-machine and it shrank to doll's size.

Miss Garfunkel, the Warden, warned them not to go into 'The Tobago Club' on South Street, but whenever they passed the door the music was pounding out - Trini Lopez sang, 'If I had a Hammer' as if the lyrics meant something - and dark figures swayed about under the dim twinkling lights inside. Men smoked and lounged near the door, and leered at them as they returned to the hostel late at night. Inevitably they went in, eventually, and found it was no different from the shops on either side, just painted black and imbued with excitement by virtue of being forbidden. The men were all 'coffee bar cowboys' and the girls nonchalant and slaggy, but the music was good.

Carol left the wholesale chemists and became a secretary at the

College of Technology, working for two Heads of Department, both older decent family men.

The relief Warden for the summer holidays arrived. She was friendly and liked to chat. She told them how, in her last hostel, in Birmingham, an intruder had climbed into the basement. When Mrs. Deck went down to check last thing at night she looked in the big laundry sink and found - the severed head of one of the girls. No-one dared to go into the laundry alone for ages.

Jean got pregnant and left to get married.

Alison moved to another city after being promoted.

New girls came, old girls left.

Gillian got pregnant and had a big expensive wedding. A year later she divorced.

There were parties and clubs and pubs and dances.

Time passed. Memories mellowed and centred on Susan's photograph which became dog-eared from its constant removal and replacement in and out of the envelope in her suitcase.

An uneasy relationship was re-established with her parents on occasional weekend visits to the village. The hostel became home.

In twos, threes and fours the girls moved out of the hostel into flats. Carol moved in with Linda and Marie to a flat in the middle of a student bed-sit area.

* * *

'I'm going to a party tonight. Why don't you two come?' Linda sat at the dressing-table in the bedroom which they shared, naked except for the damp towel draped round her hips. 'Hey mister tambourine man...' sang the radio. She claimed all the men admired her legs, which were long and slim, but her top half consisted almost entirely of rib cage and big shoulders. She drew deeply on a cigarette, balancing it precariously among the dusty heaps of make-up as she wound big rollers into her long auburn hair.

'No, I'm going out with Adam,' said Marie. 'Is Don going?'

Don was a student of architecture, the object of Linda's affections. In every pub and club in the city centre Linda knew attractive good-looking men who wanted to take her out for meals, dancing or drinks, but she was only interested in Don, with his fair hair, his couldn't-give-a-shit manner and weird sense of humour, who was off-hand and cheated at every opportunity.

'No, he's going to visit his parents. So he says, the lying bastard,' said Linda. 'Do you know what he did last night? We were sitting in the pub and he had his arm round me, breathing in my ear and looking at me really close. He said, 'Linda' in a romantic voice and I said 'Yes?' thinking, he's going to say he loves me. Then he whispered, 'You've got a great big blackhead in your ear.'' She laughed. 'So romantic. Why don't you come, Carol?'

Carol lay on her bed reading Dennis Wheatey's 'The Devil Rides Out'.

'Who, me? Whose party is it?'

'Some student from the Uni.'

'The Uni lot are all drips,' said Marie, riffling through their shared wardrobe. 'Do you think this dress is clean enough to wear?' She held up a short pink dress with deep frills round the neck and sniffed delicately at the armpits.

'Yes, it's okay. Which shoes?' asked Carol.

'These I think.' Marie held up an expensive pair of strappy French shoes in black leather. 'Can I borrow your tights?'

'Yes. Help yourself.' Marie didn't like doing her laundry and her top drawer was full of dirty knickers. Sometimes she didn't change her sheets for weeks. She spoke like a lady and had the personal habits of a tramp.

'You aren't doing anything are you Carol, tonight?' Linda spoke through the smoke of the cigarette which now dangled from her lips. She'd seen Elsie Tanner doing this in Coronation Street and was trying it out.

'No. But I won't know anyone there.'

'So - neither will I until I get there. You could wear your new paisley dress. I'll do your hair for you. Do you good to go out. The party's up near Hyde Park.'

'No, I can't be bothered.'

'Oh go on.'

Carol glanced up from the book. 'Okay then. You've talked me into it.'

* * *

As soon as they arrived Linda saw someone she knew and vanished among the dancers. Carol, feeling ridiculous in high heels and a too-short tight silky dress, sat with her drink watching the unfamiliar crowds of students. They were mostly of the type who still referred to their parents as Mummy and Daddy. The girls all dressed as if they were about fifty and had fat bums and short boring hair. The music was not loud enough, the lights too bright.

At eleven o clock she was sitting on the floor chatting to a student dentist. He had ginger hair and nice teeth, and talked like someone's dad.

At midnight, perfectly sober, she began to wonder how to find her way home alone without Linda. She sat in a room off the hall on a bed piled high with coats, smoking a cigarette and watching through the open door as people called their goodbyes and left. No sign of Linda.

Three students were leaving.

'Excuse me. Are you going anywhere near Woodhouse Moor?' They all turned to look. 'My friend has disappeared and I don't know how to get home. If I get to Woodhouse Moor I can find my way from there.'

They left together. All three were vying for her attention, joking, laughing, chattering.

At Woodhouse Moor two of them turned off. The third offered to walk her home. He was tall with fair hair which curled down onto his collar, a long thin face, and heavy black-framed glasses, like Hank Marvin. He wore a black shiny pvc coat and jeans and smiled a lot, showing his long teeth. His accent was unfamiliar, totally unlike the harsh Yorkshire vowels she was used to hearing. His voice was deep and pleasant, its timbre excitingly familiar, his manner warm and protective. A faint memory stirred, of Michael Crawford in a film, long ago, with his posh accent, pleasant manners, and blue eyes, caring and protective.

'We can't have you walking alone at this time of night.'

'That's nice of you, but you don't have to. Is it out of your way?'

'Probably, but I'm sure I can find my way back.'

'Thank you. If you're sure that's alright.'

Easy to talk to, amusing and interesting, he was an engineering student at the University, but he knew about so many other things - apartheid, politics, economics., music, Nelson Mandela. His accent was difficult to place.

'Are you Australian?' she asked, looking up at him in the moonlight. They were walking past the park and the June night was filled with the heavy scent of pollen and muted distant city noises. The after-midnight hush and unaccustomed warmth of the night air seemed exotic and foreign. Cautiously, gently, happiness beckoned her into its warm embrace.

'No, no, West London, Middlesex. Place called Eeeeling,' he emphasised the Cockney accent. Her high heels caught on the uneven paving. 'Mind the step.' He took her hand, and kept it in his.

The two mile walk was over far too soon. They stood in the doorway of Carol's flat and talked for an hour. Then he kissed her and they both enjoyed it so much they did that for another hour. Then he came in for coffee and another hour passed. Linda and Marie came home, had coffee with them, and went to bed. It was well after two o clock, and Carol had to get up for work the next morning, but there was so much to say.

Eventually, as dawn began to lighten the sky, Carol ushered him out, closed the door, and went to bed, to lie sleeplessly, hugging to herself the excitement of Paul's existence. They had arranged to meet the following evening.

At 8.o pm, only sixteen hours after she had said goodbye, she waited by the Town Hall, wearing Marie's new red suit, her eyes heavy from lack of sleep. After nearly an hour, nervousness and excitement gave way to disappointment and wretchedness. She gave up and walked slowly home, got lost in the labyrinth of terraced streets and stopped to buy chips from a corner chippy. She wandered on as night fell, high heels dragging on the uneven cobbles, oblivious to the curious glances of the natives, feeding chips into her mouth automatically, talking herself into accepting that such beautiful things couldn't be relied on to last.

The week dragged by. Then, surprise and delight, there was a letter from Paul. He had had to go home and break the news to his parents - he had failed his second year exams but intended to stay on and possibly retake them. She was thrilled. He was staying, or coming back, because of her.

Two weeks after he returned they slept together. Carol thought she would die of happiness. The fear of pregnancy was always at the back of her mind, and she wondered what she would do if it happened again.

Summer merged lyrically into autumn. They went dancing, ate out, walked in the park, saw films, and talked and talked.

It was late autumn when he said, 'If I asked you to marry me what would you say?'

She looked up at him, her heart racing. They were walking along in the sunshine hand in hand towards her flat. It was Saturday afternoon, and they had all the time in the world. She loved him, trusted him completely. She opened her mouth to tell him about Susan, as she knew she must.

The words would not come.

How could she tell him? What could she say? 'I love you but I have to tell you I've had a baby, over two years ago.' She loved him so much, her whole life and happiness was now so tightly dependent on him, she couldn't bear it if he left.

Since they'd met they had spent more time together than some couples who had known each other for years. He was kind, good-natured and amusing. His voice was fascinating, his hands gentle. His views were tinged with cynicism though he was deeply romantic. Outrageously his vocabulary included the word 'fuck' pronounced so elegantly as to give his conversation a tinge of sophistication unknown in Rossingley. There, if the boys said 'fuck', which was strictly pit-top language, it was crude and offensive. He was slim, totally unsporty and clever - the exact opposite to Rob. Even his short-sightedness gave her confidence - he seemed to think she was wonderful, which he surely wouldn't if he could see her clearly. He loved her - which he surely wouldn't if he knew about her past.

His fair hair and blue eyes held an inexplicably familiar charm. His unfailing good manners and good humour - unlike her dad - his intelligence and eloquence - unlike Rob - held an attraction which struck a chord somewhere, seemed recognisable from a previous existence. She couldn't believe how lucky she was that he loved her. Would he still love her if he knew she had had a baby? Could she risk losing him? Since they met life had become meaningful, each day had a point, she could look forward to seeing him, sometimes to waking up with him. If he went, life would return to the grey fog she knew so well. After losing Susan she had never expected to be happy again, until now. She wanted nothing more in the world then to marry him, though she hadn't allowed herself to hope for so much. Now he was asking her. Could she risk losing that?

Secrecy had become second nature. She had learned to avoid questions, to steer conversations away from possible danger, had shut away her grief into a small, tightly guarded impregnable area from which it had no escape, except sometimes alone in bed at night when she cried without waking Linda and Marie. The only two people who knew were her mother and father. She avoided discussing it with her mother because she couldn't bear the anger it aroused, and she couldn't discuss it with her father because she couldn't even pass the time of day with him without a row. How could she now, out of the blue, reverse the carefully acquired habits, throw off the defensive shell?

She could simply say, 'No, I don't believe in marriage. Let's stay as we are.'

While waiting for her reply, during the time it took for these thoughts to flash through her mind, he began to look uneasy, as if anticipating rejection. He might think she didn't love him. He might leave her.

'I think I might say 'Yes'.'

He smiled and the world lit up. 'In that case, will you marry me?''

'Yes, I will.'

He kissed her full on the lips, right there in the middle of the street.

'Okay,' he said, grinning.

The following weekend Carol phoned her mother from the call box in the next street to tell her the good news. Amid the acrid smell of wee and damp cigarette ash she forced the pennies into the slot.

'We want to get married before Christmas.' Silence. 'Mum? Hello?'

'Are you pregnant?' The line was poor, the voice thin and distant, but the clipped tones of anxiety came over clearly.

'No.'

'Are you going to tell him about Susan?' She could almost see the worn fingers tearing at a handkerchief, or twisting the phone wire.

'No.'

'You're asking for trouble. I don't know. It's bound to cause problems. Well, it's your decision.'

'Yes, it is.' No congratulations, no joy, no shared excitement. Just grinding anxiety, which squeezed all the pleasure out of every breath.

Six months after they met, one week before Christmas, Paul and Carol were married.

* * *

It was almost midnight, late spring. Carol and Paul had hitched a lift back from a visit to his parents in London. They had been picked up by a farmer's boy, in his ramshackle car which smelled of cowshit and straw. The road passed within a few miles of Nottingham, the city lights a distant glow in the darkness.

'See that place there,' said the farmer's boy. He nodded towards a cluster of lighted windows looming through the darkness of the countryside, shrouded in trees. 'That's the nuthouse. There's a place in Nottingham where lasses go to have their babies then they're adopted. That's where they go next.' He sniggered. 'They go nuts.'

Carol felt her heart pound, the heat rise in her face and spread all over her body. A trickle of sweat threaded down between her breasts. She was glad of the darkness.

She thought of Brigit, and Pam, and Tatty Liz and the others, and hoped they were not in the nuthouse.

Chapter 5

1976

A new silver N registration Rover drifted along the clean lines of the motorway through the industrial midland jumble and chaos, past the factories, cemeteries, parks, pylons and terraces, then glided without effort over the elegant tangle of Spaghetti Junction, overtook lorries and trucks and sped towards the city down the four-lane motorway spur. The stereo played softly and Carol sang, 'I'm just second-hand news, just second hand news'. The rest of the traffic was going the other way and the roads into the city were almost empty.

The car swept into the final roundabout and inched its way through the late rush-hour jostle into the station forecourt. A tall elegant figure in a light grey mohair suit, pink shirt and tie waited by the glass doors. He carried a burgundy briefcase. Paul had recently swopped his thick-lensed spectacles for contact lenses, and his beautiful blue eyes were now clearly visible to all. He looked so sophisticated and handsome Carol couldn't believe he belonged to her. Recognising the car, he moved forward impatiently and was in the front seat almost before it stopped. He kissed Carol on the lips enveloping her in a cloud of Paco Rabanne and the stale smell of cigarettes.

'Hello darling, hi kids.' She loved being called darling, which you couldn't do with a Yorkshire accent. In Yorkshire it was 'love'. The way he pronounced her name made her feel special; you could say things with those southern vowels which couldn't be uttered or even thought in a Yorkshire accent.

A tiny child with large blue eyes and dark blonde hair appeared between the front seats.

'Hello daddy, guess what I did today.'

She was wearing a red leotard and hairband, white tutu and ballet shoes, having been bundled into the back seat directly from a dancing class.

'Hello Nessie, tell me when we get home. Hi Matt. Sit back in your seats now while mummy gets us through the traffic jam. Shall I drive darling?'

'Yes please.' Carol put the brake on and scrambled over the steering column as Paul walked round the bonnet. Her long skirt caught on the gear-stick, a platform-soled clog fell off and the scarf round her hair slipped over her eyes. Paul slid back the driver's seat to accommodate his long legs. He took the car quickly through the erratic traffic of the station forecourt and onto the four-lane roundabout where it was even worse.

'Daddy, do I have to go to Cubs?' Matthew stood behind the driving seat, skinny in his Cub uniform. 'Only Arkala keeps telling me and Dibsy off and she doesn't like us.'

Paul, his full attention on the taxis and buses which were bullying the rest of the traffic snapped, 'Not now Matt. Sit down. I can't see. Sit down.' He turned to Carol in annoyance. 'You're not doing anything, can't you control the bloody kids?'

The bubble of happiness trembled.

'Sit down, love, wait until we get home, daddy's driving. Look how busy the traffic is. What's wrong with the Cubs anyway?'

'Well, Arkala makes us do stupid things and me and Dibsy want to play chasey and she gets fed-up with us.'

The car entered the main traffic jam on the approach to the motorway.

'That's what Cubs is all about, doing stupid things,' growled Paul as he steered the car off the roundabout and onto the motorway. 'Dib bloody dob, waggle your woggle.' He switched on the radio full blast for 'Brown Sugar'. Matthew, bemused and slightly shocked by the verbal attack on the holy shrine of Cubdom, sank down into the back seat and gazed out of the window at the distant football ground. The car picked up speed.

'Did you have a nice day?' asked Carol over the noise.

'As nice as it can be, four hours on the train, another on the Underground and a fucking boring meeting.' She must ask him not to swear in front of the kids – again. 'Lunch was good. We went to this restaurant in Soho. Italian. I'll take you there sometime.' He always said that. The speedo reached 95 and Paul lit a cigarette.

'Oops! You're speeding.'

'Who's driving this fucking car?' His voice was petulant and angry. 'You keep the kids under control if you want to do something useful.'

Carol's happy mood wilted, and the bubble of happiness popped under the casual viciousness. She and the children became wary and quiet.

He was tired and stressed, otherwise he wouldn't be so snappy. He'd been up since six, that was a twelve-hour day. He'd probably had too many cigarettes, and his lunch-time wine or beer had almost certainly given him a headache. This was the wrong time to try and talk to him. He loved the kids really, and her too. She loved him so much that when he was irritable and short-tempered she felt desolate, as if she had done something wrong and might lose him.

This wasn't his real personality. In reality Paul was forgiving and generous, as she well knew. When she'd told him about Susan he had been fantastic - kindness itself.

They had been in the middle of yet another row about nothing at all. Nessie was a baby, Mat was sixteen months old, and it was the day before Susan's birthday. As the year moved into early spring, - lighter nights, warmth in the air, daffodils - the ghostly echoes of those final few weeks at the Warren and the abrupt expulsion into greyness seeped into her subconscious. She didn't deliberately recall Susan, or brood, it was simply an atmosphere which gathered in spring and dispersed as May approached. Arguments and bad feeling with Paul became unsolvable, she became moody and tearful. Some instinct, some optimism, told her that if Paul understood he would be kinder and their rows would be less fierce, the aftermath easier to recover from. After all, understanding other people was the key to solving problems. No-one was deliberately nasty.

She woke early that morning, Paul beside her. The sun slanted through the curtains onto the pine-clad ceiling promising a fine day but already the memory of yesterday's arguments threw a shadow. They couldn't go on like this. Matthew and Vanessa couldn't grow up under this cloud. They'd had a terrible argument and he'd pushed her on the floor making her feel worthless and humiliated, anxious that the children should not see. He'd apologised – sort of. Since then it had simmered below boiling point, ready to erupt at any moment and she'd spent most of the time crying. She felt like an animal trapped in a cage with no possibility of escape. It was worth the risk.

'Paul.' He stirred beside her.

'What?'

'I have to tell you something.'

'What? Whassamarrer? Are the kids alright?' He wasn't very good early in the morning. He didn't wake up well. Bad timing.

'There's something I have to tell you. I should have told you before we got married but I couldn't.' Paul rolled over and was watching her carefully. She sat up in bed, pulling the sheet to cover her nakedness, which seemed inappropriate. This was not the sort of thing you could say lying down. 'I thought you'd leave me.' His stillness and silence suggested that he was listening.

'What's that then? How bad is it?'

'It is something awful.'

'Have you… have you been in the nick?'

'In prison? Are you joking? No, I haven't.' She was puzzled. How could he be so wrong? 'Nothing like that. I…I…I…before I met you, before I went to Leeds, something happened. I should have told you then, but I didn't. I had…' he waited. The struggle between the habit of secrecy and the need to tell choked into tears, 'I had a baby.'

'Christ!'

'It was a little girl. She was adopted.' Carol was sobbing in earnest. Maybe Paul would leave her now. If he did she'd be on her own with two children. She might have to go back to the village. He would be angry. She hated lying to him, to everybody. How could he fail to be angry? She had deceived him. He'd married her without knowing – if he had known he would have left her –most men would.

'I'm sorry. I am so sorry'

With amazement she felt his arm round her shoulder.

'You poor, poor - how long ago?'

Questions and answers poured out until he had the whole story. His kindness and sympathy were like balm. 'So they sent you away all on your own?'

'Yes.'

'And no-one knew?'

'No. They still don't. No-one except my mum and dad.'

'Have you seen the father since?'

'No, not since I was about four months pregnant. He's married now, I think. I don't want to see him.'

'Do you still love him?'

'No – of course not. I love you.'

'How could they do that to you? It's fucking barbaric. Why didn't you tell me?' While they talked he held her in his arms.

'I thought you'd leave me, not want to marry me. I wanted to marry you so much. I couldn't bear it if you'd gone.'

'You didn't trust me then? You didn't think much of me if you thought I'd leave you.' He reached for a cigarette and gave her one.

'Would you have?' He lit the cigarettes before answering.

'I don't know.' He blew out smoke and lay back on the pillow. 'You can't tell what you'll do - we'll never find out now.'

He hadn't said 'no'. The words sounded cynical but the tone was gentle. He gave her his hankie to wipe her eyes.

'Your parents doing that to you - it's medieval. How could they?'

She soaked up his sympathy like a dry sponge soaking up water. Each kind word raised him above her family, the rest of the world, who would condemn and blame. Each comforting hug marked him out as a man who went against convention, made his own decision on right and wrong, applied his own principles of morality and they were above everyone else's, not just acceptance of society or parents, they were in her favour. He was on her side. His kindness and consideration were soothing, healing. She felt gratitude to him for his acceptance of her past mistakes, for not making her feel like a second-class person, for not blaming her but instead trying to understand, for overlooking her lies of omission. Each utterance of forgiveness raised him higher and higher.

Whatever he said or did after that, when put into the balance and weighed against his generosity of spirit and his kindness, could never begin to turn the scales.

They dropped Matthew off at Cubs on the way home. As the car pulled up on the drive Carol glanced up at the balcony behind which Matthew's bedroom light showed. He must have left it on. Dusk was falling and the light looked comfortable and welcoming. From the drive she could see a blanket of twinkling lights which covered the shallow valley below and spread up to the horizon. Evening stars pricked through the pinks, greens and blues of the sunset. Midland sunsets could be spectacular – as the sun dropped below the horizon the last moments of daylight reflected from the low clouds of pollution. Beauty and poison - a delight to the eye, a pleasure to the soul, a poison to the body.

Vanessa tumbled out of the car and filled the house with chatter and activity. Paul went immediately to the kitchen cupboard and began rummaging about in the medicine box.

'Where's the fucking paracetamol? Have you moved it?' he demanded irritably.

'No, it's in there somewhere,' Carol said as she removed a beef casserole from the oven and set it on the table. He found the tablets and slammed the cupboard door.

'What's that? Beef stew? Fucking school dinners again. I suppose it's mashed potato as well.' It was. He swallowed the paracetamol and lit a cigarette. 'Well I don't want any. I had a decent meal at lunch time.' He pulled savagely at the knot of his tie so that it hung loose and stalked out to the lounge.

'Don't bloody eat it then,' she called after him. She'd made it from a recipe, experimenting, using red wine and herbs. She lifted the lid - it smelled delicious.

The television went on in the lounge – the evening news. Five minutes later when she looked in he was asleep, sprawled on the sofa, the tension in his face relaxed and softened. He looked pale and beautiful, aesthetic, like a monk. His skin was pale, the dark blonde hair tumbled. Her anger dissolved. As always, she felt the need for his arms round her, his lips on hers, the tenderness of his love. The cat, a blatant opportunist, leapt softly onto the sofa and nestled with precision into the warmth alongside his thigh, careful not to disturb him. She set up a low contented purr.

Carol took Vanessa and went to pick Matthew up from Cubs.

At times like this, he was impossible, but there was another side to him.

* * *

'Mummy, where do babies come from?'

Carol was straining a saucepan of potatoes and looked up as Matthew appeared at her elbow.

'Babies? I told you. They come from the mummy's tummy.'

Vanessa appeared.

'Yes, but, but….' Matthew was struggling to find the right words.

'How do they get there?' cut in Vanessa in her clear ringing voice. Matthew gave her an angry look for saying what he was trying to say and getting there first. Nessa smiled triumphantly.

Paul followed them in. Tight blue jeans, snake hips, blue denium shirt, blue eyes – he was, she thought, extremely fanciable. His sun-tinted fair hair flowed and curled behind his ears, and his skin still retained the tan from a recent holiday. He looked like a pop star.

'In a minute. Look, ask daddy while I do dinner.' She smiled at him.

'What?' he laughed.

'How do babies get into the mummy's tummy?' asked Matthew.

'Ah.' Paul reached for his cigarettes and lit one, playing for time. She could almost hear his brain ticking over. 'Well, it's a seed from the daddy.'

'How does it get into the mummy?'

'Well….. it's easy. I'll draw you a picture. Go and get your drawing book.'

They spread the book on the table, pushing aside the cutlery.

'This is the lady, and if you could see inside her you'd see…'

'Can I draw the lady?' interrupted Vanessa. 'Can I do her face, daddy?

Is she a princess?' Kneeling on a chair she leaned forward eagerly across the table, weight on folded arms, nose inches from the paper, concentrating intently on the diagram.

'Yes in a minute. Now this is the daddy. His seed comes out of here and he puts this into the lady here.' The cat jumped on the table and began padding deliberately to and fro across the drawing, seeking her share of attention.

Matthew, standing at Paul's elbow, looked up with great seriousness into his eyes. 'Oh yes, and does he do a wee in there, does he?' asked Matt intelligently.

'No, not really, no he doesn't,' said Paul as he struggled for words.

Carol, leaning on the sink, listening, raised her eyebrows as he caught her eye. She smiled broadly at his discomfort and made no attempt to rescue him. He grinned back, and his grin reached into her soul, melting her heart, creating happiness and contentment.

* * *

The gas fire flame effect flickered cosily on the lounge wall. Stylistically it was gross, like a 1950's juke box, chrome trim and plastic wood veneer, but it threw out plenty of heat. Pools of light from table lamps fell on books, plants and pictures. The window wall was curtained in a long sweep of pale Scandinavian open-weave natural wool. Pale green squirls of linen Sanderson loose covers and glimpses of olive green wall behind books on the white bookshelves added a subdued colour to the neutral creams and whites of the carpets and walls. Carol loved this room – the first one they'd furnished with things they'd chosen. Chloe, a beautiful self-possessed cream and brown seal-point Siamese, posed in front of the fire, colour co-ordinating perfectly with her surroundings. Paul sprawled by the fire in an armchair, smoking as he watched a current affairs programme which was examining the latest incidence of industrial unrest. He had already explained the situation to her in depth after the earlier news, and now he began to heckle the presenter vigorously as Carol came in fastening a towel round her wet hair. She sank into the deep sofa, swinging her legs onto the cushions. Her Japanese kimono, a birthday present from Paul, parted briefly, showed she was naked underneath. She glanced at Paul to see if he'd noticed.

'Look at that. British Management. They couldn't manage their way out of a paper bag.' She wondered if he heckled silently when she wasn't there to hear him. Carol's Open University course was in part about industrialisation and she'd have liked to listen. 'No wonder we've got problems. We've got Personnel Managers who came from the army, shiny shoes, blazers and no fucking idea about what real life's all about. They're like bloody aliens. We've got top management all from public schools, no expertise just the old boy's network. Shirt-lifters to a man. Never came into contact with ordinary people, most of them......it's not what you know, it's who you know. What a bloody shambles.'

Bored, Carol wandered over to look at the bookshelf behind Paul. A small Petri dish stood on the shelf in front of the books. It was full of stick insect eggs, collected from the bottom of the glass sweetie jar where the repulsive creature had lived until it made its escape. It now lived on the inaccessible part of the hall ceiling, coming down to feed off the ivy plant below when it was hungry and galloping back to safety if anyone approached, its little feet gripping the uneven Artex surface. She tipped the dish to look closely and the eggs tumbled in a cascade over the edge of the dish and hid themselves in the shaggy pile carpet. Bugger! Paul ranted on. She decided not to mention it, and vacuum them up in the morning.

'It's still better than the previous deal,' she offered, returning to the sofa.

'What do you mean?' Paul was unused to opposing opinions and like his mother did not appreciate them.

'Your dad was a postman, mine was a miner. You're the first in your family to go to University - even though you didn't take your degree in the end, you had the education - and I'm the first in mine to study for a degree, even if it is only Open University.'

'What do you mean 'only'? I told you, you're as clever as any of those lot at Leeds. It takes more effort to do well when you're running a home as well.' Surely that couldn't be true – Paul was much cleverer than she was.

'What I'm saying is, we've got the chance. Working class people didn't - before. If you hadn't told me I could do it, I'd never have tried. No-one told me I could, before. By the way, I had another essay back today.'

'What did you get? Don't tell me - another A for a change.'

'Yes, I have to admit it was.'

'Good. Well done.'

'I also had a form about summer school. Are you sure it's alright if I go?'

'Yes - we've already discussed this. Of course it is. Anyway it's compulsory isn't it?'

'Will you be alright with the kids?'

'Course I will. I'm not helpless. We'll be fine. When are you going?'

'August, the sixteenth'

'I'll book a week off. Where are you going?'

'Keele.'

'That's not far. Just up the motorway. You can drive yourself there, can't you?'

'I'm not sure I can do the motorway on my own.'

'Course you can.'

'I don't know. Remember when I had to take the car to West Brom up the M5. I got confused and went onto the M6 by mistake. I was hemmed in by massive lorries with wheels higher than my car, pounding away inches from my window. I've never been so scared. I didn't know what to do until I figured out I had no choice but to go on to the next exit and turn around. How will it be on my own on the M6?'

'Oh that Junction's always a bastard. Anyway, you've done it now, this'll be a piece of piss by comparison. I'll draw you a map.'

'Thanks. Do you think I'll be okay?'

'Course you will. You'll have all the blokes after you.'

If they're the same ones as at tutorials they needn't bother. Anyway, in six years I'll have a degree. Not bad, eh?'

'Course not. You worked hard for your 'A' level, you'll be okay. Why don't you apply for a full-time course?'

'Oh I couldn't do that.'

'Why not? You'd get a grant as well.'

'I couldn't do the work.'

'But you get 'A's with Open University.'

'Yes, but…'

'The standard's the same. A degree's a degree.'

'Yes but, full time!'

'Why not? As long as the kids have first call. They're both full time at school, or will be in September. What else will you do with your time?'

'I'm not sure. What if I can't do the work?'

'Of course you can do the work. You get 'A's at OU. Why shouldn't you?'

'I don't know. It might be different. I might not be able to cope.'

'You could be right.'

'What?'

Without taking his eyes off the screen he said, seriously, 'Well, you've been sitting here half an hour now, and you still haven't made the tea, so I don't know if you'll be able to cope with a full time degree.'

She laughed. 'Bugger off. You make it.'

'I've been working all day.'

'What do you think I've been doing?'

'Writing essays I should think.'

'Alright then, I'll make tea then I'm off to bed.'

She lay in bed on the chocolate brown Habitat sheets, beneath the brown and white duvet flicking through a copy of 'Playboy' which she had bought Paul as part of his birthday present. He'd never buy one himself and she enjoyed reading it. The jokes and cartoons were rude and funny, the articles, or some of them, were interesting in that whilst apparently striving for objectivity they still reflected a totally male outlook which made a refreshing change from the humourless goody goody image of women's magazines. The pictures were a turn-on, reminding her of her own sexuality and the response she could evoke in Paul. Although they did seem to be verging on the gynaecological. If the camera had been any nearer to the centrefold model it would have been taking a picture of the inside of her fallopian tubes. It was funny that pictures of men didn't make her feel sexy. She didn't fancy the women, it was as if they were expressing how one part of her would like to be if she hadn't been too inhibited. Wanton. Lustful. Beautiful.

About two hours after the central heating switched off she heard Paul stumble up the stairs. In the darkness of the bedroom he threw off his clothes and snuggled, frozen, under the duvet. On the edge of sleep, she wrapped her arms and legs round him to warm him up and he slipped his arm under her head. Their naked bodies twined together, his chilliness roused her into wakefulness again. He kissed her briefly, then again lingeringly. She ran her hand down his chest, over his stomach, lightly across his penis, which was rapidly stiffening, and curled it delicately round, cupping his testicles. He flicked his tongue into her mouth and pulled her on top of him. She kissed his lips and face gently until he was comfortably inside her, and they moved rhythmically together, slowly at first then more urgently. She pushed herself upright, knees spread widely, as he penetrated, deeper and deeper, until she felt he almost reached her throat. The cold moonlight filtered in through the white filmy curtains and the duvet fell away. Chilly air enveloped her shoulders and breasts but was scarcely noticed. She arched her back, moving strongly with increasing urgency. His hands came up to encircle her breasts. The thrusts became deeper, the mounting pleasure irresistible. The orgasm was perfectly timed - his hands on her hips held her tightly in place, and they finished together. She threw her head back, gasped as the waves of sensation swept from clitoris to vagina, swirled in a warm blossoming of pleasure in her stomach and grew out to her breasts, enveloped every nerve ending lusciously down to her toes. Her whole body glowed with satisfied desire. She collapsed upon his chest, kissed his lips tenderly, whispered, 'Oh God that was brilliant, fucking brilliant - thank you for having me.'

He kissed her back, his arms wrapped round her so tightly she could hardly breathe.

'My pleasure. Thank you for coming,' he laughed.

She laid her head on his chest and stretched her doubled-up legs out straight. Semen oozed out onto his stomach.

'Oops.'

'Here use this,' and he rummaged under the pillow and handed her a hankie.

'Virgo,' she accused, mopping herself, and handing him the hankie.

She slid off him and lay beside him on the bed, arms and legs still slippily entwined with his, his arm under her head – protectively encircling, holding her close.

'Love you.' Kiss.

'Love you too.' Kiss.

She heaved a sigh of huge contentment and nuzzled her face into his neck. Whatever doubts she had at any other time, when they were in bed she was completely, truly happy. He was hers, and always would be. He loved her and he was content, and if she had him, and the kids, she had the world. Holding in her arms everything she wanted she fell asleep.

* * *

Open University Summer School was the beginning of the end of an era.

In 1975 OU was still fulfilling its original aim of removing the barriers to higher education, before market forces took it out of the reach of the very people for whom it was brought into existence and the cost put it well beyond the means of the increasing number of unemployed and lower paid. OU still expressed the attitude of the 1960's of freedom, self-expression and opportunity, 'I think therefore I am' became 'I do therefore I can'. The courses were affordably cheap and well-designed. Students required no formal qualifications to gain entry. There were no age limits. Anyone could try, though no-one was exempted from the academic standards; a module could be repeated but a pass was required to gain a credit. Six credits gave a degree.

Traditional boundaries were challenged on all fronts and vanquished. A degree opened doors which were otherwise closed fast.

Fellow students represented the whole of the social spectrum. Regional and social accents of immense variety and purity clattered and spluttered in profusion. Glottal stops and velar plosives, bilabial wotsits and dental fricatives rendered the English language into a thousand exotic hybrids. The body language spoke even louder. Old and young met on equal and apparently amiable terms. Train drivers and vicar's daughters, housewives and accountants, lecturers and secretaries, teachers and engineers were thrown together. They discussed Hamlet and Yeats, analysed the pericopae of the Bible, sang sixteen-part madrigals – more enjoyable than it sounded - danced, met in bars, had parties and got drunk together. Many began their first steps out of their social class, which had a sad effect on the husbands and wives back at home. Many a marriage began to disintegrate under pressure of the widening gap between partners which first began to open at Summer School.

The enthusiasm for learning, the thirst for new knowledge and ideas, was like a drug, its effects as mind-expanding. For some students it was more like an aphrodisiac.

Carol slipped free from the narrow stream of domesticity and wriggled with delight into the ocean of unfettered time and space which was hers for a week. Arriving with a suitcase full of clothes, she left the mental and social baggage behind. She was not someone's wife, someone's daughter, someone's mother but merely someone - an individual in her own right. This was an intimidating thought, and lead to doubts about her own adequacy, quickly submerged by the programme which demanded full attention every waking moment. When finally she had a moment to think about it again, she found she was quite able to be an independent person with opinions and abilities and a point of view.

Groups formed and re-formed. The trade unionists drank together and told tall boastful stories about the truth behind strike negotiations. Teachers discussed schools, pupils and examination results. 'The blokes' prowled about looking for loose women and some of the male lecturers had theirs sorted out before they arrived. The girlies got together and said how wonderful it was not to do the shopping, cooking and washing up and, in truth, this lack of household responsibilities was part of the increasing self-awareness which was finding a foothold in Carol's consciousness.

When Carol glimpsed Jeanette a few places ahead of her in the refectory queue she recognised the face and voice immediately. Jeanette's non-pregnant persona was unexpectedly untrendy, even slightly old-fashioned looking, as far as clothes and hairstyle went. Instant flashbacks to the group by the fire in Mrs. Thomas's kitchen, the occupants of the chilly bedroom, the group of people round the dining table, confirmed that nevertheless this was the same person. The voice, full of confidence and now overlaid with an unfamiliar accent, was unmistakeably the same.

'He has great big feet, size 12 and he's only thirteen. You can tell his dad was a policeman, he's nearly six feet tall, and sounds like a real Irishman - you wouldn't believe he was born in England.' Carol listened mesmerised unable to tear her eyes away from Jeanette. The babble and clatter of the dining room faded to a distant murmur as her brain filtered it out and concentrated. This was her baby Jeanette was talking about.

The familiar fear of recognition, the sick churning in the pit of the stomach, failed to kick in, crowded out by curiosity, the need to hear more. This was the first link with that previous long-buried existence. Jeanette obviously did not recognise her in the 1970's disguise of Afro perm, slim figure, large owl-like tortoise-shell framed specs and brightly coloured clothes. Who would link this figure with the pale, dark-haired quiet girl with sensible shoes and brown pinafore dress, unmemorable, massively pregnant, always reading a book?

They became part of the same group, meeting in the dining-room and the bar and over the next few days Jeanette's story emerged.

She had refused to give her baby up for adoption. Instead she had taken him to London and lived hand to mouth whilst completing her teaching qualification. Then, sickening of London, she had escaped to teach in the far west of Ireland, married a fisherman, had an affair with his brother and generally scandalised the small close-knit community with her behaviour. So - no change there, still the same person.

Clearly Jeanette had had the strength of character and purpose to take responsibility for herself and her baby, to take her chances and stand up for what she wanted. She was her own person. Whatever life threw at her she made the decisions, lived by the results. She was lively, confident and, by mid-week, deep into a passionate affair with a fellow-student. Carol wondered if she was a heroine, strong spirited, admirable, pursuing her own desires, making life do as she wanted, or a trollop, causing havoc to those around her, putting her own needs first, leaving a trail of destruction behind her. It should not be necessary to make a judgement, but human nature always sought to label everything in order to understand.

Was Jeanette's story a tragedy, a comedy, a drama or a love story? It would depend on the author and the genre, which aspects were emphasised, which played down, on the audience, and the period for which it was written. Tess of the D'Urbervilles had had a baby, and the Victorian morality demanded that she should suffer for it. Jane Austen's heroines were spirited but apparently devoid of sexual appetite until beyond marriage, and then they ceased to be heroines. Cathy Linton was passionate. Did she do it with Heathcliffe? Now, in the seventies, literary heroines had sexual adventures, but didn't have babies. Values changed. The judgements became less harsh.

Jeanette's mother and husband were no doubt less than happy, and the new lover, when he was dumped at the end of the week, might not be too pleased, but she had pleased herself, decided what she wanted and had it. Her son would know his mother loved him enough to fight to keep him. She had gone against the social conventions, risked disapproval, stood up for herself.

Had Shaun's life been good? Would he have been better off adopted? You only travelled the path once, so there was no way to tell. She'd always believed implicitly in Susan's happiness. Now she began to doubt it. If she had been stronger could she have done the same as Jeanette and fought for what she wanted, had the guts and determination to take life and force it into the shape she decided on?

Carol admired Jeanette, wished she could be like her, and knew she could not be. She needed approval and the security of following the rules. Jeanette had always delighted in pleasing herself, enjoyed creating a conflict, loved to be at the centre of the storm, had the blessed confidence in herself and her survival. Where did she get confidence like that?

Susan, like Shaun, was now thirteen. Carol wondered for the millionth time where she was. Did she ever think about her mother, ask herself why she had been adopted? There was no way of knowing, no way of finding out.

The last link had been the photograph of the four-month-old baby sent to her via Matron. A few months after she had married Paul she had given it to her mother for safe-keeping. When she had told Paul about the baby she wanted to show him the photograph. On her next visit to Rossingley, choosing the moment,, she had gone into the kitchen where her mother was assembling dinner.

'Mum?'

'Yes. By, look at this leg of lamb.' She held up a roasting tin containing a raw lump of meat surrounded by peeled potatoes. 'It's from Drury's butchers. It's a beautiful piece of meat.'

'Yes.' Mrs. Stone turned away, opened the oven door and pushed the roasting tin into the heat. 'Mum?'

'Pass me that fork,' she waved a hand at the worktop, eyes on the tin.

'Right. Here you are. Mum?'

'What? What do you want?' Finally she turned and stood looking at Carol with impatience.

'You remember that photo of Susan and the letter from Matron?' Her mother looked uncomfortable and guilty. Her eyes dropped and she said nothing. 'You remember? She was four months old.'

'Yes. Yes, I do,' she said quietly, her voice weary.

'Well, would you mind if I had it back? I'd like to have it back, see it again.'

'Well, I'm sorry, you can't,' said Mrs. Stone quietly.

'Why not? It is mine, really. I only asked you to look after it for me,' said Carol persuasively.

'I've burned it.'

The words did not make sense.

'What!' It couldn't be true. 'What did you say?'

'I've burned it. I thought it was for the best.'

'Why did you do that? You can't have. What for? Why?' Mrs. Stone's lined face wobbled as the tears filled Carol's eyes. Was it a punishment? A mistake?

'I was worried in case something happened to me and someone else went through my things and found it, and found out.'

'You're joking. You can't have.'

She'd done it on purpose.

'I did,' she replied, her voice quiet, stubborn.

'It was the only photo I had. Why didn't you ask me?'

'I never thought.'

'You had no right.'

'Well, it's done now. I can't undo it.'

'Are you sure? You couldn't have made a mistake'

'No, I am sure.' She heaved a sigh, like someone bearing an intolerable burden. Carol wanted to shake her.

'Oh God! I don't believe it. I gave it to you to keep it safe. You've burned it?' Carol asked again, hoping for a different answer.

'Yes.'

'When?' she asked desperately.

'A year or two ago.'

'It wasn't yours to burn,' she accused quietly.

'I know. I didn't want anyone else finding it,' replied Mrs. Stone stubbornly. 'I'm sorry.'

It was an implacable unchangeable truth. It had to be accepted.

'Never mind. What's done is done,' said Carol, quietly, wanting to scream. Even the last little fragment had gone.

Without the photo she had only her memory, and that was now fading.

Even if it were possible to find Susan, it wouldn't be fair. She had given her up to a family who could take care of her, had renounced all rights. You couldn't let someone start a new life, then destroy it by reappearing. 'Hello, I'm your mother. How are you?' No, if they were ever to meet again it would have to be because Susan had decided she wanted to. It wouldn't be fair to cause upheaval in her life. Not that there was any choice - she had signed away her rights as a parent in the J.P.'s house in Leeds years ago. That was final, a legal document against which it was not possible to argue.

She wondered about Susan as a 13-year-old. At thirteen she had been well established as her dad's chief antagonist. They'd avoided each other, or argued. She'd started to be interested in boys and clothes, went to Youth Clubs, liked Elvis and swimming. What would Susan be interested in? Where did she live? Did she like her father? Did she have brothers and sisters? Was she happy? Did she like school? Was she pretty? Did she take after Rob or herself?

* * *

Others beside Jeanette were making the most of the freedom and anonymity of Summer School. By the middle of the week a number of affairs had blossomed. Individuals became couples, couples became inseparable, mooning over meals, bidding long affectionate farewells before separating for lectures and vanishing completely in the early evening.

'It'll end in tears,' said Betty as they discussed a couple at the next dining table who sat holding each other by one hand and eating with the other. They both looked about forty. Betty was fat with lank greasy hair and seemed to have wide mood swings. Perhaps she was jealous. Carol hadn't met a single man who could compare with Paul. They were not so handsome, or confident, amusing, well-informed, or sexy. She couldn't imagine kissing one, let alone getting into bed with one. Beer bellies and beards, sweaty smells and unmemorable faces.

The lectures and seminars, concerts and activities continued. Descartes, Marlow, Lawrence, Blake, Shakespeare - words and ideas poured out like treasure from a chest. She became a learning junkie, getting high on new ideas. She collected names and titles like a magpie collecting shiny scraps. The pieces of knowledge began to fit together with experience like a jigsaw to form a larger pattern, widening Carol's awareness of herself in relation to the world in which she lived.

The difference between the people who inhabited her childhood, who worked and lived in one place all their lives and had little control over anything that happened to them, and those who owned or controlled the offices, businesses, and organisations where decisions were made was, ultimately, education. This education was not even remotely connected to what went on at grammar school during the five years she had spent there. This education gave new insights, challenged the narrow accepted view, opened the mind to new ways of thinking.

She longed to be able to understand an informed conversation, follow an argument, understand abstract ideas and concepts. She began to grasp the wider picture of history and the social niche into which she had been born, and was amazed that she had been able to step outside it. Paul belonged to this world by virtue of his education and his job, and she admired him and aimed to follow him.

There was no turning back, her feet were on a path which led one way only. You couldn't reclaim your ignorance, unlearn awareness, unthink new thoughts, unread new authors.

* * *

The guy who gave her a lift back to the block had been eyeing her up all evening as she danced with her new best friend Judy, enjoying the music, aware of the effect of the long tight-fitting skirt and skimpy lace-trimmed bodice. He and his mate had cut in as she and Judy had guessed they would. He was a science lecturer, tall and skinny, and he somehow reminded her of the stick insect in the hall at home, although she knew that was being unfair. This impression derived from both his physical appearance and his alien personality. Knowing that students generally found lecturers irresistible, he tried hard to impress. She had accepted the lift in good faith because it was raining. They had sat in his car chatting for a few minutes and he'd suddenly pulled her head into his lap and said, 'Kiss me.'

'What?' she asked, twisting her head to look at him.

'Kiss me.' He looked suddenly embarrassed, released her head and tried a nonchalant little laugh which failed.

'How do you mean, Nigel?'

'Oh - forget it. You've been married too long.'

'For what?' she asked.

'To understand.'

She understood only too well. 'To understand what?'

'Never mind.'

'What do you mean, Nigel?'

'Sorry - forget it.'

'Okay. Well, bye then. Thanks for the lift.'

'Bye,' he muttered.

She closed the door carefully, bent down to peer through the window, smiled and gave him a friendly little wave of the fingers. He waved back with a sickly grin. He was leaning forward, arms folded across the steering wheel. Beneath the ribbed tank top in the shadow of his curving thin chest, underneath the cavalry twills, something stood up like a chapel hat-peg.

'Bye Nigel.'

She tripped lightly into the block and heard the car engine screech as he reversed savagely and roared off, probably back to the disco to see if it wasn't too late to pull another piece of totty, and rescue what he could of this last night, before going home to his wife.

Suddenly Carol remembered that she'd forgotten to vacuum up the stick insect eggs which had spilled into the carpet months ago.

* * *

On Saturday lunch-time, tired and hung-over, Carol parked the battered red mini on the drive, left the bags in the car and walked through the hall. Silence. Everything neat and tidy, no-one about.

'Hello.' No reply. The cat, sitting on the eighth stair, meowed in response, then reached out and patted her head as she passed. Eventually she found Paul in the garden mending the hose-pipe. He barely looked up as she called, 'Hi,' and gave a disgruntled grunt in response.

'Is anything wrong?'

'No. Why? Should it be?' He spoke without stopping work, or looking up.

'No. You seem - funny.' She stood awkwardly, hands stuffed in jeans pockets.

'Well I don't feel - funny,' he said sarcastically.

'Anyway - I'm home.' Tentative smile.

'Yes. So I see,' he said still without looking up.

'Don't you want to know how I got on?'

'How did you get on?' he asked in a flat voice.

'Great.'

'Good.' Silence. He walked off to connect the hose pipe to the garden tap.

'Where are the kids?'

'Playing down the field.'

'Did you miss me?'

'I suppose so.'

'Well, hello then.'

'You've already said that.'

'What the hell is wrong?'

'Don't bloody start. We've got on fine without you, you come home and you've started a row already.'

'No I haven't.'

'Yes you have.'

'Have I done something wrong?'

'You tell me.'

'Flaming hell fire, I wish I'd stayed there. At least people were civilised.'

'Why didn't you? I thought you were coming home last night.'

'Oh, so, that's it. I decided to stay for the disco. I told you.'

'Oh, right. The fucking disco. I suppose you met some hairy-arsed dick-head and stayed with him.'

'No - of course not.'

'You didn't meet anyone?'

'No. This bloke gave me a lift back to the block in his car and tried to kiss me, but I wasn't interested.'

This contribution to the conversation gave rise to twenty minutes of lively and vigorous exchange of views and personal opinions expressed in increasingly limited vocabulary. The sounds rang round the row of back gardens, echoing in the summer sunshine, enlightening the neighbours as to the precise state of affairs at No. 65.

Eventually ... 'Yeah, well - Open University Summer Schools are well known for it.'

'I tell you nothing happened. I didn't meet anyone.'

He was thawing, imperceptibly but surely.

'Right. If you say so,' he muttered, grudgingly.

'Do you want a cup of tea?' A peace offering.

'Yes please.' Peace offering accepted.

'Okay.' She turned to go into the kitchen. Negotiations concluded.

'By the way look out if you go into the lounge. I keep finding what looks like baby stick insects in the carpet by the shelves.'

* * *

Six years was too long to wait for a degree. Carol passed the A100 Arts Foundation course with OU and decided that a career in teaching was the only way to fit work and family into her life and chose a 3-year Bachelor of Education course at the nearest college – fortunately only five minutes away. Paul made his way in computer sales - a most rewarding career, financially if not spiritually.

Three years flew by – there was no time to think about the past; the present was full of everything she could want –Paul, the children, home, holidays, college.

The final year ended in its usual anti-climax. Frantic hard work leading up to the bout of examinations gave way to the unfocussed lull after the storm. Graduation day came and went. The photograph of herself in gown and mortar-board was tucked away in a drawer. The summer holiday began in earnest.

Late July. The usual weekday dullness of Park Street was transformed by roundabouts, balloon sellers, hot dog stands, groups of freshly-released teenagers, laughing and flirting, young mums with pushchairs, old ladies on their way to the market. Carol, Matt and Van ambled aimlessly through the crowd, dazzled with sunshine, absorbed with melting ice-creams. The market researcher stepped out of nowhere. Carol remembered a brief period of audience research for the BBC, before college, and the difficulty of finding the day's quota of interviewees and agreed to answer the questions. The last question was about social class.

'Professional, managerial, blue collar, white collar, manual?' the plump well-made-up redhead enquired, making her own appraisal.

Did you judge by occupation, income, accent, background, parents, husband, what?

'I'm not sure which I am.'

The red-head glanced at Matt and Nessie, now aged eight and nine. They gazed back with curiosity, uncommunicative.

'What does your husband do? Does he have a degree or professional qualification?'

Matt and Nessie transferred their blue gaze to Carol, wanting her to do well with the questions.

'He sells computers. No he doesn't have a degree.'

The woman poised her pen, ready to write. Carol suddenly remembered.

'But I do - I've just graduated and I'm going to be a teacher.'

The red-head looked up from the clipboard and smiled.

'Congratulations. I'll fill in the details for your status then.'

Matt and Nessie grinned, delighted. They were the winners after all.

The feeling of pride and independence stayed with her all day. This was the moment she first appreciated that she had a separate and creditable existence from Paul. With a degree, she even had something he didn't have.

* * *

Carol began teaching at a local comprehensive. Paul continued to be based in the large office block in the centre of the city. Matthew and Vanessa progressed through junior school. Life was busy and, with two salaries, they could afford holidays abroad, a new kitchen, cars, and all the other luxuries which money could buy.

* * *

The late October twilight was giving way to darkness when Paul's headlights illuminated the fading frost-pinched roses in the front garden. Before he could get his key in the door it was opened for him by Carol. Hair and make-up immaculate, jewellery and clothes carefully chosen to look casual but glamorous - jeans, high heeled sandals and dangly ear-rings - her face lit up at the sight of him, the first for a week.

He had phoned once or twice from the Exhibition in Edinburgh. The hotel was 5-star and luxurious, his room had colour tv, bathroom and double bed, the food was superb. The conference, exhibition and people were boring and on balance he'd rather be at home. Now here he was, the six hour drive behind him, haggard, eyes bleared, lines etched deeply on either side of his mouth. His shirt sleeves were rolled up, tie loosely knotted, jacket slung over his shoulder, hands full with briefcase and suitcase.

'Hello. Did you have a good journey?'

He leaned across and pecked her on the cheek, his attitude implying that luggage and tiredness prevented a more affectionate gesture. His breath stank of sourness and stale cigarettes.

'Yes, not too bad. Come on, let me in. I can't stand here all night.'

'Sorry. Sorry. Come in.' She stood aside. 'Shall I take your case? Dinner's ready when you are.'

'Don't want any dinner. Upset stomach.'

'Cup of tea then?'

'Yeah. Thanks. Kids in bed?'

'Yes. Gone upstairs, anyway. I'll tell them you're here.' Standing at the bottom of the stairs she yelled, 'Matt, Nessie, your dad's here.' Paul winced at the volume and the coloquial words.

They both appeared at the top of the stairs, ready for bed.

'Hello daddy,' Nessie glanced at Paul, taking in and evaluating the details of his appearance.

'Hi dad,' Matt grinned.

They came down, gave and received kisses.

'Shouldn't you two be in bed?'

With little argument they vanished back into their respective bedrooms.

Paul looked around for somewhere to put his case. The red-brown cord carpet in the hall was completely clear and spotless except for the space under the stairs where, next to the telephone table, Carol had stacked her school bag and a pile of exercise books.

'What's all this crap? Can't move in here for your school shit. Do we have to have this here?' Petulantly he slammed his case down in the middle of the narrow hall.

'It has to go somewhere. There's plenty of room.' The pleasure and anticipation of his return began to evaporate in the face of his mood.

Carol splashed boiling water into the teapot. A malevolent silence took possession of the kitchen. Waves of antagonism washed from where Paul sat slumped at the kitchen table behind her and broke upon her mind. He drew heavily on a freshly lit cigarette. His gaze was palpable, eyes flicked disdainfully over her bottom and hips, tightly encased in blue denim. The bridal excitement of dressing to please turned to the ash of self-criticism, loathing of her too-plump thighs, over-high heels.

'So - did you have a good week up there?'

'I've told you most of it on the phone. It WAS work you know.'

'Yes, I know, but a week in a five-star hotel is something different.'

'It's all superficial. A bed's a bed. Food is food.'

'Better than egg and chips at home.'

'Not better. Different. And we never have egg and chips. Why don't we have egg and chips?'

'Too fattening.'

'By the look of your arse it's too late to worry about that,' his voice and words took away the last vestiges of pretence that the careful make-up and clothes, the welcoming immaculately clean house, the fresh flowers, the well-cooked dinner and bottle of wine, were trying to construct.

'You think you're so beautiful you're entitled to criticise?' she snapped back, hating herself for the tight jeans and stupid ear-rings.

'What's this? Playground behaviour again? 'Same to you with knobs on' - since you started work at that fucking school it's brought out a juvenile streak in you. It's like talking to a bloody teenager. Your arse is fat, okay? No argument is going to change it. It's fat.' His voice was cold, judgemental, the words chosen to hurt. Panic seized her, sat in her chest. His certainty was convincing.

'You bastard.'

'Tut, tut. Childish behaviour. Oh dear.'

Anger and confusion fought for dominance. He sprawled at the table, gimlet eyes fixed on her face, enjoying his power to destroy. Insolently he drew on his cigarette.

'Why did you come back? Why didn't you stay up there in your posh hotel with your smart-arse computer-sales friends and their expense-account boozing.'

'What, and leave you here in this house that I've worked for, paying all your expenses while I live in a garret on baked beans. Oh yes.'

'What are you talking about?'

'What do you think I'm talking about'

'Have you met someone else?' Carol asked sharply.

'What bloody women's magazine crap is this? No, I haven't 'met someone else'' his voice took on a heavily mocking tone,' and if I had I doubt I'd tell you, now would I?'

Why was he being like this? She couldn't understand. Was it something she'd said?

'Who was that girl you mentioned who was on the Exhibition stand?'

'Oh God, here we go again. Can't I even speak to someone else without you getting jealous? She was a girl, okay? Young, slim, attractive, intelligent and fun. That's all.'

'Did you sleep with her?'

His eyes mocked her. He lit another cigarette.

'No I didn't.'

'Then why are you being such a shit?'

'It's been a long week. I'm tired. Leave me alone.'

He got up, walked past her into the lounge as if she was not there, switched on the television and threw himself onto the sofa.

Carol lit a cigarette and drew heavily on it, hating herself for being fat, unattractive, not fun and unintelligent - the B.Ed. degree was only an ordinary one - for wearing ridiculous tight jeans, silly high heels, cheap dangly ear-rings and too much make-up. Carol imagined herself being all those things the girl in Edinburgh was, looking different, finding another man, leaving Paul, living life. But the life she wanted was Paul. And nine and a half stone wasn't fat, not really, for a person of five feet five inches.

She followed him into the lounge. Paul was asleep on the sofa, the television flickering silently in the corner. His face was pale and the lines round his mouth deeply grooved. The sensitive lips were closed, the thick over-long fair curls needed shampooing, the lean cheeks and narrow jaw covered in stubble. Torn between loving him and hating him, Carol turned down the volume on the television and crept upstairs.

She looked in on Nessie, who was reading in bed, tucked her in, kissed her and switched off the light. Then Matt, who was making a Lego creation on the big low table by his bed.

'Come on, sausage, into bed.' She tucked him in, kissed him goodnight.

In her own room Carol picked up a book, flung herself down on the bed and pulled the edges of the duvet across her legs.

The careful diction and lightly ironic tone of Jane Austen blotted out the present. 'Persuasion'. Lady Russell's enthusiasm for Anne's cousin, Mr. Elliott, Anne's preference for Captain Wentworth, were problems of such manageable proportions, Sir Walter Elliott of Kellynch-hall, shallow and selfish - it was restful to be absorbed in them and shut out the harsh insoluble truths of reality. In Jane Austen's world, love, wealth and social position were important. Mrs. Clay represented the social climbing section of society.

Probably these wealthy, refined and highly moral characters, reflections of Jane Austen's reality, derived their wealth from coal mines, the slave trade, plantations in the West Indies manned by slaves, cotton mills, and all the other means by which the upper classes organised the lower classes to provide them with an income to protect them from the nastiness of another reality. Suitors were evaluated on yearly income - so many thousand a year - and love was fortunate if it fell where common sense and marriage dictated. Pretty manners and underneath an iron-clad recognition of what life was really about. Like a Victorian corset - all blue silk ruching and lace, covering a steel foundation.

If she left Paul, she would have to deal with reality for herself, Matt and Vanessa, all on her own. No question of running home to mummy.

Carol woke at 1.35 am, undressed, climbed into bed and switched off the light.

At 3.10 Paul shuffled across the bedroom floor, threw his clothes on the floor, tossed the duvet aside, letting in all the cold air, then pulled it over himself, his back to her.

The next morning Carol woke with Paul's arm across her, his face nuzzled into her neck. She wanted to storm away from him, take out the hurt and return it to him. But it was warm and comfortable, his hand was sliding down across her nipples, down her belly and between her legs. Against her thigh, he hardened and pressed. Gently he thrust his hips, making her aware of the rigidness, pressing it into her thigh, pushing his fingers into the warm, damp recesses of her body. Her nipples hardened, her resolve melted and the hurt and anger of last night evaporated.

Maybe she could stay a while longer. She didn't have to take Matt and Van and find a new home just yet. If Susan did look for her she would find her with a beautiful family, a successful husband, a respectable career in teaching, a lovely home, a life to be proud of.

She need never know the truth.

'Guess where the November conference is,' he murmured into her ear.

'Istanbul?'

'Nah - not far out though. Athens. How would you like to stay in the Athens Hilton?' He kissed her lips, then moved down and nibbled her nipple.

'I think I'd like that a lot.'

Chapter 6

1984

The house was overgrown with ivy. It grew thickly from roots against the wall at the back, up over the roof and half-way down the front, the windows almost submerged in the green tide. Three substantial chimneys were completely covered and bristled with healthy greenness way up in the sunshine. Long festoons drifted down from the gutters. Birds lived and sang among its thickets on the pitch of the roof: squirrels leapt confidently along the wrist-thick vines.

Beside the sweep-round drive a vast horse-chestnut spread low branches across the front lawn, fat red leaf buds glowing in the spring sunshine. Behind the shadows of the tree the house dreamed in a cocoon of verdant stillness.

It stood in a road of 1930's urban mansions, well-kept, private and prosperous, home to the town's small business-men and professional classes. Expensive cars glided along the curving road, emphasising the calm and quiet of number 46.

Despite its great size - the garage alone was like a village hall with its varnished pine slatted ceiling - the house suggested the cosy friendliness of a cottage.

Inside it was little changed in the fifty years since the builders tore up the fields and set about developing this farm-track on the edge of the town. Olive green, chocolate brown and cream predominated. Dark panelling, stained glass windows, plate-rails and open fireplaces added the charm of a past age.

On their first visit, after a tour of the ruined splendour which was number 46, Mrs. Holland, who may have been old but knew a thing or two about salesmanship, sat Carol in the lounge in front of a crackling, fragrant log fire. Seated in the red velvet armchair, she sipped Earl Grey from a china teacup, nibbled home-made shortbread, and had a perfect view down the length of the garden. Every possible nook and cranny was filled with a glorious carpet of daffodils which danced and bobbed in the spring winds. The magical vista easily outweighed the smell of the leaking toilet pipe, the sight of leaded fanlights welded ajar by rust and giving off icy draughts, the dim mustiness of a purple and olive green bedroom, and the expensive sizzle of ancient electric radiators.

In the pub afterwards Paul was enthusiastic, like all salesmen a sucker for a good sales pitch.

'Did you see that garage roof? It was like a school hall - and the size!'

'Yes, and the garden was lovely.'

'It's the best road in the entire town. Everyone wants to live there.'

'What about this flat in France. Do you still want that? Carol asked.

'It's a better way to spend money than a flat in France. This way we'll be living in it, enjoying it all the time. A holiday flat - well, you can rent it out, but you only enjoy it for a few weeks a year. It does need a lot of work though. What about that purple and green!'

'Too right,' she agreed.

'Still, when Ian surveyed it he said it was 'Rolls Royce construction'. He is impartial - after all he is your brother. He seemed impressed.'

'So he should be - I'm impressed too.'

Anyone in their right mind ought to have run a mile. Three and a half years later, when she was cooking the Christmas turkey in the original 1930's Cannon gas cooker, left for them to use temporarily until the kitchen was redesigned, Carol wished they had.

Gradually, slowly, it changed. Five men took two days to remove the ivy. Builders turned several small rooms and pantries into a spacious twenty four foot kitchen with cherry-wood doors, red lampshades and Laura Ashley curtains. Dark panelling was painted white to reflect light. An oak inglenook fireplace in the lounge was painstakingly stripped, the bathroom refitted, bedrooms transformed, dining room made elegant and beautiful.

The bay window of the main bedroom looked out over half an acre of garden. Here, several years of work restored to their prime masses of roses, delphiniums, cranesbills, peonies, Solomon's Seal, daffodils, poppies and a pergola of climbing roses. Stone staddles and bird bath, Italian rockery and, in the distance, a tennis lawn, apple trees, poplar and sycamore completed the image of a perfect timeless English garden.

In their first new year in the house a pedigree Gordon Setter puppy joined the family, and began systematically weeing on all the carpets. Beautiful, totally daft and untrainable she was, in addition, spoiled and indulged by everyone. No animal ever had such enthusiasm for life, or capacity for destruction, as did Molly.

It was the perfect setting for a happy family life. Its size and glowing charm made the house a natural setting for a party.

The housewarming party was wild - few carpets and nothing to spoil, lots of space, masses of food and drink and two hundred guests. By Mat's 16th birthday party there would be hall carpet and white panelling. By Nessie's 18th, the kitchen would be done. Carol's 40th and the dining room would be complete. New Year's Eve 1987 the lounge would be resplendent in apricot and pale green. Two 21st birthdays would be celebrated in turn, but by then Matt and Nessie would be only visitors. By Silver Wedding Day the house would be complete, children and love gone, gone, gone.

* * *

The poppy red front door opened and Carol emerged backwards. Inexpertly she pulled after her over the doorstep a wheelchair containing an old man. The winter jasmine growing by the door brushed against his heavy overcoat and the plaid blanket which covered his knees, releasing perfume into the cold air. Sunshine splashed through the copper leaves of the horse-chestnut, glinted on the leaded and stained glass windows. Carol's mum waved from the kitchen window as they made their way past the cars on the drive down to the road and the pavement where they turned left.

Carol gripped the handles of the wheelchair tightly and exerted all her strength to guide it in a straight line over the tree roots which extended like frozen snakes and distorted the pavement. The autumn wind whistled through the branches overhead, whirling down the remaining brown leathery leaves of the beech trees which lined the road. The little grey head in front showed signs of agitation, the loose skin on the neck creased into folds as the head turned, showing a gaunt lined face and milky blue eyes.

'Watch out for those tree roots,' he instructed testily.

'Okay.'

She struggled on against the wind. A heap of dog mess loomed up ahead. Should she go to the right, the left, or over the middle? He pointed with his stick.

'Watch out for that dog shit.'

He replaced the stick across his knees. 'Must have dogs like bloody elephants round here.'

'Yes, yes, okay Dad,' she didn't have enough breath left to argue.

The wheelchair had a mind of its own and began to lurch towards a brand new Jag parked by the kerb.

The tortoise neck craned out of the carapace of over-coat, the voice rose an octave.

'She's trying to run me into the bloody kerb. Watch out for that car!' he called indignantly.

The voice rattled instructions and complaints as Carol continued round the block.

As she got the hang of wheelchair management she needed less concentration and tried to imagine how it must be after a life-time of independence and activity to rely on others to take you out for a breath of fresh air - particularly a daughter who had never been exactly close. It was necessary to make an effort to think so positively and charitably because her natural instinct was to throttle the old bugger.

He had always been a dominant, fear-inspiring figure. She remembered a few occasions, when she was very small, when they had been close. Once she sat on his knee and he told her about Hitler, and how if he had won the war all Europe would have been slave states. Another time he'd explained how the sun was a bright star, growing all the time, and would one day swallow up the earth. Carol, at the age of four, became very worried for some days about her unknown, unborn, distant descendants, whoever they might turn out to be. And then there was the small matter of his insistence on the adoption of her daughter: had it really been his decision, or her mother's? She would probably never know.

In the thirty year war which was her parents' marriage, her loyalties always lay with her mother, whose shadow stood figuratively, and often in reality, between them, moulding their interaction to a shape she found acceptable, working on them individually until each regarded the other as a malign influence, the cause of Mrs. Stone's undoubted dissatisfaction and unhappiness.

Once Patsy had been born, Carol felt that any interest her father had in children was directed towards this pretty blonde little sister. 'Daddy, pull my tickers up,' she would lisp as she waddled out of the bathroom with her knickers round her ankles, and he would smile fondly, foolishly as he knelt to help her. Fancy having to ask for help for a thing like that, Carol had thought in disgust.

In fact she, as first-born, had been claimed body and soul by her mother, her father subtly elbowed out and dispossessed. With the arrival of a second child in the house he no doubt had to be allowed more involvement and he became fond of the curly blonde toddler, while she, the older sister, dark and probably surly, observed and noted each sign of his affection, and found it incomprehensible.

As she grew older his influence, always slight, waned and they bickered continually. He was a pigeon man, and all his free time, spare money and filial interest had been expended on three hundred or so prize pigeons which lived in the splendidly ramshackle loft which covered three-quarters of the small back garden. They received all the detailed care and attention which belonged, Carol thought, to herself, her sister and brother.

She remembered one day when she had been visiting with Paul and the children. Her dad was standing by the back window of the tiny kitchen washing his bird bowls in the sink her mother dodging round his huge bulk trying to cook a meal, nagging and fussing about the muck on his boots and the mess he was making. The kitchen was full of steam and cooking smells, the surfaces covered in flour, bowls, vegetables and pans. He took no notice whatsoever. Dirty water splashed. The Saturday television sports programme was on full blast so that he could watch it for a few minutes every half hour or so, when he tramped in to wash another item of his encrusted pigeon equipment in the sink.

Raymond Glendenning's manic monotone leached from the telly, 'And they're off. And it's Blue Flash on the outside…'

His attention was captured by something in the back garden. He stopped dead in the act of rinsing a drinking trough.

'Here, Ian,' he called above the noise to Carol's younger brother. 'What's that under t'loft window?'

Ian, then a slender youth in his mid teens, sauntered into the kitchen, hands deep in his pockets and craned his neck to see down the garden.

'Er, um, looks like a ferret. Yes, a ferret, I'd say,' he said calmly, well aware of the effect his words would have. He nodded sagely, confirming his opinion.

Raymond Glendenning screamed, 'And they're neck and neck now. Crown Glory is in the lead, and Blue Flash….'

Mr. Stone stood there, massive and motionless in his wellies, overall and cloth cap, breathing deeply, unable to take in the sheer awfulness of the situation. Then, with a grunt of rage, he headed for the door. He seized a home-made solid steel coal shovel from beside the coal bunker.

Someone turned the telly off.

The ferret, clinging to the wire mesh of the loft window, mesmerised by all those delicious, terrified, rustling birds and taken by surprise, was dealt a death-blow of such ferocity that his little white furry body fell to the ground in two separate pieces. He never knew what hit him. His tiny ferret soul must have been surprised to find itself disembodied so swiftly at a moment of such intense satisfaction and anticipation.

Mr. Stone snorted in righteous indignation, the murder weapon still in his hand, and glared at the bloody corpse. The entire family watched in open-mouthed silence from the kitchen window at this display of unbridled passion. The warrior in full tribal dress, defending his territory.

A head bobbed above the hedge which bordered next door's garden.

'Sid. Sid, have you seen anything of a ferret?' Mr. Stone looked up aghast. 'A white one? Only our Chris's lad's staying with us for a few days, and his pet ferret's gone missing, and he's right upset. We can't find it anywhere. Have you seen it? I thought it might have been attracted by the pigeons, like.'

A quick estimate suggested that Joe Rawlings' line of vision over the hedge did not extend to the wooden platform on which Sid Stone stood, where both pieces of the recently departed ferret lay. He cleared his throat.

'Er no, no Joe, I haven't,' he said as he carefully nudged the body over the edge of the platform and further out of sight with the toe of his wellie-boot.

In the kitchen the laughter was quickly suppressed when the back door opened. An elaborate pretence that they had not seen what happened was pantomimed. Mr. Stone came in, blue eyes wide in a most unaccustomed affectation of innocence.

'Well, I didn't know it was a bloody pet,' he said apologetically to no-one in particular.

His natural dominance, his bulk, even his height, seemed to diminish as his illness developed. The giant all-powerful figure of Carol's childhood was reduced to the frail pathetic person in the wheelchair, snapping helplessly at everything within his range. He was no longer a threat. Maybe he never had been.

Sensing Carol's lack of attention the wheelchair took a sneaky lurch towards a beech tree. She fought for control as the wind whipped her scarf into her eyes.

His words could be heard above the wind.

'Bloody women drivers.'

Carol heard a dry rasping noise. His shoulders shook. He was - laughing!

* * *

Later, Mr. Stone sat on the sofa in the lounge. By his side, and firmly restrained, was his Yorkshire Terrier, Candy. Chloe peeped round the door. Seeing the dog, her pose altered minutely and changed from relaxed to watchful. Observing Candy's lack of freedom, Chloe strolled slowly, with supreme elegance and grace, without even a glance at the dog, into the middle of the carpet where she sat down. She yawned with studied nonchalance and began a careful and thorough wash. Her eyes seemed focused inwardly upon the task, but flashed wickedly when her sapphire gaze rested briefly on the dog. If a cat could laugh she would have been chuckling, holding her sides and roaring.

Mr. Stone's big hands, disfigured from years of working the coal face, gently grasped Candy's tiny body which was rigid with fury. Her eyes started from her head, and probably, under her fur, her veins were bulging. She was far too suffused by emotion to bark but small inarticulate whimpers forced their way through her drawn-back lips.

'Look at that bugger.' He looked at Carol and nodded angrily at Chloe. 'Just look at her. Bloody dog's nearly busting.' His voice expressed all the grievances felt by the dog.

'Sorry. I'll take her away.' Carol picked up the cat and carried her into the kitchen. Paul was chopping salad by the sink.

'Why did he have to bring that sodding rat? Couldn't he leave it at home? I've had to shut Molly out, and she's upsetting the cat.'

'The cat's alright. Actually she was teasing the dog. He couldn't leave it, there's no-one to leave it with.'

'You've always got some excuse. It's the same every time they come. They won't like the food -'foreign muck, that lasagne, give me a nice plaice and chips,' he mimicked the accent cruelly. 'It's always the same.' He was looking for an argument, some excuse to cause unpleasantness. If he was in this mood, he would manufacture something before the day was out. He'd already done the usual routine of creating an argument before they arrived, so that Carol had either to apologise or have her parents arrive to an atmosphere of malevolence

'You agreed they could come,' she replied and was relieved when he didn't answer.

Mrs. Stone, always appreciative when someone else did the cooking, sat down eagerly to lunch.

'By that smells nice. What is it?'

'Lasagne,' replied Carol. 'It's Italian food. Minced beef, onion, tomato, herbs and pasta and a cheese sauce.' She began to serve. Mr. Stone looked at his portion suspiciously, but said nothing.

'It smells right nice. Did you do it?' she picked up a fork, stabbed a mushroom and ate it.

'Yes, Paul did the salad.'

'That's nice an' all. Right posh. Did you find this on one of your business trips?' she smiled.

'No – Sainsbury's,' Paul replied witheringly.

'Where have you been this year then?' she enquired, oblivious to his rudeness.

'This year? Germany. South Africa. I'm going to Scotland soon.'

Molly, scenting food, put her nose onto the edge of the table, waiting her chance, sniffing deeply, checking the layout of the food.

'Go away, Mol,' said Carol sharply. Mol didn't move but rolled her eyes.

'Down, get down,' shouted Paul. Molly obediently removed her nose from the table, pretended to walk away, then doubled back and quickly plonked her front legs on Nessie's lap. This gave her a good view of the entire table and she began to drool, a sight which drew cries of disgust from everyone at the table. Nessie protested, her skinny arms trying ineffectively to push the heavy dog away.

'Get her off, Nessie, put her down,' yelled Paul, as if Nessie had any choice.

Paul leapt out of his chair and stood over the dog. 'Get down, get down.' Molly drew back her lip and snarled gently.

'Don't do that to me,' he yelled. He reached for her chain collar, she snapped, Nessie squealed, Molly lunged at a bread roll. Paul seized her collar and yanked the dog off Nessie's lap and almost off her feet.

'Out, out,' he shouted angrily. Molly crouched and snarled quietly, still holding the bread roll in her teeth. 'How dare you. Get out,' he yelled. The dog made for the hall door. Paul seized her collar and dragged her, snapping and snarling, to the outside door. 'You'll do as you're damn well told.' He threw her out and returned to the table, 'And you shouldn't encourage her,' he snapped at Nessie. Nessie's protests were swept away.

Having proved he was master over the dog he was now ready to eat.

'Well, now you've all had yours is there any left for me?'

The salad was passed, his glass filled and he proceeded to entertain the company with a detailed account of some incident which illustrated his sheer wonderfulness in the world of computers.

'They say there's a recession coming, said Mrs. Stone.

'Yes, they say we'll have another ice age as well, but it won't be just yet,' Paul replied with assurance.

'Molly has figured out the pecking order in this family,' observed Nessie to change the subject. 'And I wouldn't mind, except that she's too accurate.'

'What do you mean?' her grandmother asked.

'She knows that dad is the boss, then she puts mom next, and Matthew after mum. What I don't like is that she thinks she comes next, and I'm last. She bullies me.'

* * *

That evening, when the visitors had departed, driven by Mr. Stone in his neat little motobility car, Carol and Matt began clearing away.

'I have a Parents' Evening at school on Monday,' said Carol. 'I'll be late back.'

'Don't look at me – I'm going away on Monday morning and staying overnight.'

'Well, I guess Matt and Nessie will be alright for a few hours on their own. Where are you going?'

'Nowhere that concerns you.'

She stopped stacking the dishwasher and turned to look at him. He sat at the kitchen table smoking a cigarette, flicking through the Sunday supplement.

'Are you going to leave a phone number in case there's an emergency?'

He stubbed out his cigarette and walked to the door, letting the silence grow.

'Get off my back,' he snarled, as he left the room.

'Bastard,' murmured Matt.

Mat and Nessie went to bed, Carol followed.

She lay in the dark, thinking about Susan, about her home, about where she could go with Matt and Nessie if she left, about divorce, about whether it was better for children to live with parents who argued or with a single parent. Matt's GCSE was only a year away, the following year would be Nessie's, then his A levels, then hers. Hardly fair to cause upheaval for the next four years.

It was a long way from Rossingley to where she lay now in this spacious bedroom, in a lovely house, surrounded by beautiful things.

There was a price to pay, of course. Paul was increasingly arrogant and overbearing. Frequently their arguments ended when he said she was 'acting like a child' and he 'smacked' her or was 'forced to restrain' her. This usually meant a fierce push and pull struggle as he grabbed her wrists or twisted her arm up her back. He was abusive - remarks about her appearance - weight, hairstyle, clothes, - or cooking, or friends - 'why can't you choose attractive friends instead of those frightful bloody teachers'- scathing and insulting. He seemed to hate teachers – perhaps because she was one.

It was a long way from Rossingley, because even in his worse moments her father never ever hit her mother, never abused her like this.

* * *

Carol sat at the desk which Paul had built for her in the loft. The fan heater made little impression on the winter cold in the unheated roof space. The ancient blue carpet and piles of junk stretched away from the pool of light around the desk lamp into the gloom. Outside the wind howled round the roof in the Sunday afternoon darkness. Sitting in an armchair, zipped into a sleeping bag, most of her was warm except hands and face. She was marking a set of fourth year essays, wishing it was finished so she could go down into the central-heated warmth of the house. Paul didn't like the house littered up with school books so he had put this desk and shelves up here so she could work undisturbed. But just now it was damn cold.

* * *

The candles on the dining room table burned low. The port bottle stood among the ruins of the cheese board, and a litter of liqueur and chocolate wrappings. Paul came in from the kitchen with the coffee. Molly and Eric lay contentedly by the bay window.

'Bad week last week,' said Keith. 'Nearly chucked it in. Visited this small firm – we put their system in about six months ago and it still has teething problems – mostly because the department manager, the guy I was visiting, doesn't know what he's doing. He was giving me hell. I thought well, mate, there you are on 20K, and I'm on 100K, so who gets the last laugh?'

At the far end of the table Paul began a long story about his recent visit to America. The four guests, mellowed by food and drink, listened without interruption, laughing on cue. Carol had heard the story, several times. She sat now, listened to the rather nasal tone of his voice, watched his hands as they waved limp-wristedly, emphasising a point, raising a cigarette to his lips. His laugh was light and somehow unpleasant.

Before the guests arrived they had quarrelled over choice of food. He always wanted top-quality restaurant-standard, something he expected to see on a menu, so a dinner-party was usually an expensive business.

'Look, this is a dinner party, not fucking school dinners. You can't invite people for dinner then serve them some crap - mashed turnips and cabbage.'

'Soup instead of avocado and crab isn't school dinners. Why can't we have soup for a change? We always have avocado and seafood.'

Matthew and Vanessa arrived back from their evening out, pink-cheeked, happy, the fresh night air clinging to their outdoor clothes and displacing the fug of food and cigarette smoke. They were introduced and scrounged a few delicacies, joined the wrinklies for a short while then, bored with the conversation, went to bed.

Watching Paul, a feeling of weariness crept over her. The effects of a busy week and too much alcohol, no doubt. He was successful, by anyone's standards. Still good-looking, he had a glamorous job, made lots of money, ran an expensive car, dressed well. He was articulate and charming to his guests, well-thought-of by his colleagues. He owned a fine home, had lovely kids, handsome pets. They had holidays in exotic places, visited the theatre, ate out.

She felt her wrists where he had seized them last night. If they disagreed, and they always did, it often ended in this mild controlling violence. Tonight he would probably fall asleep on the sofa again and not come to bed. The space between them was increasing. She knew there was no way back - but a future without him was a yawning black chasm, the idea of him being happy with someone else still hurt.

He offered no affection or tenderness. He rejected any attempts to give him any. It was as if he no longer needed human warmth. He was basking in the glow of his success, up on his pedestal, absorbing the admiration like a flower absorbing sunshine. He seemed to dislike physical closeness, to avoid touching or cuddling. They still had sex, gave and received orgasms with expertise born of practice, without passion. Conversation was one-way - he chose the subject, gave his opinion, tolerated no other viewpoint. People listened, or if not, they faded away.

He was faithful. Carol truly believed he was. To her, physical bodily faithfulness was important, and he was, truly, faithful. Of course, he was often away from home, and sometimes he wouldn't tell her which hotel he was in, or give her the number. He said he didn't want her pestering him with phone calls, jealous, checking up on him. Of course he was faithful. He said he was. But he no longer said he loved her, refused to say the words, or allow them to be said to him. And he became more arrogant and overbearing, less loving and kind.

Yet, even so, he was still understanding about Susan. He hated her parents, on her behalf, because of the way they had treated her.

She didn't hate them for it any more. Finally she had seen that her mother was not responsible for making her pregnant. She did that herself, with Rob, of course. Her mother had simply done the best she could, trying to ensure that her grandchild didn't suffer the stigma of illegitimacy, her daughter didn't have to endure the label 'unmarried mother'.

Logically, you could see why.

In mining villages in the 40's life was lived quite close to the edge. Money was scarce, the men earned a living, the women brought up the children, ran the home. There was neither example nor precedent for any other pattern. A woman with a child, and no man to support her, was a burden to her family. The shame was rooted in not only morality but also practicality. The pregnant girls in the village married their boy-friends - and stayed chained to the village, the family, the pattern of existence which renewed itself with each generation.

She had escaped that. She had an education, a job, a family, a lovely home. Everything, however, has a price. She had a choice, like everyone else. She chose to pay the price, because the alternative was to return to the wastes of loneliness and uncertainty which lay between the village and marriage - The Warren, the hostel. Rootless, homeless, lonely, wanting a life and love. Well, she had the home and family, career and marriage. She was lucky. She didn't have the life and love. You couldn't have everything. Sadly Paul seemed to have no love, no respect for her, or anyone.

Increasingly he was an enigma. His reasons for staying were hard to understand - unless he positively enjoyed his deliberate cruelty. They could probably afford to split up and live separately. So why were they still together?

'What's the matter with you, dear?' Paul's mocking voice floated across the debris upon the table, the guests turned and stared. 'Had one too many have we?' The chorus laughed dutifully.

'No I'm fine thanks.'

'You look like you're falling asleep. Why don't you go to bed? We won't mind. Will we?' he looked round, they murmured reassurances - no they wouldn't mind, go on, must be tired.

She went.

Tumbling into bed she reached for the top book from the pile on the cupboard beside the bed. If she didn't read to the point of sleep, concentrate her mind on something outside herself, she would get into that downward spiral of worry and wakefulness which could last until dawn. Evelyn Waugh 'Men at Arms' should do the trick. Shakespeare was best - one page and zonk, out like a light. If it was a really good book she could be awake for two to three hours anyway, but then it wouldn't matter because her mind would be elsewhere.

The sound of goodbyes floated up from the hall. The front door closed, Paul's footsteps mounted the stairs, the bedroom door opened.

'What are you doing? I thought you came to bed to sleep. You were supposed to be tired.' She laid the book down.

'I am tired, but I can't sleep unless I read.'

'Don't argue. Give me that.' He took the book from her hand, closed it without marking the page, put it on the pile and turned off the light. 'Now, go to sleep.'

Protests rose to her lips but died there. It was too late to oppose him because that would lead to an argument and she hadn't the energy to hold her own.

The door closed behind him, his footsteps receded down the stairs.

* * *

Daniel Simms' dad was a charmer. Medium height, chubby with greying dark hair, he hadn't Paul's elegance, but his smile was warm, his eyes reflected his interest and it wasn't confined to his son's academic progress. His was one of the last appointments of Parents' Evening. He was a teacher too, and a widower.

They discussed the play showing at the Rep Theatre. Another set of parents arrived and sat waiting their turn. Carol and Daniel's dad - Dave by now - talked about a new film they'd both seen, a pop concert at the NEC which they'd both heard. He was being very amusing about being the oldest person in the audience of teenyboppers. Another parent joined the queue and the first ones looked pointedly at watches, glanced and muttered. With many smiles and goodbyes he left.

By 9.30 pm the bar of The King William was jammed shoulder to shoulder with teachers. Since they were all colleagues it was easy to pass from group to group. Conversations varied. Pat was telling a joke of mind-boggling filthiness to an attentive audience. Brian, skinny and balding, was being waspish and witty, acting out his fantasy of being Irish in the manner of Sean O'Casey. When very drunk, this alternated with wittiness of the Oscar Wilde variety. The Head was, as usual, remote and isolated, talking to his Deputy, a man with a serious personality by-pass, enigmatic and James Bondish. Silvia led the girl-bonding anti-male corner and Lucy shepherded and controlled her carefully selected little group of insecure sycophants. Carol enjoyed mildly flirtatious conversations with many of the men, secure in the knowledge that no-one was going to take it any further. In short, everyone was having a good time in the way that pleased them most.

Suddenly Dave was there, soon he was part of the group. Then they were a separate group of two. People began to leave, calling, 'Goodnight Carol,' meaningfully. The car park was empty. He sat beside her in the car and they talked.

He kissed Carol briefly on the cheek when he left.

The following week he whisked her away from school for a lunch-time meal and flirted across the table. She rediscovered the squishy feeling in the stomach which comes in the early stages of a love story. He chattered on about nothing, his eyes warm and admiring, his words tinged with flattery. Her body responded with enthusiasm, longing to feel his lips on hers, his hands on her breasts, his naked body in contact with her, from top to toe, the curly hair on his chest, which she could see peeping from his open-necked shirt, rubbing against her soft nipples, his….

'Coffee?' Her eyes focussed on his face.

'Sorry?'

'Would you like a coffee? With cognac?'

'Yes, please. Yes, I would like,' she smiled slowly, 'a coffee. With cognac.'

He reached across and took her hand.

'It's a pity you have to go back to school.'

'It certainly is.'

* * *

'We don't have sex any more. It doesn't bother me.'

Another dinner party.

Annette stretched a pudgy hand across the breakfast bar and flicked cigarette ash into an overflowing ash-tray. The overhead spotlight flashed rainbow colours from the large diamond on her middle finger. A string of fat lustrous pearls nestled between the generous creamy breasts and enhanced her plump blondeness.

'Nor me. I can't be doing with it,' replied Sonia. Her un-made-up face and work-roughened hands contrasted with the designer-label dress, expensive but subtly old-fashioned. She helped out in the factory when they were short-staffed. The expensive clothes she wore to work were frequently splashed with soldering.

'What about you?' Annette's bright black eyes looked challengingly into Carol's blue-green ones. Carol dropped her gaze.

'Well, you know.'

'Jim goes out and he doesn't get back until three or four in the morning. I'm in bed by ten,' said Sonia.

'Don't you mind?' asked Carol, curious.

She shrugged. 'No, he's just drinking with his mates at the bowling club.'

'Why don't you go?'

'Why? Because it's boring.' Jim was twenty years older than his wife, a shy and taciturn man.

'Don't you mind not having sex?'

'Paddy's too pissed most nights. I'm not bothered. I've got my house and my garden, the kids and my car. I'm alright.' Annette said.

'But sex is so important. It's one of the best things in life. How can you do without it?'

They looked at Carol blankly, then at each other, and laughed.

'Easy,' said Sonia.

'No problem,' said Annette. Her sharp milky white teeth gleamed. She lit another gold-tipped cigarette and sat with folded arms on the high stool, a dumpy figure with lovely skin and beautiful clothes - like a gilded Buddha -contained in her cocoon of dissatisfaction.

An echoing burst of laughter from the dining-room drew their attention. The dinner-party had reached the stage where people began to leave the table. The six guests were neighbours and could walk home, so drinking and driving was not a problem. Consequently, most of them were drunk.

Sam appeared in the doorway. His meaty hand grasped the door post as he adjusted his balance, and the vast bulk of his body swayed ominously. He burped gently and closed his eyes, then opened them and lurched round the breakfast bar to Carol's side.

'Hello, gorgeous,' he breathed into her ear. The widest point of his waistline pushed gently into her side. Paul emerged from the dining room.

'Are you groping my wife again, you bugger?' he asked lightly as he passed by on his way to make more coffee.

Sam's hand, surprisingly gentle and sensuous, slid down her back, following the contours of her waist, over the hips, and came to rest on her right buttock. His eyes, half closed with excesses of food and drink, blinked slowly, his fat red lips curled into a satiated smile.

'Yes,' he murmured.

Carol twisted away out of his reach, and he watched her go, reluctant but unresisting, like a large tired child whose favourite toy is taken away when he is too sleepy to retrieve it. He exhaled heavily and thoughtfully, and turned his gaze to Annette and Sonia.

'What were you ladies discussing with such interest?' he enquired with the careful courtesy of the practised drunk.

'Sex,' said Sonia, wishing to capture the conversational initiative and resorting to the easiest method available.

'Ah ah,' said Sam, his eyes flicking over her in assessment. He appeared to consider coming round to her side of the breakfast bar then apparently decided not to put himself to the trouble.

His wife emerged from the dining room. Rowena's expensive green silk trouser suit was crumpled and hung about her thickened figure in unattractively wrinkled swathes. Her skin gleamed unhealthily, like uncooked pastry.

'Sex. Did someone mention sex?' she asked in a shrill little-girl voice, and laughed a nerve-grating laugh of singular shallowness and lack of humour. Her narrow too-close-together eyes gleamed, and she clasped her hands under her chin in a grotesque imitation of childish glee. 'What are we saying? Who? When? Where?'

Sam gazed on his wife, sighed a deep sigh and ambled back into the dining room. The soft chandelier light fell on his bald head and sweaty face. He reached for the cheese-board, then the port bottle. Paul, bearing a jug of fresh coffee, followed him in'

'Shut the door,' said Annette, and Rowena obliged.

'We were just saying that we weren't interested in sex any more,' said Sonia. 'Except Carol. She's still quite keen.'

'But we ain't bothered that much,' laughed Annette. 'What about you? Is Sam still up for it?'

'Oh, he never misses a day,' moaned Rowena. All eyes turned in astonishment to see if she was joking. 'Every. Single. Bloody. Day. Never misses. Twice sometimes.' There was a silence as they all matched the recent spectacle of the overweight, drunken, groping figure of Sam, and this first-hand testament to his powers of physical performance. Carol decided that if ever tried to live up to his publicity, he would be dead in a week. Then she remembered the feel of his hand on her body. 'He's always been the same, since the day we were married, and that's, let me see, twenty years.'

The conversation faltered, hesitated, and petered out. You couldn't call the woman a liar, and further enquiries as to how her husband looked so unhealthy if he was such a sexual athlete were not possible. Perhaps she didn't fully understand what sex meant - sex as in bonking, a shag, doing it, a good seeing to - but as she had four children you had to assume she did. Maybe he had help from a third party, someone to assist him. Maybe he took the more passive role, and she…..The three women sat gazing at Rowena as chasing thoughts showed clearly on each face. Rowena flushed, giggled and wandered back into the dining room.

'In your dreams, chuck,' murmured Annette.

* * *

Ten days later, on a quiet Tuesday evening, Carol answered the door to find Jim standing there, hands in pockets, shoulders hunched. Jim had never, ever knocked on their door before. He accepted the invitation to come in, and joined herself and Paul in the lounge, but declined a drink.

'We haven't seen you since the dinner party,' said Paul, politely switching off the television.

'No, we've been busy,' replied Jim. Never articulate, he seemed particularly word-bound this evening. Odd, because he'd obviously come over especially for something.

'Us too,' Carol offered. 'We've been decorating this house since we moved in. I suppose it will be finished one day.'

'Yes. As fast as one bit gets done, something else falls to pieces,' said Paul.

Jim nodded but said nothing. The light glinted on his specs, hiding the expression in his eyes. A small silence began, and stretched.

'So what have you been doing? Anything interesting?' asked Carol.

'Well, I don't know if you would call it that.' He appeared to be searching for words. 'Sonia's in hospital. I came to tell you.'

'In hospital?' Carol was puzzled. 'I didn't know she was ill. She seemed fine last Saturday. What's the problem?' Jim's face, never expressive, was unreadable.

'She's been in since Tuesday. She had a breast removed last Friday. She has - had - breast cancer.' He sat uncomfortably on the edge of the sofa, elbows on knees, hands clasped, looking from one to the other as the stunned silence lengthened and deepened.

The words bounced around Carol's brain as she tried to make an alternative meaning from the one she had immediately understood but rejected.

'Oh my God, I can't believe it.' Tears gathered in her eyes. 'It's so sudden, so awful.'

'Christ,' said Paul. 'That's terrible. Poor Sonia. How is she?'

Carol drew the back of her hand over her eyes to wipe away the tears.

'Don't you start crying. You'll set me off,' said Jim gruffly. The idea of the quiet, impassive Jim expressing his emotions in tears was one which lent veracity to the dreadfulness of the news. 'If you want to visit her she's in a private ward at the Abbey Hospital.'

* * *

'Come in, come in,' called Sonia as soon as she heard Carol's knock and saw her peeping round the door. The dark room overflowed with expensive flower arrangements. Roses, lilies, carnations, freesias, all released their perfume into the warmth of the small space. Opposite the door, sitting up in bed, Sonia looked and sounded exactly like her usual vigorous, cheerful, uncomplaining self.

'Hello, how are you?' Carol approached the bed and leaned carefully over to kiss Sonia's cheek. Her upper left arm was bandaged. The white folds disappeared into the sleeve of her nightie and could be seen at the neck, the crisp, clinical layers contrasting with the normality of the soft folds and frills of the M and S nightie. Estee Lauder and Savlon fought for dominance against the smell of flowers. Her skin was warm and soft, still golden with the Mediterranean tan from the summer.

'I'm fine. Can't wait to get out of here. Just look at this lot.' She waved her right arm to encompass the banks and waves of blossoms. The dark eyes glittered, the smile was tight and determined, the words and body language sent a message - no pity, no sympathy.

'I brought you some flowers, but I think you have enough here to start a shop.' Carol placed the slim cone of yellow roses on the bed.

'I think everyone I know has sent flowers,' Sonia's voice was raspy and rough. 'Some are from business associates. Those from mum, the roses from the boys, that from Jim.'

'They're beautiful. Really beautiful. How do you feel?'

'Fine. No different, really.'

'Does it hurt?'

'No, I can't say it does.' She shook her head and shrugged.

'I was so shocked to hear. One minute you were at the dinner party, the next thing I hear you're in here and its all happened.'

'That's how it was. I was showering on Monday and felt this tiny lump almost in my armpit. I asked Jim to feel it and he said he didn't know what to make of it. I saw the doctor on Tuesday, in here on Wednesday, tests on Thursday, surgery on Friday. All over.' Her face expressed acceptance, the shrug acknowledged the unexpected twists and turns in life's path - no more.

'What did the doctor say?'

'He said they weren't sure about the lymph gland. I said, take the lot. No messing about with lumpectomies - get rid of it. No chances. Take it all out – lump, gland, the breast, the lot. So he did.'

'What did Jim say?'

'He's having a hard time. He can't deal with it. He brought the books in this morning for me to do. He's lost, he doesn't know how to cope. It's a bad time for the business. I said, bring them in, I'll do them.'

'You shouldn't be doing that. You should rest, not worry. Take it easy.'

'I can't be doing with that.'

'Do you have to have any more treatment?'

'A bone scan. Anti-oestrogen tablets. I'll be on them for the rest of my life. No chemotherapy. The tests showed it was in the lymph, so they were right to take it out. Get rid of it.' Her voice never wavered, no trace of tears, fear or self-pity. If that was me, thought Carol, I'd be a jelly. I'd be so scared I'd never stop crying. How can she be so brave? Maybe she has a closer friend who she tells how she really feels.

'I think you're very brave. With a positive attitude like that, you'll be as good as new in no time.'

Sonia smiled - natural buoyancy and optimism.

'I wish I had your guts. I think you're coping really well – I admire you.' Carol squeezed the right hand which lay on the counterpane. The nails were bitten and traces of soldering still showed on the square, capable fingers. The squeeze was returned briefly, the eyes softened for a moment and some glint of the ultimate loneliness of her position showed far back. A frightened child looked fearfully out at the ordinary, trapped by a trick into occupying this extraordinary position at the centre of attention. The comforting acquisitions of the journey down the primrose path, friends and family, money and possessions, when face to face with mortality, were powerless, provided no refuge for a mind confronting wider possibilities.

'If it was me I'd be a gibbering wreck.'

'No you wouldn't. I'm just concentrating on getting better.' The assurance and confidence resurfaced, glossing over the uncomfortable, unspeakable, yawning uncertainty which had been allowed to show for a while.

'Is Jim taking you away on holiday?'

'He might. The business needs him at the moment especially with me in here. He can't do my work.'

'Sonia - give yourself a break. You can't just go back. You must rest, give your body time to recover. Sod the business. Put yourself first. It's important. You're more important than the business.'

Sonia looked at her, preoccupied, as if she were turning over a new idea, looking at a familiar object from a different angle.

'Yes.' She nodded. 'I know.'

Carol changed the subject. 'Have you had many visitors?'

'Yes - dozens. It's like New Street Station.' She laughed. 'Jim and the boys, mum. People from the Cricket Club. Business people. The vicar. A woman from the self help group. She was nice. She's had one - a mastectomy. Funny, when it happens to you, suddenly everyone else knows someone who had one.'

'Yes? It's like that with hysterectomies. Since I had mine, everyone I talk to has either had one, or knows someone who had one. Sometimes you think practically no-one over forty has a womb.'

'Or two boobs.' They laughed.

'What did the vicar say?'

'He was very good. The RC priest was better.'

'Yes? What did he say?'

'Hard to explain - but you feel better when he's said it.'

'Yes? That good, hey?'

'Yes. You see my palm. My life-line - there - a big break in it, then it rejoins and mends and goes on as strong as ever. That shows a serious illness in mid-life, then a recovery.'

Carol examined the palm, soft and dry, 'Oh yes, I see. Do you believe it?'

'Well you read palms. You tell me.'

'Only at school fetes.'

'You have to believe in something. Maybe one thing is as good as another.'

'If it serves a purpose and makes you feel better, why not? Who can say one belief is better than another. Who knows for sure?'

'I know what I think. When you're gone, you're gone. So enjoy what you've got while you've got it.'

* * *

Da da da dum de di dum dum diddle di di di diddle dee Dah

The band romped into the final trills of 'Whistling Rufus' - six middle-aged men, sweating and straining at their instruments, slaves to the blood-stirring music and wild magic of jazz and show biz, made real, brought to rip-roaring life in this regular weekly orgy of escape from routine and respectability. The trumpet player, an accountant in real life, paused and grinned widely at the couples on the little dance floor in front of the low stage. His wife twirled and spun in front of him with her partner, an old school-friend . Carol knew her slightly. Earlier, in the Ladies, she had told Carol that she didn't wear knickers or tights, her doctor recommended stockings and lots of fresh air. The hem of her skirt twirled vigorously at mid-thigh. A man sitting at one of the tables at the edge of the floor appeared to be doing his best to check this out - his eyes never left her hem and twisting, twinkling knees. He had a thoughtful expression, 'I could have sworn I saw....'

The banjo player, a car mechanic in his nine to five existence, launched into the next number and the dancers adapted to the new tempo.

The low room was crowded and smoky. Its walls were covered in fake plastic bricks, like a real cellar, the spotlit stage and dance floor surrounded by the gloom and intimacy of grouped chairs and tables which reached into the distant darkened corners. Some of the couples at the tables were married and virtually ignored each other, companionable but separate, having exhausted their conversational potential years before. Carol recognised some as older versions of couples encountered at PTA dances. Others tried hard to conduct a conversation against the deafening cacophony of music and chatter. A shadowy crowd stood before the bar watching the dancers and musicians, nodding and swaying to the music.

Most of the dancers on the brightly lit floor were women. The majority of the figures standing watching them from the shadows were men. The women, mostly married, lived locally. The men, also mostly married, were guests at the hotel of which this room formed the basement bar. They were on business trips and lived far enough away to justify an overnight stay and to ensure anonymity. Hungrily they watched the dancers, and some of them even ventured onto the floor themselves.

It was the village youth club, thirty years on. The fresh-faced fifteen-year-olds had developed beer bellies and bald heads, wrinkles, dyed hair and sagging breasts over the past thirty years, but their enthusiasm was undimmed, enhanced now by self-knowledge and determination to enjoy the ability to enjoy, which after all would not last for ever. The gaiety had an irresistible quality, like a tank in Tiananmen Square.

There were recognisable youth-club characters; the rather unattractive chap who danced like a dream, and was in constant demand as a partner; the long-established couple, not married but known to be together; plump easy-going Jennie, never without a drink in hand, who had seen the inside of most of the hotel rooms over the years, and was pointed out to the new blokes by the regulars. After a disastrous marriage she was out to enjoy her freedom, but seemed to be creating a new kind of self-punishment. There was the bloke who was keen, but a rotten dancer. Jock, a giant Scotsman, was sociable, loud and friendly, just out for the company. In his shadow was Jim, small and shifty, on the look-out for the passing liaison with any female who seemed willing. Around this warm and ebullient character and his icy companion were the less confident satellites, attracted by the sheer carnival and the reawakened teenage ganging instinct.

From her seat Carol could see Sonia on the dance floor, the liveliest and most carefree of the dancers. She spun and twirled on the end of the arm of a clothing rep from Northampton, a man of middle height with thinning dark hair, a foxy expression and, at home, a wife and three kids. He passed through about every four weeks and was fond of female company, dancing and eating out, and not averse to a quickie in his room, said Sonia.

From the other end of the bar Sonia was watched hungrily by a stocky grey-haired man, now on his second whiskey - Joe. Sonia and Joe had met the week before, spent hours on the phone during the week, and arranged to meet again in the bar - and here he was! The dancing display was for him, though Foxy-face didn't yet know it, and so was the radiant smile which flashed out when their eyes met, when Foxy-face whirled her out towards Joe's smouldering possessive presence. She was his woman. He was her man. No-one had done anyone wrong yet, but they were about to, given half a chance. They were aware of each other across the crowded floor, drawn by the ancient irresistible force of attraction, and even his wife and her husband, had they been present, could not have stemmed the flood of feeling and passion which was building up. The steady security of a long marriage was nothing compared to this hectic bubbling of happiness, the long-forgotten joys of lust and desire.

Feeling conspicuous and out of place, Carol cast a glance at the men around her. They were all between forty and sixty, in various stages of physical decomposition. Grey hair predominated, as did designer casual wear, sloping shoulders and, in some cases, oddly substantial chests. The level of oestrogen in the water system must be reaching emergency level. All those women, on HRT and the pill, peeing pure hormones, all that water recycling round the system to re-emerge into cups of tea and pints of beer, with ever-increasing levels of oestrogen - no wonder male impotence was endemic. As the women were becoming more confident and less dependent, the men were turning into androgens. Attacked on two fronts, by their own body chemistry on the inside and by the rising tide of female crap-resistance all around them, they were doomed.

Whether this was true or not, the sad but undeniable lack of virility which age brings was apparent; these were old pussy-cats, devoid of claws and teeth, all mangy fur and old battle scars. That old-time reek of rampant hormones was missing, replaced by Paco Rabanne or Pour l'homme. Some had come here, genuinely, to hear the music, others eyed the women, still open for the possibility of a pull, a piece of totty, and hoping for the strength to carry it through if they got lucky.

Carol decided the secret of being chatted up must be in the body language. Her feelings must be showing in her face. Here she was, forty-seven, not too awful looking, a stone and a half overweight, bored, disillusioned, with a career she disliked, a husband who had become a hostile stranger. Why, she asked herself, am I here? I don't like jazz. I don't want a casual affair, I don't know, or want to know, anyone here.

Her thoughts drifted to Dave. Did she want him? He made her pulse quicken, but she could not pretend she felt anything like the attraction which pulled Sonia and Joe together. Sonia was intent on experiencing everything life had to offer before her body chemistry threatened her again with eternal oblivion. She valued every moment, lived every second. The years of obedient domesticity were behind her, the boys, Jim and her mother could accept it or not, as they pleased, but she had her own path to follow, her own separate existence to take care of. She had finished her mothering, and was giving away nothing of value to Jim, who wanted only a quiet life, his bowls, his pint and his dinner on the table when he got home from the factory.

Well, she thought, looking around, this may be Sonia's highway to happiness but it's not mine.

* * *

The phone rang in the Hall. Carol paused on the landing above listening to the ringing, and heard Paul pick it up. She froze in anxiety, hearing her heart beat heavily inside the wall of her chest, heard him call, 'Carol'.

'Yes,' she answered, her voice fighting for normality.

'It's your mother.'

Not Dave!

Relieved exhalation, collapse of sick prickling feeling, run down stairs lightly, take phone, 'Hello, Mum.'

* * *

The dream is real. She needs to wee. She goes into the bathroom, pulls down her pants, sits on the seat. Is it real? Am I dreaming this or is it real? Bladder muscles grip tight, under control. She needs a wee. Her bladder is full. Am I awake? Is this a dream? There's the sink and tap, here's the loo paper, these are my knees. It's real. Am I sure? Yes, it's OK. She releases the muscles. Warm liquid flows out, runs over the thighs and floods the mattress.
Carol woke up and flew out of bed into the loo across the landing. Fucking hell fire. Now she was awake, really, and the bloody bed was wet. Paul hadn't stirred. Am I awake now? Hold it. Am I? Am I? OK

then. Yes OK.

What now? She sat on the seat, long after she'd finished. This was beyond a joke - the third time this week, probably. She could hardly remember in the morning. Usually it seemed worse than it was - luckily, because she could hardly wake Paul and change the bed. What could she say? 'Sorry, dear, I've wet the bed.' He would not be amused. He had little enough patience for the ordinary calamities, he'd have none for this.

In the darkness she ran her hands over the bottom sheet. Dry - one wet spot the size of a penny. Not so bad. Cautiously she slid into bed, careful not to wake the deeply-breathing figure beside her. Gradually her body relaxed and slid again into an anxious shallow sleep.

* * *

She saw Dave again, across the wine bar, with another woman, a few weeks later. She was with friends from school. She waved. He grinned and waved back. He wasn't so gorgeous, really. Not worth wetting the bed for.

* * *

Matthew took his A levels but didn't like the results, so spent a year at an FE college re-taking them.

The following autumn he and Vanessa left, within a day or two of each other, for new lives at distant universities – one to Reading, one to Leeds.

The house, which was perfect for a family, ideal for parties, was now a silent shell. Even the dogs, lacking the stimulation of voices and activity, lapsed into sleep, drowsing the days away in wicker baskets next to the kitchen radiator.

Unlike the predicted ice-age, the recession arrived, bringing with it a widespread and all-pervading despair.

'What's the point in learning how to do a c.v., Miss?' asked Grant Perry in Year 11 Careers, 'we all know, there ain't no jobs out there.' Carol couldn't argue with him, she felt his despair.

The recession settled in and got into its stride. The Midlands' economic base, the manufacturing industry, 'tin bashing', cornerstone of national wealth for two centuries, faltered..

Paul was commuting to London, to the southeast honey-pot, which was still plodding gamely on, like a soldier on a battlefield whose legs have been cut from under him, but he doesn't yet realise. He left early to catch his train and returned late, living on coffee and cigarettes. At weekends Mrs. Thatcher and her economic theories were discussed bitterly over dinner. Perhaps not so much a discussion as a one-sided rant in which Paul vented his feelings, as much in fear as in anger, because he, like millions of others, was quite helpless.

'I hope I live to spit on her grave,' he snarled every time her smiling, confident, condescending face appeared on the news. Was any woman, anywhere, any time, so hated, Carol wondered. It was tragic that the first woman to achieve the break-through of political power to the extent of becoming Prime Minister should be so uncaring, oblivious to the destruction of lives and families which came as a natural result of putting her unproven ideas into practice.

The interest rate reached 15%, and the mortgage on the house zoomed up. Stupidity and incompetence, hand in hand, were in charge. 'Negative equity' a new concept in house ownership, began to be heard daily on the news, along with 'repossession', 'redundancy' and 'unprecedented levels of unemployment'.

Paul's eventual redundancy, though inevitable, was nevertheless a great blow to his pride, his self-image and his confidence. His life-pattern changed abruptly from tightly-scheduled commuting, meetings, reports, deadlines, to daily empty horizons, a mental desert of isolation and hopelessness with no green oasis of hope to be found anywhere.

Futile visits to job clubs alternated with hours of preparing c.v.'s, applying for the kinds of jobs, so few in number, which his age, experience and expectations told him should be obtainable. The result left him high and dry, enraged, unable to accept failure. The evening news on television confirmed on a daily basis that thousands of applications were received for every job advertised. The message was – there are very few jobs and you're not going to get one.

The dogs were the only beneficiaries. Every day they romped through the damp autumn leaves in the park with Paul, their delight and joy in living contrasting sharply with his heavy tread and stooping shoulders.

The housing market slumped, at about the same time as the ability to meet the mortgage payments on Carol's salary alone became clearly impossible.

The house, never so desirable as now, cleaned and polished to a level of perfection rarely seen outside the covers of a magazine, redolent with the welcoming scents of new-baked bread and freshly made coffee, adorned with fresh flowers, was thrown open to prospective buyers. They arrived, in pairs or, in one case, in an extended family group, and invaded every room, inspected every crack and crevice. Some, Carol was certain, couldn't even afford the asking price and just came out of curiosity.

Paul and Carol had worked long and hard on the house – it had, for ten years, been their hobby and their passion. Paul in particular mourned its imminent loss. For him the house was an expression of who he was – successful, a man with a place in the world, to be envied.

For Carol the house had lost much of its charm when Matt and Van left home. For her, at that point, the life went out of it. It was merely a series of large empty rooms, costing the earth to heat and maintain. At each stage of transforming the house from its original bleak and dowdy condition to the present level of comfortable luxury, she had imagined it through Jessica's eyes. She had seen Jessica arriving, seen herself welcoming her at the poppy-red front door, seen them all eating a family meal, happy and smiling, showing her round the garden, taking her case up to the spare bedroom, welcoming her into her new family, introducing her to her half-brother Matthew and half-sister Vanessa. Now she would never see it. And her happy family was, she had to admit, a myth as well.

* * *

On a dark January afternoon, after school, a knife-edge wind whips over the slowly freezing slush of half-melted snow in the gutters outside the solicitor's office as Paul parks the car. He breaks the silence which has extended, intermittently, since Christmas.

'Don't slam the fucking door.'

Cold neon lights shine on the cadaverous features of the unlovely Mr. Milnes, Solicitor, of Milnes and Baker. His smile begins and ends with the lips, and he has a cold.

They have lived in the last house for eleven years and, coincidentally, the same in the one before that. If she signs the papers spread before her on the desk, it could be a further eleven long years with Paul. Can she bear to think about it? Selling the house had not been easy – Mrs. Cotton must have been the only punter in the market with that much money to spend, and she'd got herself a bargain.

'So once you've signed the papers you can move in in four weeks,' says Mr. Milnes, his voice a smooth pond concealing the depths of his real feelings.

'Good. Let's get it done then,' says Paul. He glances at Carol sitting in the chair opposite, her gaze fixed unseeingly on the wall.

What if she just says no? Perhaps sign the papers to sell the house, and then put the pen down and say 'I've changed my mind.' No – wait until Paul signs both sets, then sign the papers which sell the house, then say it. 'No, I've changed my mind.' She likes the sound of the words. What would happen then? Mr. Milnes would be politely surprised. Paul would be incandescent with rage. He'd shout, no doubt. She should have thought this through and acted sooner – seen a solicitor, got some divorce papers, whatever they were, maybe wait for him to sign both, then sign the one herself, then hand him the divorce papers and say, 'I've changed my mind. Here, have a read of this.'

'Hello, are you with us?' Paul's voice, with an edge of annoyance. He is standing, holding the pen. He's signed already.

'Sorry....what?'

'The papers.....sign?' he holds out the pen.

Slowly she comes to her feet and takes the pen - a gold Parker fountain pen, she notices.

'Here,' Mr Milnes points, 'and here.'

She looks at Paul. Under the neon light his face is grey, lined, unwell. Too many fags, too much coffee, not enough sleep. His mac swings open showing the dark business suit, the one he hasn't needed to wear for months.

Throw the pen down and run for it. Get out – go. Where to? What about the kids? Her job?

Both men are waiting, one puzzled, one with evident irritation.

Hands not quite steady she signs, and hears Paul's sigh of relief.

Chapter 7

1995

Carol opened the oven door. A blast of hot air melted her mascara into clumps, and pores all over her face opened wide, oozing perspiration and letting in Prescriptives Soft Beige 02 foundation make-up.

She slid a roasting tin containing a 12lb turkey to the edge of the oven shelf. The skin was brown and shiny, stuffing oozed out of one end and the smell was divine.

'Mum?' Matthew called.

'Yes?' she placed the turkey on the bread-board and picked up a sharp knife.

'Where do you want the garden chairs and table? On the patio or the lawn?' he was at her elbow, hanging over the turkey, 'smells good.' Fair hair flopped across his eyes and he had left a fallow patch on the jaw-line when he'd shaved. His shirt and trouser-tops met in a loose bunch around his middle in a way which suggested that if he were to stand up straight his trousers would immediately fall round his ankles.

'It is good. What do you think? I think the lawn.' She stuck the knife into the leg and clear liquid ran down the golden flanks. 'There'll be six adults, two children and a baby. We won't fit on the patio.'

'Okay. Do you need a taster for that?' he reached out to pick at a leg.

'No I don't. Get your hands off,' her smile softened the words.

Paul came in. Before he spoke a word the atmosphere altered. Neither of them turned, but both were acutely aware of his presence, and waited for the inevitable nerve-grating abrasion which passed for his social contact.

'Who's putting the garden furniture out?' he stood in the middle of the kitchen, hands on hips, chin out, 'and did you know it's going to rain? There're big black clouds over there.' It wasn't the words, it was the tone - aggressive, truculent, demanding submission or confrontation.

'Oh no,' Carol wailed, having chosen submission. She didn't have time for the confrontation. 'It can't. I've planned everything so we can eat in the garden.'

'Well - you can if you want but you'll be on your own, and you'll be sitting in a thunderstorm. What time are they due?' he peered out through the window. He knew perfectly well when they were due to arrive.

'12.30 to one o clock. About half an hour.'

'You'd better set the dining table indoors. It's going to pour down - oh – hear that?' Thunder rumbled in the distance, threatening a storm.

'Okay then, yes, I suppose I'd better if you think so.' She looked round at the clutter which covered every surface in the kitchen and wondered how she would find time.

'Don't blame me - I'm just telling you what it's like.' He seemed almost pleased at the disruption of her plans.

'Yes I know. Are you nearly ready? Have you showered?'

'Don't start bloody nagging. I'll be ready. Look at you - and how long will the fucking turkey be? And you can't even decide where we'll eat.'

Carol poured hot fat over the turkey. A feeling of dread was building up. Paul had decided to be awkward. He frequently did this before visitors arrived, especially if they were her side of the family. Sometimes he continued after they'd arrived, if it was someone whose opinion he did not esteem. And today was so special - nothing must go wrong. The anxiety level rose. They must like him, like the family.

'Yes I can - we'll eat indoors. I'll set the table. I'll just put this back in the oven for half an hour.' He disappeared upstairs.

'Ignore him. He's an arse-hole,' said Matthew. She closed the oven door and went to stand in the cool air by the back door. The top half stood open and she leaned her elbows on the bottom half.

The lawn sloped gently down to the apple tree. Borders which four weeks before had been perfect were now past their mid-summer peak. The dogs, shut into their pen at the bottom of the garden, expressed their disgust by whining. Molly banged on the gate with her paws. Eric stood at her shoulder like the sweet dope he was, copying his mum. Huge drops of rain began to fall, knocking the petals off the yellow full-blown roses round the door, filling the air with the metallic taste of summer storms. The shower turned into a deluge and the delphiniums and foxgloves by the back fence began to bend under the weight of rainwater trapped in their petals. Yellow rose petals floated in the puddles which formed on the patio. The dogs retreated into their kennel.

'Look at that.' Carol was almost in tears as she turned to Matt who was leaning on the doorpost, his long frame stooped to her level. 'I really wanted the garden to look good.'

'Never mind,' he grinned. 'We won't be able to go out in this to look at it anyway.'

'I bought two new garden chairs as well.' The rain slowed into a steady downpour.

'Don't worry. It'll be okay,' he smiled, full of confidence.

'Is Vanessa ready yet?'

'No but she will be soon. It'll be fine. Don't worry.' He nudged her arm and grinned. She smiled back. 'Think positive.'

He began to roll a cigarette, licked the paper and lit it. His friendly and companionable silence soothed her nerves.

'How do you feel about meeting your half sister for the first time?' she asked.

'I don't know,' he replied slowly, choosing his words with care. 'It's hard to say. I don't know her.' Honesty, and no false promises.

'I hope you like each other.'

'You can't force these things,' he said. 'I don't know her, she doesn't know me. We'll have to see how it goes.'

Carol nodded. 'The rain's stopping,' she said. 'Maybe the sun will come out and we can eat outside after all.'

'You'll be lucky,' Matthew peered up into a bank of black cloud. He tipped his head to one side, 'Can you hear a car?'

Through the front kitchen window Carol could see a large white saloon drifting slowly down the drive.

'Oh God, it's them. They're early. I'm not ready. The salad's not done, nor the Pavlova. Your dad's not ready. Where's Ness? Go and let them in.'

'No, come on, mum, you have to go and let them in,' he spoke with gentleness, like a fond parent.

Jessica was going to see a family which she would love, and to which she would be happy to belong. The stage setting was splendid - a charming cottage, brand new but with the appearance of antiquity, stable door with the upper half standing open, surrounded by roses, neat lawns and gravel drive. Waiting to greet her - mother, father - or was it step-father? - two charming, though adult, children, two handsome dogs. Perfect. The characters knew their lines - the question was, would they remember to deliver them convincingly?

Afterwards Carol's recollections of this day were fragmentary, brightly coloured scraps of images and conversations. Later, months and years later, she came to understand that this was the day when the fantasy and the reality met, head on. For weeks she had thought of this day as a development on from what went before but gradually she began to see that this was the watershed, the point at which a dozen, a thousand, little individual nuances were put into the balance and the scales began, imperceptibly, to hover, then to incline and resolve their direction. No one incident was the cause. It was, rather, the sum of the interaction of six adults, three children and two dogs, all with different expectations and aspirations, the weather, two totally separate family cultures, and a video camera which captured much of it on film in inarguable images, to be digested later, instead of being remembered with the gloss of the hopes which had been part of the occasion.

It was unrealistic to have expected it to be otherwise

Something about the look in Jessica's eye made Carol hesitate to greet her daughter with a hug. She introduced Matthew and Vanessa with a feeling of absurdity - they all knew perfectly well who they all were. They kissed shyly, with forced smiles.

Uncertainty and lack of confidence made it hard to strike a balance between the warmth of a relationship between mother and daughter, brother and sister and the polite distancing of complete strangers. Physical contact was uncomfortable, so all the cuddles and hugs were channelled into baby Lucy, Ben and Jamie, where they were more naturally accepted.

Ivan was pleasant and charming, Paul unusually reticent and watchful. Matthew, bemused, deferred to Ivan with the natural carefulness of a recent student towards a head teacher.

Ivan took out a video camera, and panned across the living room capturing the stiff poses and wariness of six adults on their best behaviour.

Vanessa and Ben fell in love with each other immediately. At six he was ready to be charmed by a pretty new auntie with long blonde hair who was happy to draw pictures with him, let him help to make a salad, and blow bubbles which bounced all over the room.

The children were delighted with the presents Carol had bought for them. She had missed Jessica's childhood, but now here was a second chance with her children. A little train engine, a toy piano, and a teddy.

'You're trying to buy their affection,' Paul had said when she showed him what she'd bought, effectively destroying her pleasure and excitement.

Jessica was very quiet. 'She must be shy,' thought Carol. 'She must be overwhelmed by meeting so many new people.' It was very brave of her to come at all.

Soon after the visitors arrived the storm broke. Over dinner thunder and lightning raged in the garden as they carved the turkey, passed the salad, poured wine and made rather formal conversation.

'We found the people in Turkey were very friendly. And the place is stuffed with antiquities…' Paul was telling Ivan over the soup.

Later - 'And the staff room morale is as low as it's ever been….' said Ivan as he held his plate out for turkey.

Ben had eyes for only Vanessa. 'Vanessa, can we paint another picture after dinner?' he whispered.

Jamie ran round the table to sit on his mother's lap, and she had to try to eat her dinner with one hand.

'Would you like some salad?' Carol offered the dish to her daughter, feeling that she should be able to say something more significant

Watery sunshine and a rainbow appeared with the Pavlova and apple pie.

Paul allowed the dogs into the utility room, where they barked, whined and scratched at the door, providing a fractious chorus as a discordant background. The Roses kept a careful watch on their language, editing out the more colourful vocabulary which they were accustomed to use with friends and each other. Words were weighed and measured before being offered up to the conversational construction which was their joint social creation of the afternoon.

Carol sat next to Jessica on the sofa and was aware that every word they spoke was soaked up, evaluated and placed in a pattern emerging in the mind of each separate listener which was labelled as their relationship. She felt like a pet mouse in a cage, with everyone peering in to see how she and Jessica performed. Words dried up.

'Why don't you show Jessica the photo album?' suggested Paul.

Over coffee it seemed bright enough to contemplate a walk to the park swings. Ivan busily videoed as Carol raced about pushing swings and roundabouts.

As evening fell they stood on the drive to say their farewells.

'You must come and visit us, one weekend soon,' said Ivan. ''We have really enjoyed today – it was great to meet everyone.'

The car pulled away. A last wave and they were gone.

'I feel like I still don't know her. She's an enigma,' Carol said to Vanessa as they stood, arms linked, waving at the last glimpse of the car.

'What's an enigma?' asked Vanessa.

'A puzzle wrapped in a riddle,' replied Carol.

'You will,' said Vanessa, ignoring this descent into Eng. Lit. 'It takes time. You can't build a relationship out of nothing. When you've seen each other a few more times, you'll get to know each other.'

'I feel that she's so much like me, but I don't know her well enough to say for sure.'

'She doesn't say much - it's hard to tell.' Vanessa squeezed her arm. 'It was her decision to come and visit us. She didn't have to drive all this way. She wouldn't have come if she didn't want to.'

'That's true. Do you think she liked us?'

'I don't know - she's a bit quiet. At least we all behaved well - even dad. And we didn't swear. Or argue. Of course Molly was a div, but then she always is.'

'What did you think?'

'I think she's nice. Very quiet but nice.'

A week or two later, at the beginning of the new term, Ivan sent a copy of the video. The first part showed Jessica's other family, together with her children in the garden. It was a family at ease with each other, relaxed, enjoying each other's company. The latter part, in the garden after dinner, in the park, showed clearly what Carol had been trying to understand. The body language spoke loudly, though it had not been heard at the time – between the chatter and smiles were folded arms, averted gazes, gaps between people, awkwardness and silences. The contrast was obvious. And devastating. They were strangers, forced into the role of family. As time passed, as they got to know each other better, they would relax, learn to read each other, to know each other's mannerisms and expressions – learn to love each other. Other visits would follow, and the web of relationships would grow. At last they had all come face to face – from now on they would become more familiar, become a family.

* * *

The new academic year began in its usual way - a flurry of paperwork, meetings, new students, new schemes of work. The staff, refreshed after a break, were stress-free, the absence rate low.

Jessica wrote and sent photographs of the children, but no mention was made of a visit.

By October the rain had set in, and the cracks in staff morale were beginning to show in the form of absences with colds and other minor complaints.

Carol arrived at school early and parked near the tennis courts as usual. Instead of jumping out of the car and hurrying into school she sat listening to Radio 4 and gazing out at the low grey clouds and spatters of rain. The motorway thundered fifty yards away, beyond the pylon which sizzled in the drizzle, beyond the dripping hawthorn hedge, an uninterrupted flow of high-sided lorries, like a procession of fairground rides, or the moving targets in a rifle-shot side stall. Bang. You disappear. Bang. Another one gone. A cold wind blew a tide of rubbish across the tennis courts. The bottom of the dividing fences was thick with ancient litter, the discarded wrappings from a million lunches and breaks. In places the plastic coated wire mesh was pushed up from the bottom, or squashed down from the top, or just bulging between posts where the kids had piled up against it. Ragged nets hung slackly on loose wires, or flopped on the ground in puddles. Six boys in school uniform emerged from a hole in the fence and ran across a court, clambered halfway up the opposite fence and scrambled over it as if they were on an assault course, legs cartwheeling joyfully in the air. Quite expert, really. Bang, you're gone. Mentally Carol picked them off, one by one.

A youth on a motorbike roared up from the bottom end of the school field near the canal bridge from the direction of the council estate. A sitting target - bang, blow him away. He did wheelies and slide turns all across the rugby pitch and a sliding turn on the Redgra, churning up what was left of the worn-out red surface into a spray. Then, standing on his pedals, knees flexing to absorb the bouncing, he did a cross-country style traverse of the hilly bits between the pitches. Finally he turned, opened the throttle and roared away across the pitches towards the towpath under the motorway, leaving deep tyre tracks in the rain-softened grass. Some of the watching kids cheered.

Reluctantly Carol lugged her bags out from behind the seat, locked the car and picked her way along the path through the mud-puddles and litter to the door by the English Office. The window to the English Office was boarded up, suggesting that there had been another break-in over the weekend. The burglars were unlikely to appreciate anything they'd find in there - books on teaching English and sets of 'A' level texts.

The first thing she noticed when she unlocked her classroom along the corridor was the board over the back window. There was no sign of damage. Since her keys had gone missing from her desk during the course of Friday afternoon's lessons, she had to ask Jane from the Maths Department to open her cupboard door. Sure enough the computer keyboard and printer, portable television and video and four SLR cameras were gone. It would be at least nine months before the insurance claim could be processed and they could be replaced. Whoever stole the keys had had an easy time. She had reported them missing at the time but no-one had seemed interested. Since they were attached to a foot-long plait of coloured wool, they had certainly not been picked up by mistake.

A fat-bellied scruffy man with red shiny lips and shifty blue eyes slouched into the room.

'Hello Mr. Simms,' said Carol. 'I see we've had burglars again.'

'Ar.' The caretaker was a man of few words. 'Thum cut the glass art and purrit round the side, like, so no-one could see it. Someone who's done it afore.'

Carol had suspected his involvement in the frequent burglaries ever since a large Victorian dining-table had vanished without trace from the Hall stage one weekend.

An electric bell shrilled in the corridor and a crowd of twelve-year-olds, lethargic, hyperactive, squabbling and pushing, surged into the room and the school day began.

Carol had her horrid Year 8's for Period 2.

In a class of only nineteen low-ability kids Joey Jeeves stood out as achieving levels of anti-social behaviour which could astound even an experienced teacher. He was always covered in mud from his last footy game - before school, break, dinner-time, even between lessons -

and his uniform was almost in rags. He had bright shiny brown eyes and his chestnut hair was cut like a bowl above his ears and across his forehead, and shaved below that. He was as fit as a flea and had about as much common-sense. Even his eye-brows looked full of health and vitality.

The lesson chugged along in its usual fashion - superficially chaotic but with an underlying level of orderliness perceptible only to the initiated. Within the limits of their capabilities the class, mostly boys because it was a bottom class and current interpretation of equal ops said children must not be streamed or set for balanced gender, only for ability, were working. To the untrained eye, this looked like a scene in a pub but without the beer. The support teacher, Leanne, was busy doing one-to-one with a quiet kid in the corner. She would creep in like a mouse, work with one or two at a time, ignore the wider class situation, then creep out again when the bell went.

Carol became aware of an intensification of the level of buzz in the classroom. These boys would normally communicate in terms of teasing, confrontation and abuse but at the moment the content was more than usually acrimonious and the volume was attracting attention from the others. The boy sitting next to Joey Jeeves, a pale, stringy, fair-haired boy with protruding blue eyes, was shouting and pointing at his chair, pushing JJ in the chest, holding his head in his hands and walking in a circle, coming back and pointing at his chair.

'Miss, Miss, Oh God, it's disgusting. Miss. Look, Miss.'

JJ stood grinning foolishly, hands in pockets, but with a hint of pride at the level of disruption which he had generated. His glance took in the whole class, assessing their reaction, seeking approval and admiration for his latest effort.

'What's the matter, Craig? Settle down. It can't be that bad. What is it?'

'Miss, Miss, I was getting a felt tip pen to do my leaflet and when I came back -look, I could have sat in that.' Having a legitimate grievance he was making the most of it.

'What?'

'Look what he's done. There. Oh, Miss.'

Arms folded, Carol approached the chair with caution. 'Where? What?' She peered, seeing nothing, not knowing what she was looking for. She looked more closely.

'There Miss, look. He's put a big bogie on it.'

'Oh my God.' Carol recoiled in repulsion, feeling sick. There it was - huge. Did all that come out of one head? 'Oh no.'

The rest of the class, by now paying far closer attention than they ever would have done for the lesson, craned closer to see and, following Carol's example, turned away with groans of disgust, cries of, 'Oh man,' and retching noises.

To restore order Carol gave Craig another chair and sent Joey to the next classroom to borrow a cloth and some cleaning liquid. He then took the chair into the corridor and cleaned it until it shone. He obviously preferred this to an English lesson. Then he sat at the front and wrote a statement about what he'd done. This took ten minutes and the spelling was wonderful. By this time the lesson was almost finished so, ignoring her fleeting look of terror, Carol left Leanne in charge of the class and took JJ to find his Head of House, the person responsible for his pastoral care, to make the point that his behaviour was unacceptable. On the way they met Mark, who happened to be JJ's tutor.

'Well, well, what have we here?' Mark was good with the rough kids - said he used to be one himself. 'What have you been up to now?'

Mark stuck his hands in his pockets and rocked back on his heels. His pale face was alert with pleasant anticipation.

JJ stood there, and blushed. Such sensitivity in one so hardened to public opinion!

'Go on, tell Mr. Dawson what you did. Take your hands out of your pockets and tell him.'

Deprived of a place to hang his hands Joey stood awkwardly and hung his head instead, a bashful smile on his red lips showing perfect white teeth. 'Aw Miss, I can't say it.'

'Well, you managed to do it with no problems. Go on, tell him.'

'Miiiss,' he wheedled.

Mark took the statement and read it in silence. In a voice overlaid with theatrical outrage he said, 'I put a boggie on Craig's chiar.'

JJ laughed, despite the disapproval all round him.

'Yes Sir, a bogie. I spelt it wrong.'

'Chiar?'

'No Sir, 'chair' Sir. I spelt that wrong as well.'

'And you still think it's funny? I think, Mrs. Rose, we should get a pair of pliers and pull all the rest of his boggies out.' JJ looked alarmed. It was so disgusting it was funny and JJ suspected this, but wasn't sure whether he was allowed to laugh. He looked closely from face to face, an expert reader of human mood, and risked a shamefaced grin. Whatever anyone did wouldn't make a scrap of difference to him. At 35 he would probably be putting boggies in nasty places at work, in the men's locker room of some blokie workshop. This child had, thought Carol, been born in the wrong time and place. If he'd happened to have been born on the Canadian frontier two hundred years before, he could have been a national hero - a Davy Crockett. People would have sung songs about him.

Mark took JJ off to spend break picking up litter and probably hatching his next outrage.

The day staggered on.

After break the Year 10 Literature class had a test on their examination text - 'Kes'. They had only read the beginning, but Carol wanted to see if they could write about what they had read and discussed in class. To see if they could write at all, really.

After the usual amount of flapping about the class settled, miraculously, to work.

Zeon, who had attended perhaps three lessons that term and was commuting from a children's home at the other side of the city, began whispering loudly to Jake. He was supposed to be reading his book to catch up. He was a competent reader, although he wouldn't read outside school, and had lost two copies of the book already.

Martin sat on the front row, crouched over his paper. The pen which he held clenched in his teeth, bounced up and down as he bobbed his head in concentration. At the very least sign of distraction he would look round, sweeping the room with a big smile, his handsome coffee-coloured face alert for diversion. The paper on the desk before him was covered with spikey badly-formed handwriting in mangled sentences. He would laugh out loud whenever possible, not always for any particular reason. When the class had watched the video of 'Kes' he had nearly fallen off his chair, beside himself with glee, watching Billy being beaten by his brother Jud. His mother was mortally ashamed of him. She was a powerful, big lady, and had hoped for more from him. Martin said that when he was ten he had watched his cousin being born, an experience which, in Carol's view, may have deprived him of his wits.

The door burst open and bounced back against the wall. Julie came in, thirteen minutes late, and Carol's heart sank. She stalked across the room in her skin-tight lycra leggings and expensive high black leather boots - neither were school uniform but her Head of House was a psychology graduate to whom confrontation was anathema and understanding the child was all. Carol had already had a lively discussion with Julie's parents at the last Parents' Evening about classroom behaviour, and they had decided she was picking on their daughter, and complained to her Head of House.

Carol looked pointedly at her watch. Without a word of apology, ignoring Carol completely, Julie sat at the desk immediately in front of Carol's and began a verbal exchange with Jake. She liked to sit under Carol's nose so that Carol could be fully aware of how little notice she took of her teacher.

By now the test atmosphere was in tatters. From the moment she entered the room and swung her gigantic bosoms across the line of vision of the boys the testosterone level had shot up and most of the boys were mesmerised. Julie's period seemed to be over, thank God, or she wouldn't be wearing the lycra leggings, so she wouldn't be pre-menstrual and vicious. However, as she began to tell her mate Ginny, she had a rash, probably arising from a particularly active post-menstrual sexual encounter (though these were not Julie's chosen words) shared with her boy-friend the 'hard man of the school' some five years previously, and, Carol suspected, the rider of the early-morning motor-bike on the games pitches. The street-cred arising from broadcasting information about her sexual expertise to selected friends with a wider eavesdropping audience was incredible. Julie's ability to manipulate an audience was enviable. This latest piece of news was so riveting that Carol was tempted to abandon the test and listen herself, along with the other twenty occupants of the room.

After all, she reasoned, in her role as teacher in charge of sex education this information could be relevant.

Instead she attempted to get the lesson back on track.

'Julie, you're fifteen minutes late. I think you owe me an apology and an explanation.' The tone was pleasant and reasonable and did not betray the trepidation with which Carol attempted to impose some classroom discipline.

Julie turned slowly and deliberately. Beautiful liquid dark eyes raked Carol from top to toe and back again. The pouting well-made-up lips expressed contempt as she drawled, 'Sorry Miss.' Turning her back she resumed her conversation.

Sam, a spotty white youth who laboured under the burden of a clever and well-motivated older sister and Ezra, a toothy black youth of strict religious background, sat side by side across the room. Both had anoraks wrapped round their bums, the sleeves tied round their waists. They began every lesson like this and after a five- or ten-minute wrangle could be persuaded to untie themselves for the duration of the lesson. Today Carol couldn't be bothered to make the effort. In identical poses they hung forward over the desk, grinning, hands in laps, heads nodding, emitting short sneery nasal laughs, looking at each other, repeating key words of Julie's conversation, stamping feet in appreciation of particularly spicy bits. They particularly appreciated Julie's put-down of their teacher. Their role-models were clearly Beavis and Butthead.

The situation glided smartly beyond Carol's control. A great wave of inadequacy rolled over her head, leaving her floundering. She checked her watch and sighed. Fifty minutes to go.

'Come on class. Settle down. You only have fifty minutes left and you must attempt both questions. Martin, turn round please. Jake, pick your book up off the floor. Come on, you girls on the back row, stop chattering now, try and do some work.'

With reluctance pens were picked up, papers shuffled, preparatory to starting work.

Carol droned on. 'Don't forget you may refer to the text for your answers. Do try to use quotation to illustrate your point. Julie, turn round please. No book? Well, use mine then. No pen? Here have this one. Now settle down please.' This last remark, though intended for Julie, was aimed at the class in general in an attempt to avoid antagonising her.

Julie's career plans centred on nursing. Carol prayed that she would not find herself, in old age, delivered into Julie's tender care.

Amazingly there followed a five-minute spell of work - they were all writing. The sun shone through dirty glass, splashed with mud, streaked with rain, emphasising the dark shadows by the boarded-up window. Bright sunlight illuminated the layer of dust which sat on every surface, and the pot of pink chrysanthemums on Carol's desk among which nestled, she now noticed, a Crunchie wrapper. The new cleaning contract did not include dusting and the floor could only be 'spot-cleaned' which meant a wet mop on any actual mark such as squashed sandwich or, perhaps, boggie. Consequently the room was filthy. The weather was warm and the smell from the boys' toilet, across the corridor, could be faintly detected if you were unlucky enough to sit by the door. Most afternoons some deranged little chappie would turn on the taps, block the sink with bog roll, and flood the place. Fortunately Martin had chosen the desk nearest the door so he could wave to any mates who happened to be roaming the corridors during lessons, and he didn't seem to notice the pong.

A chair scraped and Jake waded out to the front of the class. The laces of his gigantic over-sized black boots bunched loosely over the tongue, the untied ends trailed on the dusty floor. Voluminous trousers fell in folds around his boot tops, which reached half-way to his knees, shirt-tails hanging down like Wee Willie Winkie's below a torn blazer. The school tie hung loosely, the knot resting somewhere near his left nipple. Jake was a man of style. Carol had had numerous run-ins with him over school uniform and decided to let it go this time in the interests of getting some work done.

Jake wanted paper. He was actually quite bright but had less self-discipline than Eric and Molly who had a concentration span of approximately thirty seconds. His work was improving and so was his attitude. Last year he'd been in Winnie's class. She was away for long periods, and when she was there she was more interested in decorating her classroom, running the Tuck-Shop and telling anyone who would listen about her sex life than she was in teaching. Apparently her Careers advice to her Year 11's was 'Basically, you take your GCSE's then you fuck off.' This was hearsay, of course. The kids in this class who had been in her class in Year 8 and 9 were ruined. They had been quite outraged when Carol expected them to write in class and to hand in homework.

'Write, you want me to write?' Butthead had demanded in disbelief.

There was a ripple of conversation while Jake got his paper and carried it back to his desk, dropping it only once and creasing it only slightly, then they settled down again. Tuey, thank God, was quiet. She had this immensely complicated behaviour report which took five minutes to fill in at the end of each lesson. She would stand at Carol's desk, by her elbow, towering ten inches above her, monitoring the comments which were entered on the report sheet, arguing and bargaining for ticks and praise, disputing anything negative, while the next class clamoured in the crowded corridor, waiting to be let in. She was supposed to have been expelled six months before. The Governors had told her mum and the accompanying gang of aunties that Tuey had one more chance, then she'd have to go. This was about the sixth chance since then. Tuey was the winner, she was running the staff ragged. They were cantering round in circles, writing reports on her every time she walloped someone, smoked, swore, broke the furniture, bullied or intimidated other pupils. They sent in report slips to the Head of House, gave detentions which were ignored, and Tuey remained untouched by it all. Rumour was that she was permanently affected by the pall of cannabis smoke in her home. The rumour was generated by her cousin. In the first year Tuey had been accustomed to sitting on the back row in the Science labs next to boys who were inexplicably frightened of her. The reason why they were frightened turned out to be the grip on their testicles which Tuey used to subdue any signs of disobedience to her orders.

Carol was frightened of her, and so were most of the other pupils. She wondered how she was going to survive for another ten years in this mad-house, trapped in a living Breugel landscape of gross humanity, each individual encased in their own little hell, shoulder to shoulder with the next lunatic, together but separate.

Gemma was bored now. She tapped her feet, called out, tapped her pen on the desk, laughed, obviously due to erupt any minute. Ten minutes to go, Carol estimated, five to collect papers. Try to keep them writing five more minutes. This was after all the most productive lesson they'd had for weeks - apart from Meena who had done nothing. Carol decided she wouldn't complain. She still felt bad about Amendip. Shortly after her parents had received a complaint about lack of homework and handing in an essay copied from another student, Amendip had disappeared, banished to Pakistan, and was now, apparently, married with two kids.

The bell shrieked, and five seconds later the dust settled on an empty classroom.

A lunch-time meeting had been called and would begin in ten minutes at the other side of the vast school site, in the drawing office. Carol packed her bag, abandoning her classroom to the fifty or so kids who would eat their lunch there, and leave their uneaten food for her to clean up before the afternoon session.

Forty teachers, the members of one of the four teaching unions in school, sat on high stools at the drawing desks, eating sandwiches and listening to their leader, Don, a slight man of about forty five, with a pronounced nervous twitch to the shoulders. The big windows looked out over fields and the canal, and it was quiet and peaceful on this side of the school, away from the kids.

The subject of the meeting was the school budget deficit. This was, apparently, so enormous that the only way to deal with it was to make redundancies. Voluntary redundancies would be preferred. There was silence as they heard that a special package was on offer - anyone over fifty could apply for early retirement with redundancy. If enough people decided to accept this, the jobs of younger colleagues who had more pressing commitments to dependent families and mortgages could be protected.

There was a general looking-round as rapid off-the-cuff age assessment was carried out on everyone present. No-one looked at Carol, and she remembered that most of them thought she was about forty five. She expected that a subtle pressure would be felt by older members to take the offer and reduce the pressure on younger teachers.

'God I wish I was eight years older,' said Robin from Business Studies.

'Wish I was twenty years older,' muttered Jeff from Modern Languages.

Most of the teachers were caught in a trap, something which Carol knew, but this situation brought the realisation home clearly. Schools taking on new staff were looking for newly qualified teachers, at the bottom of the pay scale, not older experienced ones who would cost more and push up the salaries budget. Anyone who had been teaching for more than five years had effectively priced themselves out of a job, unless they were ambitious and competitive enough to be joining the fierce battle for promotion. Jane in the Geography Department had been short-listed and interviewed by nine different schools for positions as Deputy Head. One day soon she would succeed, if she didn't fall beside the wayside in exhaustion in the meantime. Jobs outside education were almost non-existent. It was a clear choice of continuing in teaching, or joining the ranks of the unemployed.

These people were wishing their lives away, envious because they were not old enough to apply for early retirement.

Carol looked round at her colleagues and saw the hang-dog expressions, nervous mannerisms and prematurely aged faces. The predominant mood was hopeless defiance. If I don't seize this chance, she thought, I may have to stay here until I am sixty - a long dark tunnel, ten years before I reach the light. I'd have a small pension - not enough to support all four of us, but it's about time they all began to support themselves anyway. I can't stand much more of this.

On the way back from the meeting she passed two little Afro-Caribbean boys who were standing in front of a large poster display on drugs. She had only put the posters up the day before. This was one of three with diagrams of a body showing all the internal organs with notes attached describing the effects of a particular drug. They were reading the one on cannabis. Leaning on each other for support they were in fits of laughter, pointing, reading out the labels.

'No man, that ain't true. No man, no way. Who is this dude? He ever try it?' spluttered the smaller boy.

'Hey man, look at that - you smoke a spliff you can't get it up no more. You tell that to my daddy,' his friend replied.

'Look, it turn your brain green. Oh man, this is great.'

'Who write this stuff?' demanded the second one in a falsely high squeaky voice. In an exaggerated pantomime he held his stomach, bent double and staggered in a circle, laughing fit to burst.

Carol crept past. She'd thought the posters were good - until now.

* * * * *

The next morning there was a letter from Jessica. Carol picked it up from the hall carpet as she was leaving and, seeing the postmark, put down her bags, sat in the rocking chair and tore open the envelope.

The first paragraph had some news about a trip out the previous weekend. Then the bombshell.

She had told her mother, Jane, about their visit. Jane had been deeply upset, and this had brought on high blood pressure – particularly dangerous considering her fragile state of health. She believed that blood being thicker than water, she was about to lose her daughter and grandchildren. She would never try to stop any contact, but had told Jessica that she didn't want to know about it, it was too hurtful. Jessica had therefore decided that any further contact must be limited to herself. Her mother must on no account be upset. If the children were to visit they would naturally talk about it to grandmother. Young children could not be expected to keep secrets - Carol knew well how crippling secrets could be, and would not have wanted that - so there would be no further visits.

Well, thought Carol bitterly, you have to hand it to Jane, she's handled it well. She effectively cuts off close contact whilst remaining the good guy. This woman was clearly an expert operator.

Carol sat on the hall chair, coat on, ready to leave for school, with the opened letter in her hand. Her eyes were drawn to the oil painting on the wall opposite, a brightly-coloured still-life done by Vanessa, based on a Mary Fedden which they'd both liked at the Royal Academy Summer Exhibition, but she didn't see it.

'These are your grandchildren,' she thought. 'Look, aren't they lovely? See how pretty and lively they are, like me in the childhood you missed. Now - sorry - you can't see them again. But I'll send you photos, so you can appreciate how lovely they are as they grow up, so you can see exactly what you've missed.'

It wasn't as if the woman had anything to fear. Your mother, your real mother, is the one who nursed you through childhood illnesses, shared your problems, made you cakes and fancy dress party outfits. Your mother helped you learn to ride a bike, put plasters on your grazed knees. The reward for all that was the child's love and trust. Jane was undisputedly Jessica's mother. The two of them must have a strong relationship based on their life together. But I, thought Carol, I have the biological link, which will never fail - how could it? She was part of me. I feel she belongs to me in a way which, if I never see her again, cannot be dissolved. In a way which her mother can never know.

She had visited her brother Ian and his wife Celia the previous weekend. Celia had said, 'If I was her mother I'd be upset if I thought her real mother was going to come back and step in. After I'd brought her up, spent money on her, given her my time.' But that was Celia. Did she really think it was that simple? Had her mother bought her, body and soul, with money and time?

Having children was not a business, a profit and loss concern, a balanced sheet of disparate items. 'I'll give you food and shelter, you give me allegiance and loyalty. There is only a finite amount of filial love and yours belongs to me because I have bought it with years of love and money and care. Love is a limited commodity. You cannot love more than one person, you would have to take away a portion of love which you have given to me in order to give a little to another. The pie is all mine - you can't give a slice to someone else.'

'Love isn't like that,' Carol said to herself. 'You don't have to limit it. It's like knowledge - the more you have the more it grows.'

'I gave her my baby,' thought Carol, 'because I didn't have the means to keep her. I was overjoyed that it had been a success, all that I'd hoped for. Jane has had a life filled with the fulfilment of my child. Couldn't she spare a tiny bit for me? Is she so insecure despite all their years of family togetherness that she has to feel threatened by my existence, and use these subtle emotional blackmail control tactics to ensure that her family remains tightly bound to her, with no divided loyalties?'

She read the letter again. All she wanted was to get to know her child as a person, to meet her often enough to build a relationship, to feel that she knew her. The most basic prerequisite for this was time - time and interaction. If Jessica took that time, her relationship with her mother would be threatened, which would make her unhappy. The last thing Carol wanted was to cause conflict in her life - she had done enough damage already.

Paul came downstairs, fastening his dressing gown, and saw Carol sitting in the hall, wearing her outdoor coat, school-bag at her feet.

'What's the matter?' he asked. 'Is anything wrong?'

Carol handed him the letter. He took off his thick-lensed specs and peered closely, making the effort to read the tiny handwriting.

'Yes, well,' he said. 'I guess you have to expect it.'

'I know,' Carol replied in a low voice. 'But I didn't.'

'You must look on the positive side. You know where she is, that she has had a contented childhood, has a family of her own. She's happy, she wants to keep in touch, she writes regularly.'

'Yes, I know. But I wanted,' she blew her nose, determined not to cry, 'I wanted to get to know her. And my grandchildren. To find out what kind of person she is.'

'Look on the bright side. She seems to care about your feelings. Give it time. It's early days yet.'

'Yes, I know, you're right,' and logically she knew that he was. But emotionally it was a different story.

'Do you want a cup of tea before you go to school? Or are you staying at home?'

'No, I'm going.' Carol folded the letter and placed it in her handbag, where it remained all day, pricking at her mind at odd moments, like a snagged nail which pulls down to the quick and catches on your clothes when you forget to protect it.

'She is a closed book to me,' Carol thought, 'and it looks as if she will remain so.'

She picked up a handbag, a heavy school-bag and a pile of GCSE folders, and opened the front door.

'See you,' she called.

'See you,' came the response from the kitchen.

She closed the door and climbed wearily into the car.

* * * * *

Chapter 8

'Dinner's ready.' Paul's voice drifted upstairs from the kitchen. 'Can you hear me?'

'Yeah, yeah,' Vanessa called from her room.

Carol lay, fully clothed, on top of the duvet in the darkened bedroom, her eyes on the small square window, her mind picking remorselessly round the contents of the letter which lay in its envelope on the bedside table. The bright hopes which had carried her through the last thirty years now sat heavy and almost dead in her heart.

'Wake mum up,' Vanessa called.

'Okay.'

The bedroom door opened, letting a slice of yellow light into the darkened bedroom.

'Mom, you awake?'

'Yes.'

'Dinner's ready.'

'Okay.' She sat up and swung her legs over the side of the bed, groping with her feet for her slippers. Tantalising smells of good food drifted up the stairs, and she realised how hungry she was.

The kitchen was full of noise from the television and the extractor fan.

Eric lay under the table, head on paws. He'd been dejected ever since his mother had died, at the end of the summer holidays. The only member of the family who felt her loss more than he did must have been Paul, who didn't say much but had mooched about for weeks looking miserable. Steam from the recently-boiling pasta obscured the window-panes at front and back, behind the Laura Ashley curtains.

The pine table was laid with blue patterned plates. Vanessa and Matthew were already sitting at the table, picking at a bowl of precisely sliced and artistically arranged salad which stood at one end. A saucepan of pasta rested on a trivet in the middle, and a bread-board with two sticks of garlic-bread at the other end. Paul placed a bowl of bolognaise thick with mushrooms, tomatoes and fresh herbs on another trivet. He took a bottle of wine from the fridge and poured some into Carol's glass.

'This looks scrum-diddly-umptious,' she said, trying to inject into her voice some of the enthusiasm which she knew his efforts deserved.

'Okay, that's it. Get stuck in,' said Paul, taking his seat.

Matthew yawned widely.

'My God, you'll break your jaw if you do that,' said Carol with disapproval, reaching for the pasta.

'Sorry. Couldn't sleep last night. I lay awake until four o clock, then I couldn't get up this morning.'

'Poor old you,' said Carol, sarcastically, 'it must be difficult to remain unconscious for more than sixteen hours a day.' Matthew looked wounded. She handed him the bowl.

'Well, I haven't got anything else to do.'

'You could try looking for a job.'

'There are no jobs,' Paul cut in. 'Do you think I'd be here cooking your dinner if I could get a job?'

'Have you been to the Job Club this week?' she knew he had before she asked.

'Yes. Three times. It's full of men my age, chasing jobs which don't exist.'

'Why don't you get a job in a bar or something. Just temporarily. At least it's money.'

'I've just worked for two years to get a Business Studies degree. Why should I work in a bar?' Paul was angry. Again.

'Have you applied for employment benefit, or whatever they call it these days?'

'Yes. I'm your dependent, and as such I am not entitled to anything. You know that, I told you.' There was an edge to his voice which suggested that it would be a good idea to choose her words carefully.

'It's so unfair. How many thousands of pounds - hundreds of thousands, I bet - did you pay in tax and all the other things when you were working?'

'Yes well, I'm not an unmarried teenage mother, or a black lesbian prostitute, so I'm not a deserving case. It's clever. You both pay tax, then if one of you has a job, the other can't claim anything. By the way, there's no money left in the pot.' He was referring to the teapot where the housekeeping money was kept. Carol kept it topped up, but sometimes it ran out.

'I put fifty quid in there on Monday. Where's that gone?'

235

'Sorry,' said Vanessa, 'I took five quid yesterday for some fabrics for uni. I need them for my new project. Silks. I got them from the Indian shop in the Rag Market. Dead cheap.'

'You're supposed to get things like that with your grant,' said Carol.

'You're kidding. I've had to buy new brushes, a load of hand-made paper and new fabric dyes this week. If my grant cheque doesn't come through soon I don't know what I'll do.'

'Give up smoking. I can't afford to,' said Paul, bitterly.

Matthew looked uncomfortable. He smoked twenty rollies a day.

'Thank God this is your last year. You'll be virtually finished by Easter. Then we'll have a degree each, and one bloody job between the lot of us which, unfortunately, is mine.' Carol knew she was pushing her luck, but there was a feeling that life was so awful at this moment that it couldn't get any worse. She was wrong.

'Don't blame me, blame the fucking Government that decides the only people who matter are those who subscribe to the Tory party funds. The rest of us can go piss up a rope as far as they're concerned,' Paul's anger was translated into the timbre of his voice, which grated on Carol's nerves more than the words.

'Have you applied for anything lately Matt,' Carol asked to change the subject from one which they'd all heard before several million times.

'Haven't seen anything advertised. At least I'm getting some experience at the drop-in-centre. I mean, they only pay me ten quid above dole rate, but it's better than nothing.' He did voluntary work at a legal drop-in-centre in the city. 'You should see some of the people who come in there. You think we've got problems!'

'Why don't you get an evening job? You could earn some extra money, help out.'

'There aren't any. You have to have a NVQ in Waiter Skills or something, or be on a Work Experience scheme so the employer doesn't have to actually pay you anything.'

Carol thought about the lunch-time meeting. It was bad timing, but she had to raise the idea some time.

'We had a meeting at lunch-time today.'

'Do we have to hear about your school? Don't you think we've had enough of it?' asked Paul. 'We've heard enough about the demented psychopaths you teach. Spare us, please.' He stuffed his mouth full of salad and chewed viciously.

'They're talking about redundancy.'

'And that's the end of the national news. Here is Midlands Today,' the television blethered into the sudden pool of silence which welled up around the table.

'And?' said Matthew.

'And before they make anyone compulsorily redundant, they're asking if anyone over fifty is interested in voluntary redundancy. With early retirement.' No-one spoke. 'I'm over fifty.'

'So what are you saying? That you've applied?' asked Paul.

'No. I'm telling you about it, to ask your opinion. Before I make a decision.'

'Oh great,' said Vanessa. 'I'll chuck my degree and get a job. Thanks mom.'

'If I did apply it wouldn't be immediately. It would be for Easter. Or the summer. And the last thing I want is for you to give up your course. You know I want you to get your degree as much as you do.'

'More pasta anyone?' Paul offered the bowl around, noted the shaken heads and piled the remains of the tagliatelle onto his plate. He began to eat as if the conversation held no significance for him.

'What do you think Paul?' she asked.

'Who me? Don't ask me. If you give up your job we'll have nothing to live on, but if that's what you want, I expect that's what you'll do.'

'Well, no-one else seems obliged to do what they don't want to do. Why should I spend any more of my life in that hell-hole?' Her voice was rising. Carol knew that the disappointment of the morning had a lot to do with the way she was handling this, but her feet were set on a path, and a blazing row seemed appropriate for the way she felt.

'It's not what you're saying, it's the way you're saying it,' said Vanessa.

'Does it matter how I say it? The bottom line is, I work and support you lot, I hate it, and I've had enough,' she shrieked. Eric climbed out from under the table and looked from one to another in confusion. He shook himself, and gave a muted, disconsolate little howl.

'Here we go again,' Matthew put his fork down. 'Even the dog's joining in.' He pushed back his chair, stood up and walked out of the room. The front door slammed.

'Nice to see you all care so much,' she yelled.

'Come on Eric,' Paul stood up, took the dog into the utility room. A few minutes later he mooched past the back window in his tattered old Barbour, hat jammed on his head. Eric's cheerful woofs and throaty rumblings faded away and the gate banged shut.

'You've done it again, mum,' said Vanessa. 'I hope you're happy.'

'Fucking ecstatic,' snapped Carol bitterly, head in hands.

Vanessa stood up, pushed her chair back. 'As soon as I finish my degree, I'll be gone.' She turned and her footsteps could be heard on the stairs, followed by the sound of her bedroom door banging shut.

Carol looked at the ruins of the meal on the table. She felt that her case was reasonable. Why couldn't they all discuss things like adults, instead of shooting off into angry words every time anything came up which required any degree of negotiation. Did it always have to be like this? She felt trapped.

The week crept by. Paul was silent and angry, avoiding her whenever possible. On Saturday he agreed to drop her off in town. They only had the one car, and he needed it to pick up some paint from the DIY store. They barely spoke.

In the High Street a car pulled out unexpectedly and without warning from the kerb. Paul slammed on his brakes.

'Is he a taxi? he yelled. 'I'll take his number and report him. There's too much of that sort of thing.' The anger which he directed at the other driver was only a drop from the vast reservoir which lurked inside him, waiting to spill out at any convenient target. The feeling of dread and panic in Carol's chest rose. She longed to jump out of the car and escape.

She decided to change the subject. 'The Union rep, Ed, he's been making enquiries, and my first two terms of teaching supply, back in 1978, won't count towards a pension, if I apply for early retirement,' she offered.

'Your Union rep shouldn't let that happen,' he shouted. 'You can sue the Council for that sort of thing.' As if!

His mood had still not improved by the evening. The icy silence which he had maintained for most of the week remained intact. Vanessa was getting ready to go out for a meal with friends and Matthew had disappeared for the weekend, leaving them to eat alone together.

Carol cooked dinner without enthusiasm, wondering how to answer the letter. What could she say, after all? She called Paul in from where he was painting the window-frame at the back of the house. She waited for him to clean his brushes and wash his hands. He walked into the kitchen and peered at the dinner on the table.

'School dinners again! It was the same last week. You have decent food all week when I cook the dinner and do the shopping. You cook and we're back to fucking school dinners. Mashed potatoes,' he sneered.

So - he didn't like the potatoes! He began poking the desert with a fork, as if it was a dead rat.

'What's this - cheese?' he yelled, stabbing a piece of apricot which lay on a bed of strawberries.

Panic, a physical hurt in the stomach. It was like Year 10 all over again. Another situation which Carol could not control but for which she was responsible. There was no way out. Whatever she did or said it would be wrong. Anger replaced panic. Tossing caution aside, surfing expertly upon the rising wave of fury, she yelled back.

'I've worked all fucking week to provide you with your living. I'm sorry it's not up to the high standard you have come to expect. I can't be a teacher and Delia-sodding-Smith as well as the cleaner, laundry-maid, gardener and floor-washer. What do you want - blood?'

He was standing, fist drawn back, eyes bulging, ready to punch her in the face.

'I'll go to jail for you, you stupid fat ….'

She wanted to cry but wouldn't give him the satisfaction. His words cut like razors.

'Go on, do it - once. Go on,' she taunted. 'You can't do anything else right. You don't work, you don't screw, you won't go out anywhere, you don't like anyone, you're lousy company - there's no point to anything about you.'

He turned and stalked out into the back garden. Carol had won, and she hated herself.

Vanessa appeared at the kitchen door, arms folded, face a mask of derision. She leaned on the door jamb.

'Nice one, mom. Yeah - real nice.'

'What do you think I am - Mother-fucking-Teresa?' Carol snarled. But she knew she'd handled it all wrong. He was wrong but so was she. He was deliberately refusing to share the responsibilities, leaving her to carry them alone. He was clever, easily able to do anything he chose, and he chose to sit about at home, watching tv, playing computer games, wallowing in pity, and blaming everyone except himself. He could afford such self-indulgence - because she was doing a job she had come to loath simply so that they could all have some security. She didn't miss the big important house, the luxurious lifestyle, but God, she resented the feeling that she was the only one rowing the boat.

The following weekend, to escape the oppressive atmosphere which invaded every corner of the house, she accepted an invitation to Saturday lunch back home with June and James. The lunch was in the

Director's Box at the football stadium - corporate hospitality. It was an important match - she didn't know who was playing, she wasn't interested enough to find out. There were only two tickets, and June had invited herself and Vanessa - another indication that people were beginning to count Paul as not important any more. She and Vanessa had settled their differences almost immediately after the events of earlier in the week had settled down a little. Carol wished it was as easy to end the antagonism between herself and Paul.

June wanted Vanessa to approve her new interior design plans, so she had been invited instead of Paul. As if to emphasise Paul's lack of importance he was invited to join them for drinks after the match if he should happen to be around. Carol wondered if June expected him to travel a hundred miles then hang about outside until summoned inside to receive her bounty.

June and James were perfect hosts, charming and hospitable. Both of them managed to wear a number of large diamonds, and labels were not worn on the outside of clothes, exactly, but could be deduced by the quality of the cloth and cut. Unfortunately they couldn't bring the Merc into the box, but everyone knew it was there, parked outside. Ian and Celia were in another hospitality suite up the stairs with their corporate invitation. He was a Senior Partner of his company now and drove an Audi. Funny, thought Carol, how things change. Ten years before she and Paul were the affluent yuppies of this family, now they were the poor relations. She was the only one in the family with a job. She drove a modest Renault 5 and Paul had rediscovered public transport - which showed what an education could do.

Truly, she didn't begrudge her family their good fortune - they all worked very hard - but Paul was bitter. She also had a nagging feeling that she herself was envious. He hated visiting them. Someone always asked him what he was doing now, and listened with disapproval when he had to say he had no job. They thought no-one needed to be without a job, even if it was only £2.00 an hour. They couldn't see that it was demeaning – nor was it available, because there were hundreds of students hustling for low-paid jobs.

June and Vanessa had a good natter about colour and styles. June's ideas on style were all derived from expensive hotels she'd stayed in, so the finished results tended to be somewhat over the top. She was the perfect corporate wife - well-groomed, auburn hair, controlled weight, slim, thick enough to make James feel comfortable - and that took some doing. He professed to like Pavarotti and Hemmingway, and to read The Guardian, because he thought they were suitable for his image. Carol suspected he preferred Eddie Cochrane and The Sun. Patsy was no better - the Earth Mother, devoted to her family, contented, wearing shawls spun from pure honey, all detectable brain activity directed towards her kids - all four of them, five soon. A baby machine.

Carol gazed unseeingly at the twenty two handsome young men racing about on the sunny green pitch below, sipped on a gin and tonic, and did not hear the roars and chants of the crowd as the ball hit the back of the net. Inside her head black and gloomy thoughts revolved. The reunion with Jessica, for so long the reason for denying present disappointments and focussing on the future, was not going to be the way she had imagined. Bitterness etched deep gouges in her soul. The best-loved people in her life were reviewed, condemned, and their images coated in poison. Deep inside she knew she was on a path to destruction, but she was powerless to change the direction of her steps.

Inexorably, the pattern laid down for the next few months unrolled and revealed itself. It was unstoppable. Fortunately Carol could not see the precise details of her immediate future, or she might have decided not to participate in it at all.

In December, by arrangement, she met Jessica again for lunch. Just the two of them. She drove for an hour and a half to meet her, and found that Jessica had brought Ivan and the baby as well. The moment she arrived she knew it was wrong. The atmosphere was chilling, and she felt that Jessica was there by coercion, her coercion, not choice.

'How did it go?' asked Paul when she returned.

'Fine. It was alright,' she replied, and lapsed into a depressed silence. To discuss this with Paul would only make it worse. His support consisted of handing out advice which, if not taken, was made the subject of further argument. He was sympathetic, she knew, but the idea of listening sympathetically would never have occurred to him

She sent Christmas cards containing money to the children, expecting Jessica to open them.

The following week she had a letter which asked her not to send cards addressed to the children, because Jessica did not want them to know of her existence until she chose to tell them, when they were grown up.

Carol took out a book from the library about adoptive children. The writer said that adoptive children, at puberty, either rebelled fiercely, or became compliant and eager to please, feeling they must be better than the child who was given away. The first reaction of an adoptive child to a reunion was to reject the mother, but the mother must not allow this to happen, and must hang on in there for the child's sake. The child was testing and must not be rejected a second time.

The whole subject was complex, and Carol felt she had done everything wrong from the beginning. She had been too needy, wanted everything too desperately.

She bought a copy of the book and sent it to Jessica. Jessica returned it a few weeks later with a note saying she had glanced at it, and it was quite interesting, but she hadn't had time to read it thoroughly. Fair enough, thought Carol – who had time to read boring books with three young children to look after?

The autumn term drew to a close in a welter of Carol Concerts, school pantomimes and special assemblies. After Christmas lunch in the Dining Hall Registers were taken and the children dispersed, full of bounce and high spirits, to the bus queues. The staff meeting which followed had the usual speeches and presents for departing colleagues. If she decided to go, thought Carol, she could be standing there making the traditional thank-you-and-goodbye speech at the end of the summer term. She dreaded the speech, but wanted to be the one leaving. In the gloom of the early afternoon of December 21st, Carol locked her classroom door.

'Coming up the pub?' called Dave from Maths as he passed the end of the now-empty corridor.

'No, I have some shopping to do,' Carol called back with a cheerfulness she did not feel. 'Have a good Christmas.'

'You too. See you in January,' called Dave and the outside door banged behind him.

The house was quiet when she arrived. Carol took off her outdoor clothes and climbed the stairs. She closed the bedroom door, laid on the bed and wrapped the duvet round her legs. A navy-blue sky with a few early stars could be seen through the window. She wondered about Jessica, and her children, who would probably be getting more and more excited about Christmas. She remembered Matthew and Vanessa when they were little, how they loved the excitement of putting up the tree and the decorations. This year she hadn't done anything. Vanessa had put the tree up, and Paul was making the trips to the supermarket for all the Christmas food, making decisions about turkeys and wines and all the other details of the feast. All she had to do was provide the money. It was all too much trouble. Big tears rolled down her cheeks and she fell asleep.

At Paul's invitation Carol's mother came for Christmas. The day before Christmas Eve Mrs. Stone sat in the lounge watching television. Paul and Carol were preparing dinner. He took out five lamb chops from the fridge and began to lay them out on a baking tray.

'I thought you said we were having the fish today and the lamb tomorrow,' said Carol.

'What is this? Are you trying to control me again?' snarled Paul.

'No. I am asking you if you've changed your mind,' she replied.

'No you're not, you're just looking for a damned row.' Carol was glad her mother was deaf and couldn't hear this. She had a heart condition, and became stressed and breathless at the least sign of agitation.

'Can you keep your voice down. My mother will hear you,' she asked, her voice as cold as ice.

'Hear me? Hear me?' he yelled. 'She'll hear me. I'll bring her in here and show her what you're really like. Bullying me, control freak. I'll hurt you through someone you do care about. You don't care about anyone, except your mother. I'll bring her in here.'

'No leave her alone,' said Carol alarmed. 'She's ill, she can't deal with this. Why punish her?'

'Don't tell me what to do.' He pushed her aside, and had his hand on the door knob.

He was actually going to get her mother in here, and involve her in this awful, pointless row! On top of school, on top of having to swallow her hopes of a happy reunion with Jessica, he was going to hurt her mother.

Inside Carol something snapped.

She launched herself at him. With the strength of demons she smacked his hand off the door handle and pushed him away from the door.

'Get out, you bastard,' she growled quietly, the voice coming from far back in her throat. She pushed sharply with all her strength, with both hands, at his chest. He stepped back but caught the force of it. She aimed another.

'I'm sick of you and your evil temper,' she ground out. 'You leave my mother alone or I'll kill you, you nasty evil bag of rubbish.' He began to struggle back, but over-whelming anger gave her strength, and his surprise weakened his blows. Vanessa was upstairs and Carol hoped she couldn't hear. 'I'm sick of your picking and picking at me. You think the world owes you something. You sit here at home day in and day out, you let me earn your living. You should be ashamed of yourself, you're not a man, you're a pathetic, snivelling little excuse for a human being.' She pushed him again. He looked frightened. 'You go anywhere near my mother, and I'll rip your bloody head off. You won't know what's hit you.'

Her anger spent, she leant exhausted and crying on the worktop, her knees ready to collapse and pitch her onto the floor.

Paul's lips clenched into a tight white line.

'You mad cow,' he spat out. Then he walked across the room, opened the door and went into the hall. The lounge door was still closed, and the telly could be heard. He picked up the phone. Vanessa came down the stairs.

'What's going on?'

'I'm going to call the police. This is domestic violence.'

'What is? What are you talking about?' Vanessa demanded.

'Your mother is bullying me,' he reported.

With cold dread Carol saw him begin to dial. Surely this was a trick to frighten her. He wouldn't really do it. Would he?

She could have taken the receiver from him, and put her finger on the ringer, but she didn't. Her mother would certainly hear any fracas out here. He completed his dialling as Vanessa and Carol watched him, silently, aghast.

'There is an incident of domestic abuse. My wife is beating me, and I am afraid she might do some serious damage. Could you send a policeman round please?' He gave the address.

The three of them stood in silence, waiting. Eventually an absurdly young policeman came crunching up the drive, and Vanessa let him in, brought him into the kitchen, and shut the door behind him.

He listened to both sides of the story for over an hour.

'Three years ago I filed for divorce. Then, afterwards, it was like I was facing a black hole, and I couldn't go through with it. I went to Relate and found he was already going there. We discussed it and decided to have another try. Stupid decision. Ever since then he's been trying to manufacture a situation where he can do the same. I don't regret what I did - then or now. Before I did that he used to hit me and say it was my fault. He hasn't touched me since then. Instead he uses verbal abuse - I went to see a divorce lawyer this summer. I will divorce him. It's just a matter of timing.'

'She's mad. She's trying to make out she is scared of me, that I'm a bully, but she is the one who is violent. I'm the one in danger.'

The policeman listened patiently, occasionally breaking off to answer the squawk from his brick sized mobile phone. Then,

'I'm going to go now. If I am called out again this side of Christmas, one of you will spend the remainder of the holiday in a cell. I have one piece of advice. You have a nice home here. If you do get divorced, do it in a civilised fashion. If you begin to argue through solicitors, they'll have most of the value of your house, and neither of you will have anything left.'

Vanessa let him out, came back into the kitchen and shut the door. The three of them stood in silence. Anger was palpable. The door opened. Mrs. Stone popped her head round , her face fuzzy with sleep.

'Where's everybody got to? I was watching the film and I fell asleep, and I've just woken up. I thought you'd all gone out.' She looked from one to another. 'What's the matter? Is something wrong?'

'No, of course not,' Carol smiled. Paul said nothing, and left the room. Mrs. Stone turned her head to watch him go. 'Would you like some tea? And a mince pie?'

'What's up with him? Have you had an argument?'

'Don't worry about him. Tea?'

'Oh yes, please, go on then. And I'll have a mince pie as well, please,' said Mrs. Stone. She took her hearing aid from her ear and shook it. 'Blooming thing. I don't know what's wrong with it. I can't hear anything.' She knew something had happened but if they wanted her not to know, she wasn't going to insist.

They followed the ceremonies of Christmas Day, with the three course lunch which had been planned. Carol went mechanically through all the motions of serving and eating the food, making conversation with her mother. When she was alone, the tears coursed freely down her cheeks. She did not sob, her face did not distort into a grimace, her mouth did not pull into the howl which she felt inside, but now and again the tears slid out from under her eyelids and ran down her cheeks. And inside her chest was a desert of isolation and devastation.

This, she knew, was the end. In her mind's eye she saw Paul's hand on the receiver, saw him speaking into the phone, and knew that she had no business staying with a man who could do that.

He was tied to her with cords of dependence which he resented but was powerless to break. He didn't have the strength of character to stand on his own two feet, he wanted her support, but he resented his dependence. Knowing he had no control of his own life, he wanted to control hers. Knowing he had no life of his own, he wanted to live hers, dictating each detail, exerting his will with ruthless spitefulness. Had he planned this? The first step had been to invite her mother for Christmas, which was his suggestion. He had created the row in the kitchen, he had threatened her mother, and he had called the police. Was it all planned and she had followed his plan like a lamb?

The next day, with no sign of the events of the previous day, with great friendliness and politeness, Paul took Mrs. Stone back home to Yorkshire. While he was gone, Carol had time to think about her situation.

As her hands automatically cleared away the debris of Christmas and loaded the washing machine and dishwasher, her mind ground into overdrive. She felt that she was at the bottom of a deep well, and drowning. Vanessa was in the last few months before her finals. She was not going to be deprived of her chance because her mother and father could not act like adults. A change of house and a divorce would disrupt her. It was out of the question. Matthew would not be long at home. He would soon find something he wanted to do, and go. She could wait until the summer, for Vanessa's sake.

After Christmas, she went to see a solicitor to check on her obligations and expectations. She needed information, to know how things were done, how long it would take. But inside was such misery, such grieving for the death of the marriage to the one person she had ever really loved. Without Paul, she felt, her life would be nothing, she would be nothing.

The new term began. Carol walked into school, and began to cry. The tears would not stop. They flowed, seeping out and running down her cheeks. Hopeless. She went to see the doctor. He listened, aghast. She felt shame at telling him all the sordid details, but it couldn't be helped.

Dr. Welsh gave her anti-depressants, and sent her home. He didn't give her a sick note. He said she'd be better off at school.

The next few months passed in a daze.

Superficial working communication was gradually established, like new skin which grows over the septic depths of a badly tended wound. Matt applied for dozens of jobs, anything that came up, and got something in London. He arranged to stay with a friend until he could find a place of his own, packed his bags and left.

Vanessa continued with her studies and projects.

Carol kept in touch with Jessica by letter, but never suggested another meeting, aware that all her previous suggestions had been met with an excuse as to why it couldn't happen.

She began to see that there was a certain hurtfulness in the way Jessica had let her in, raised her hopes, then shut her out. Her own fault, no doubt. There must be something she'd got wrong, something wrong with her as a person. She seemed to mess everything up.

On Jessica's birthday she sent her a present, a piece of jewellery, and a card. She hoped Jessica would like it, but had no knowledge of her tastes, so couldn't be sure. Her photograph was on the wall in the Hall next to Carol's Granny in her splendid gold frame. She saw them both every day. Her Granny was dead, and Jessica was equally beyond reach. She still worried, when she wrote to Jessica, that she would say the wrong thing, and never receive a reply.

As the end of term approached, Nessie applied for jobs in Milan. The fashion industry had many opportunities for her talents there. Carol joined a gym - it gave her somewhere to go to get away from home without imposing on friends.

Nessie got a first. The family celebrated with meals out, superficially polite and friendly, but only ever three words away from confrontation and disaster.

July approached, and Carol's retirement party took place in a pub in Birmingham. The upstairs room was gloomy and vast. The stained-glass window had a bullet hole in it - whether the bullet was coming in or going out she did not know, but it was a drug-dealing area so it could have been either.

Paul accompanied her and was polite to everybody. He had known them for years, superficially, but never wanted to mix with them - or they with him. Slick computer consultants with lots of money, his previous incarnation, and impoverished, stressed teachers were not given to mutual admiration. Ironically they were now affluent compared to him - he had no income whatsoever and showed no inclination to do anything about it other than complain bitterly about the government.

The last links with school were severed on 21st July, Carol's fifty-first last day of term. The seventeen years she'd spent here seemed to have passed in a flash. 'I should have left ten years ago,' she thought, 'while I was still enjoying it and had a sense of vocation.' The last few years had been dreadful. She knew she would miss the money, but nothing else, except the staff, some of them.

July turned into August. One Wednesday Carol returned from the gym, exhausted. Paul was sitting, as usual, watching television. She washed the oven trays which she had left soaking and put them in the oven to dry with the heat switched on.

Paul came in, his face like thunder.

'Why have you put the oven on?' he demanded.

'What do you mean? ' she asked, confused. She knew this was another manufactured row, but could not see how to avoid it.

'You always answer a question with a fucking question.' He swore in every sentence now. 'I said why have you put the fucking oven on?'

'To dry the trays.'

'You've put them in there,' he shouted, 'using electricity. Why can't you dry them with a cloth?'

'I can but I'm doing it like this. My mother used to do it like this. What's wrong with it?'

'What's wrong with a fucking cloth?' he screeched. 'Why can't you do what normal people do and use a tea towel?'

'I could have done that but I decided to do this.' Her stomach was churning. He was beside himself with rage.

'You say we haven't any money and you put the oven on to dry trays. That's perverted.'

'That's an extreme way to describe it.'

'You're mad,' he screeched.

'I'm mad because I switched the oven on for five minutes?' Carol asked, putting as much over-patient disdain into her voice as she could

'Yes - you're fucking mad - and perverted,' he screamed.

'I am not mad - and I don't think switching the oven on makes me perverted,' she answered back.

She picked up her coffee and walked over to the window. Inside she was quaking.

In a cold voice he said, 'My solicitor phoned me up yesterday to follow up from last December.'

'And?'

'I have a meeting next week.'

'Oh.'

'I'm destitute. I haven't a penny. And you switch the fucking oven on to dry a pan. It's like waving fivers under my nose.'

'Have you - did you actually fill in a divorce petition last December?'

'No I didn't. You know I didn't,' his voice was angry and accusing, as if she was testing his patience deliberately.

'What is the meeting about then?'

'I told you,' his voice rose, 'don't you fucking listen? It's a follow-up. I'm destitute. You tell me we have no money and you go having your eye-brows dyed and going to gyms and God knows what. You're waving fivers under my nose. I haven't a penny.'

'I've offered to put money in your bank account. And the joint account. There's money in the teapot in the kitchen. I've offered to buy you new clothes, new shoes. You say no. Short of handing you my bank account what more can I do? The best interpretation I can put on it is that you're depressed. I think you should see a doctor, but you won't. What do you want from me?' She tried hard to keep a level, neutral voice.

'You put the oven on,' he yelled.

'I don't understand. We were alright yesterday - well, as alright as we've been for years. Then this solicitor phones you up, stirs you up and we have this.'

'I haven't any money.'

'You haven't any money because you haven't worked since God knows when.' Her voice was rising, she heard it from outside her head. 'You spend two years at University then you go to the job club and piss about reading business magazines. I'm supporting you completely, paying all the bills. What do you want exactly? When we run out of ready cash I'll go and do supply work - I'll get paid because I'll go and do a job I hate, so I can have money. You can do that too. You can phone an agency and ask for work, just like I can. You choose not to. What do you want from me?' She was screeching too.

'You can't shut your gob, can you? You can't fucking shut up. You're mad. You're demented. You're worse than my mother.' He was almost sobbing.

He seemed in two minds whether to hit her or walk out. Fortunately he chose to walk out.

Carol stood rooted to the spot, shaking. The walls seemed to be ringing still with the echoes of all the bitter words. Life was never meant to be like this.

All the stress in her life had been gradually clearing. The dogs had passed peacefully away taking with them their mess and their old-age illnesses. She missed them, very much, but life was undeniably easier without them. The kids had belatedly found their feet and their independence. It was in the nature of things that they should. Her job and the peculiar brand of lunacy surrounding the school was a rapidly fading memory. The knowledge that she need never step inside the school gates ever again gave her immense pleasure.

She was beginning to get the message that Jessica wanted her to know that she was alright but beyond that there was no place for her in her daughter's life. This had been a bitter pill to swallow. Thirty years of optimism had to be relinquished. True it was replaced with the peace which came from knowing that Jessica was safe, happy, had a satisfying life, lovely children and a happy marriage. But she was never going to be a part of that, and she had to accept it as a fact of life.

'Nothing is as it is but thinking makes it so.' Where had she heard that? She had to make something positive from it. At least she could build on certainties now, instead of being tormented with possibilities and speculation.

As other problems began to vanish the remaining life-long intractable mess of her marriage became more and more clearly a disaster area. If she was prepared to accept it, this would continue until she was an old lady - if she ever reached old age.

Carol looked round at her lovely home - picturesque, well-cared-for, containing a life-time of possessions all with their special meanings and memories. It was a long way from her bed at Mrs. Thomas's, with all the other pregnant girls. Here were her books, her garden, her colour schemes, pictures, photographs, ornaments, cooking things - her life linked intimately with every detail of the house. It was an extension of her personality. But in the end it was only bricks and mortar. All these things could be recreated elsewhere eventually, if she needed to. At any event, possessions were meaningless without the peace of mind which could make them enjoyable. If she stayed here she would crumble.

She had lost Jessica, now Matthew and Vanessa were gone, standing on their own feet. Paul didn't want her - he needed her, to hide behind, to be a barrier between him and reality, but he hated her for it.

Paul's figure vanished round the wall at the top of the drive. How long would he be gone? Where had he gone? Was he coming back? She didn't know the answers.

With unaccustomed blinding certainty she realised that of course he would come back. And when he did she didn't want to be there, and didn't want to share his immense problems or let him share hers.

With a sense of frantic urgency she ran upstairs and threw open the store cupboard at the back of the spare room. With energy born of desperation she hauled out a suitcase and a holdall. In the bedroom she stuffed them full of clothes and make-up. She swept armfuls of clothes, still on their hangers, from the wardrobe, ran downstairs past the wall full of photographs, the framed impassive gaze of Granny Stone and Jessica's cool stare, and threw them directly into the back seat of the car. On her way back upstairs she grabbed the two photographs, wrapped them in clothes and placed them in the suitcase. What to take? The terracotta elephant! She wrapped it in underwear and stuffed it into Granny Stone's black jug, a prized possession which, she was sure, would come to grief when Paul took his revenge. Passport, cheque-book, bank statements, computer discs, specs, all went into a plastic carrier bag. Shoes - dozens of them - went into another. Frantically she searched her mind - what else? Nothing! Thirty one years of marriage and that was all she needed. The rest was excess to requirements.

There was no sign of anyone on the drive. Carol flung everything into the boot, slammed the front door, jumped into the car and jammed the key at the ignition. Heart thumping she fumbled for the key-hole. With a screech of tyres the car shot off backwards up the drive. A quick three-point turn and she roared away before Paul could arrive back and stop her.

Six minutes later she was beyond his reach. The car bounced down a steep country lane between high hedges and she forced herself to slow down and drive more carefully, concentrate on keeping the car on the road. Her hands were trembling on the wheel, her knees were weak, her foot shook on the pedal.

The September afternoon sun lay across the countryside. Birds flittered drowsily, poppies nodded in the hedgerow. The car was stuffy and she opened the window, letting in the cool air. She switched on the radio, to Heart FM, and heard The Eagles singing 'Tequila Sunrise'.

As she left behind her house, her life and her husband, Carol's heart became light. The further she went, the lighter it became. Heavy weights fell from her shoulders. The frown on her face lifted - she felt it go. Her stomach ceased to churn. She did not have to face any more bitter arguments, no more threats to punch her in the face, kill her, go to jail for her. She could decide what to do without the certainty of having her plans opposed, having every thought checked as soon as it was uttered. She could smoke, if she wanted to, which she didn't, have a drink, make decisions. Freedom and confidence began to creep cautiously back into her soul.

She turned the car northward. Where else would she go at a time like this but home - back to where she came from, back to her mother.

Chapter 9

The afternoon sun lengthened into evening as Carol drove into the village. The faint smell of coal smoke hung in the air. Where it came from was a mystery, so many years after the Clean Air Act. Like the local Communist Party, she thought, which lingered on in the village years after it ceased to exist in Russia. She steered the car onto the narrow driveway and squeezed out of the barely opened door, by the rose hedge.

The back door opened directly into the kitchen, redolent with the rich scent of freshly baked chocolate sponge. Her mother, plump and white-haired, stood by the sink, vigorously drying cake tins. At the sound she turned, and assumed an expression of surprise.

'Why, it's our Carol,' she said. 'What are you doing here?'

She knew - the question was rhetorical. Carol kissed the wrinkled cheek and felt the soft moustache on her face. It was like kissing a comfortable little hedgehog.

'I've come to stay a few days. Is that alright?'

'Course it is,' replied Mrs. Stone stoutly and unhesitatingly then, to show that she wasn't going to make a fuss, she wandered off to get some icing sugar from the pantry.

There was no comment when Carol carried in suitcases, carrier bags and armfuls of clothes on hangers. She installed herself in the double room which she'd shared with Patsy before she left to join the WRAF.

The family showed no surprise at her arrival - Ian and Celia, Patsy and Michael, June and James, the nieces and nephews, uncles and aunties, all knew she came to stay for a few days from time to time, when things were not going well with Paul.

Carol phoned Matt at his office in Battersea.

'I'm staying with your Gran for a while.'

'Oh. Okay.' A keyboard rattled somewhere near the phone.

'Yes - your dad and I….'

'Look, I don't want to know.' The keyboard had stopped.

'What do you mean?'

'I mean I've heard it all before. I don't want to hear it again.' The keyboard resumed.

A defence mechanism, Carol reasoned. It was only fair to leave him alone, let him find his feet without burdening him with her problems. She changed the subject and the conversation was soon over.

Rainy August drifted into a sunny September. The days were long, and peaceful once school began. This year the turmoil of the new academic year, in a classroom with crowds of kids, was not her concern. She was free. She fell into the week-long rhythms of the village. The barely-detectable pulse of every day, the stress-free shapeless afternoons, became part of her life again. The freedom from constant bickering with Paul, the awareness of the buoyant benign web of family relationships were soothing.

As her stay lengthened into weeks, the web began to renew. She went for walks with June and her two cocker spaniels, for bike rides with

Patsy. The three sisters went swimming in the village swimming pool on Ladies' Night. The middle of the pool was full of whale-sized permed ladies, immersed to the neck, bobbing gently up and down whilst they nattered, the modern manifestation of the corner shop gossip.

The hairdresser, she discovered, was at school with her sister, played golf with her brother. The conductress of her childhood, her hair still in bleached sausages under her cap, still worked on the bus. Mr. Potter still ran the shoe shop.

Mrs. Stone climbed eagerly into the car for visits to relatives, jaunts to the shops, afternoons out, pleased to have a chauffeur and company. They visited Auntie Doris in hospital. Mind gone, she wandered about like a ghost, puffing on her cigarette, childlike but happy. Uncle Albert was bone-thin but still active and alert, with a girl-friend in the next village who looked and sounded like his dead wife. They were going to Tenerife for Christmas. Auntie Mabs was ninety and greatly overweight, but still retained enough ego to be bothered to boast about her numerous offspring, the only product of her long life.

Carol ran errands. One was to the village butcher, Tommy, a classmate from junior school. His face lit up when Carol walked into his little shop. She asked how he was, and he told her – in detail.

'Well, I've not been too well.' As he spoke he unwrapped a block of ham and placed it on the slicer. The spatulate hairy fingers arranged the ham near the blade. 'I've just got back from holiday and I haven't been well.'

'What's the matter?'

'I had this stomach-ache.' His left hand held the ham in place, his right hand pressed the switch.

'I had diahorreah.' He raised his voice above the whir of the machine.

A slice of ham fell from the blade. He caught it expertly and laid it on a sheet of wrapping paper. His nails were very clean.

'It went on for days. I tell you, it were really bad.' Another slice of moist pink meat.

'To tell you the truth, I've had a bit of trouble down there. It were so bad I've got piles.' Carol raised her eyebrows to indicate concern, surprise, disguise the speechlessness. He described his visit to the doctor, the pain, and the treatment with a wealth of anatomical details.

'Well - I hope you're feeling better soon.' She felt unable to contribute anything else to the conversation. There were now sufficient slices and he turned off the machine and wrapped the meat. His fingers touched the cold slices. Carol wondered about the hand-washing facilities in the shop.

'He does lovely ham, does Tommy. He boils it hisself,' said Mrs. Stone when she unwrapped it later. Carol decided to have a boiled egg with her salad.

Paul did not phone. Matthew might have told him where she was, though on reflection they probably didn't bother to contact each other very much. Maybe Nessie had mentioned it.

The village had changed. A whole new community had grown out of the fields, across the inter-city railway line from the old village. New houses, privately owned. Her sisters and brother lived in the picturesque executive-type houses near the old church, in twisting green lanes which ran between spreading sweeps of lawn and conifers.

Many of the pit houses in the old village had been bought by the occupants and now had new windows and doors, well-tended gardens, satellite dishes, cars on the drive. The Co-op, once a large-well kept store full of chatter and the clatter of over-head change-machines on wires, the centre pin of village shopping, was boarded up, the windows covered in graffiti. The only detached house in the village now crouched beside a vast new supermarket, its rose garden tarmacked and covered in cars. The row of beautiful mature oaks which had marched some five miles from the extreme perimeter of one side of the village to the other were long gone, parts of the quiet lane which they had shaded now a dual carriageway. The cinema had vanished, replaced with an ugly row of shops and a Chinese take-away which sold the most disgusting food known to mankind. The Golden Dragon did a roaring trade - lumps of stringy batter-covered micro waved meat covered in a violently red jam-like goo, heaving with E-numbers.

The Friday market was a shadow of its former self - a few stalls flapping in the rain on the triangle of tarmac under the wall of the Working Men's Club. Some of the faces were familiar. Women Carol knew by sight as a child still went decently about their business, now in their seventies or eighties, shrunken, wrinkled but still respectable, straight-backed and wooden-faced. These and others were the unknown people whose awareness of her pregnancy was so carefully avoided. According to gossip, it seemed every one of them now had children, grandchildren, nieces or nephews who were single parents, divorced or living together, changing partners as often as they changed cars, having children with different people, so that family relationships were a snarl of half-brothers, full sisters, step-fathers and mothers, aunties, uncles and cousins.

'Carol? Carol Stone? Hey, din't you recognise me?'

Jean Taylor - a friend from Grammar School. Jean had married a local lad and stayed in the village all her life. She had been a mother at sixteen and never worked outside her home. Her face was pleasant and open, and expressed delight.

'What you doing back here? I thought you'd moved away for good. Are you back to see your mam? I saw her on Tuesday and she said you'd come back for a bit. Retired then have you? Come back to see how the peasants are getting on? We're still the same, nowt ever changes here. Same old market, same old people. No I don't go out much. Me Mam died you know. Yes - heart attack. Well a stroke first, then a heart attack. It were quite quick really. You what? Go out for lunch? Yes, great, sounds right posh. I'd like that - I never go anywhere. It's right nice to see you again. Yes, Tuesday then. Half past eleven. Ta rah.'

Conversations with Jean always felt as if they were one sided.

They had lunch together and it was just like old times, except that in the old times they never went out for lunch.

One afternoon Carol drove her mother to the remote graveyard beside the path which meandered to the river. The pit-tip, rounded and greened with high-tech grass, like a real hill, looked benignly down on the sunlit spaces. It was a place her father had known well as a boy. Across a field of honey-scented yellow rape the thick woods of her childhood were struggling to new maturity after being denuded during the miners' strike. A village which ran on coal which was part of your wages needed a substitute when you weren't getting paid.

The caretaker's house, by the gate of the cemetery, had been sold into private ownership by the Council, and the new owner now kept two rusting cars up on blocks beside the path.

'Just look at that - it's disgusting,' said her mother.

The granite block which marked her father's cremated remains was one of a long line beside the path. His school-mate and life-long friend was buried nearby, a neighbour next door but one, Auntie Win two rows away. After a lifetime of bitter arguments and apparent extreme unhappiness Mrs. Stone tended the grave with astonishing regularity. Once a fortnight in all weathers she undertook the two mile walk. She's probably checking to make sure he hasn't escaped, Carol thought. Mrs. Stone removed the dead flowers, took a duster and spray polish from her plastic bag, and knelt to begin work.

Carol stood watching.

She closed her eyes against the dazzle of the sun and a breeze carried skylark song and the overpoweringly sweet smell from the adjacent field. Under that stone lay what was left of a father she had not spoken to for thirteen months before his death. Her mind could summon up clearly the anger in his eyes when Rob told him she was pregnant, and the memory still churned her stomach in fear and anxiety.

She remembered their last meeting. She had taken one of her precious half term days to drive up because he wasn't well. They talked, then argued. What about? Politics, probably. Her mother helped create the situation, stood between them, protested every comment either of them made, her anxiety winding them both up, instead of leaving them to talk. She left, turned in the doorway for a last comment. Despite his illness he leapt from his chair with the agility of a young man, caught her unawares. His heavy walking stick crashed down onto her breast, the pain spread in a hot tide. Stunned, she sank to her knees and it crashed again into her cheekbone.

From somewhere she summoned up a final act of defiance. 'You....' she couldn't find a word, 'you will never, ever see me again,' she gasped, keeping the sobs at bay, refusing to cry.

She had not set foot in the house again until she reluctantly attended his funeral.

Should she feel some emotion now? She waited, examined her feelings. Nothing. No regret for the life-time of lost opportunities. No sadness at his absence - his presence had never meant much to her anyway, except looming fear. No memories of warm hugs, shared laughter, help with problems, affection. And he was the force behind the decision that her baby must be adopted. Wasn't he?

She vividly remembered seeing him at the funeral parlour, in his coffin. The giant figure of her childhood had looked small and slightly disreputable, a faint shadow on his chin, sparse hair combed neatly back. This was not the dominating John Wayne figure in blue overalls and flat cap, shaking his pigeon-corn tin, building his rambling wooden structures which covered the back garden, or sitting in pit-clothes, eating his dinner before going reluctantly off on afternoon shift, hardly noticing her. She was certainly not important to him. Now he was not important to her.

She began to see that he was not the hugely powerful figure of her mind. He was in fact a rather weak and helpless man who dealt with problems by roaring at them. She had been a problem who roared back. She was employing the same technique with Paul. With the same effect. What difference would it have made if she'd listened instead? Or thought what it must be like to walk round in his shoes.

Mrs. Stone gave the gravestone a final rub with the yellow duster.

'There you are Sid, all clean and tidy again.' She fluffed out the bronze chrysanths once more, stuffed the spray polish and dusters into a plastic bag and struggled to her feet.

Her mother leaned on Carol's arm as they walked back to the car. Should she ask the question which had been itching away in her subconscious? She probably wouldn't get an answer, but she could ask.

'You remember before Jessica was born?' The question was swallowed by the silence of the graveyard, and Carol began to think her mother hadn't heard.

'Yes.'

'Where did the idea of adoption come from?'

'Eeh, lass, I don't know. I can't remember, it's so long ago,' she replied, her voice heavy with weariness.

'You know I've told Ian, and Patsy, and June.' It was a statement, not a question.

'Aye, I do.' She removed her arm from Carol's and walked on unsupported. 'I don't know what you told them.'

'Not a lot.'

'Well, so long as they don't talk to me about it.' It may not be a secret any longer, but it was still not to be discussed, apparently.

Back home, Carol put the kettle on and started the washing up. The window above the sink looked out into the back garden, once a maze of pigeon-sheds, pens, storage sheds, and aviaries and now, finally, restored to the lawn and borders which Mrs. Stone had always craved. One large shed remained, isolated and stranded by the fence half-way down one side. Once part of a grand design, it now resembled a wrecked boat tossed up on the sea of vivid grass, its paint flaking and peeling, the concrete steps crumbling between borders of yellow and pink chrysanths. Inside in the gloom dozens of tools, tins of nails and screws rusted under layers of dust and cobwebs, untouched from season to season, the air full of the metallic taste of rusting iron.

'Tea's made, mum.'

She ambled into the kitchen and stood looking at the two beakers, one large and one small, which stood by the kettle.

'I could have made it. I can do that washing up an all. I don't know why you have to do it. Is the big one mine?'

'No.' Carol hated washing-up but this time she'd insisted. She'd had a dishwasher for the past twenty years. She could feel the nail polish peeling away.

'Which one is mine then?' She wasn't joking.

'The small one.'

Mrs. Stone turned and looked at her daughter, like a small child being chastised. Carol felt uncomfortably thrust into the role of adult.

'The small one?' she asked in a little-girl voice.

'Yes.' Incomprehension. 'You asked if the big one was yours and I said no, and there are only two there so it must be the small one.'

'Oh you and your complications - why don't you just give me a straightforward answer.' She took the beaker, trudged off to the sofa and picked up the newspaper. Carol was left feeling she had bullied her - she was unsure how this had come about but she'd seen her dad squirming in this position many times and, as onlooker, assumed he was the bully.

Carol got to know her mother again but now the roles were subtly reversed. Her mother had for her whole lifetime been engaged in a vigorous game of 'Victim', until deprived of her partner. Now, unexpectedly, she'd found a new partner, albeit unwilling and untrained, and began working the game up again.

Carol found her needs were served before she had formulated them. If she wanted tea, a newspaper, a blouse ironed, shoes cleaned, it was done before she'd even acknowledged the need to herself. She began to feel oppressed by this mind-reading subservience, as if her mother wanted to live her life for her. Carol became the reasonable adult, her mother the intractable, questioning, cute child. Carol stood between her and the world, like a protective parent. Casual answers were referred back to as if handed out as a dictat by some powerful force.

'You don't want tea with your dinner.'

'It's a glass of water isn't it?'

'You want East Enders on, don't you?'

The questions came thick and fast.

'Which vase shall I put these flowers in?'

'Which coat shall I wear?'

'Will these shoes be alright?'

'What shall we have for dinner?'

'What's that man doing on telly?'

'Will it rain tomorrow?'

Aunt Lily came down from Selby to stay for a week. She was as thin and dark as Mrs. Stone, Iris, her younger sister, was plump and fair. One hot afternoon they sat in the living room in the net curtained, furniture polish scented shade, over tea and cake. Inevitably they reminisced.

As they talked Carol could see clearly Granny Vincent's kitchen, the black iron range with its little doors and knobs and trivets, the kitchen table with velvet cloth and starched white tablecloth, the big polished sideboard with backing mirror.

'I remember Granny Vincent – she was thin as a stick with immaculate white blouses and pinched lips. She hardly ever spoke to me,' Carol contributed.

'She had a very sad childhood,' said Auntie Lily. Even her lightest comments managed to convey judgement and disapproval. 'As a baby, coming back from her christening, a storm broke and they all got soaked. Her and her mother took a chill, and it turned to pneumonia. Her mother died and she survived, the youngest of three. They were brought up by her father's parents, who didn't want them. She was always sickly after that. She went into service at fourteen.'

'That must be why she always had everything neat and tidy, proper household linen, china and glass – not like Granny Stone – chaos.' said Carol. She liked Granny Stone's chaos, and Granny Stone.

Mum cut in, keen to add her bit. 'Aye – we had to do her work when she were ill. I remember kneeling on the hearth, on a clean tablecloth, kneading the bread dough in a big pansion – that one I still use. We had good food, and we never went without. Chapman's next door, their kids couldn't go out when it snowed. They had no shoes.'

'Was she a cuddly, affectionate person?'

'She was sharp tempered – there were no cuddles, no bed-time stories. The four of us were put in bed, and the candle taken away for safety. In the dark I told the others stories about three girls, Thin, Fat and Greedy. You three, laughed yourselves silly,' said mum, and she won a smile from her vinegary sister.

'How old were you when they had the miners' strike?'

Carol never had the chance to talk to the two of them together, and probably never would again.

'I were nine,' said mum. 'It was a hot summer. We were given meals at school, soup and bread, or bread and corned beef. The men went to the pit tip to rake for cinders because families needed a fire to cook. Police came to the pit yard.'

Just like 1984, thought Carol, when the village was full of police and virtual civil war broke out – though no-one outside the coal-fields seemed aware of it.

Auntie Lily chimed in, 'The men were given vouchers from the pit to spend on food. Grandad Vincent would walk eight miles to town each week, because you could get more food for your ticket there. After the strike the miners went back to work on lower wages and had to repay the value of the food tickets, and their rent arrears, from the 9/11d a shift at the rate of a shilling a week.'

That was ten per cent of their wages.

Carol thought of the laughing, warmly dressed, well-fed middle-class youths in old newsreels who turned up to break the strike and play at driving trains and buses before going home to meals cooked by servants, and wanted to punch their lights out. The Government had been afraid of Communism and revolution – it was after all only nine years after 1917, the Russian Revolution and the Winter Palace, but if the threat existed, no awareness of it filtered through to the children.

'The miners met in the Drill Hall, and us kids were shooed away. Life went on. We had hopscotch, rallyco, Sundays at chapel, and practice for the Whitsun concert,' said Auntie Lily.

'What was the depression like?'

'Our dad kept a pig on an allotment, to give us food in winter,' said Lily. 'We saved all the household scraps to feed it, nothing went to waste. Then there was an outbreak of swine fever.' It sounded like a script from Monty Python – except it was real.

'I were there when the inspector came,' mum cut in. 'I'll never forget me dad's face when he declared his pig condemned. He were condemning us to a winter with hardly any food. He told me dad how it was to be killed and buried,' her voice broke. 'Even after sixty years I can still see the tears rolling down his cheeks.'

'Then we had a meningitis outbreak....' began Auntie Lily.

'Spotted fever,' interrupted mum.

'Yes that's what we called it then, but it was meningitis,' corrected Auntie Lily, the patient older sister. She was getting into her stride now. 'There was no treatment. Mrs. Kilgallon, next door, lost three of her eight children in one weekend – a teenage daughter, a small son, and a baby.'

It was unbelievable.

'What was school like?'

'We learned to read at school, but were never interested in what we were learning,' said Auntie Lily. 'We didn't fill the scholarship forms in. Me mam said, 'I can't keep you. You're going into service when you're fourteen. And it's no good your running away and coming back. You'll go straight back again. And don't come here with any bundles in your arms, or you'll go in the workhouse.'

The bundle....that must mean a baby. If you come home with a baby you will go into the workhouse.

Auntie Lily paused. Carol glanced at her mother, who avoided her gaze. Clearly her mother's shame extended to exclude her own sister from the secret of Jessica's birth.

Both sisters went into service, because Granny Vincent did not want them to become coarsened by factory life. Iris was sent to Southport, 144 miles away from home, at fourteen, because Lily was already there, with another family. The two boys remained at home to work locally and be spoiled by their mother.

'One day I was in school, the next at the other side of the country, all on me own.'

'No I was there,' corrected Lily.

'Yes, but I worked from early morning until late at night, skivying, and we only had a half day a week to meet up. Me mam didn't even tell me about periods, nobody did.' She was still angry.

'I thought you knew,' said Lily.

'When I found blood on Christmas morning, I thought I was dying. The woman I worked for, she gave me a towel and belt. I'd never seen one before, so she showed me how to use them.'

Both girls sent five shillings a week home, keeping one shilling for themselves. 3d of this went on a postal order and stamp, leaving 9d to squander on idle luxuries. Granny Smith furnished her front room very nicely on the girls' money. The boys, of course, worked in the pit and lived at home.

At eighteen, Iris was in service in Leeds. She wrote home to say she wasn't sending any more money. Her father, sent by Granny Vincent, arrived on the next train to find out why. Perhaps Granny Vincent was afraid that her daughter was going to be returning home with a bundle, thought Carol.

'I told him, 'I want some nice clothes.'' She won, and had the nice clothes.

'I remember, you looked lovely in that coat –mustard it was – with your fair hair.'

'I felt like Lady Muck on my day off,' she said proudly, her emotions, as always, reflected in her expression.

Her employer, a lady doctor, knew Iris was interested in nursing, and offered to get her a place to train as a nurse at a big teaching hospital in London.

'However,' she was told, 'it might be prudent not to mention that your father is a miner. The other girls are from very middle-class homes and it will be easier for you if they don't know.' Lizzie, headstrong, unable to take the long view, proud of her father, refused to go.

'I told her, 'My dad's as good as anybody. If I'm not good enough for them, I'm not going.''

Instead the war came along, and young women made a choice between the land army, the armed forces, factory work, or nursing. Grandad Vincent did not want his daughters to be 'groundsheets for soldiers' so they both took the opportunity to be nurses, though in less exalted circumstances than those offered by mum's employer. Sid Stone, in the reserved occupation of mining, was one of her patients.

Aunt Lily was clearly the assertive, dominant older sister, mum the impulsive, attention-seeking cheeky younger sister, always fighting to assert her independence. She was sensitive, emotional, proud, and eternally the child. She hadn't changed.

* * *

'Gloria Smith is organising a school reunion at the Village Hall. We're all going, and you're coming as well,' announced Patsy. They were all drinking tea in mum's living room.

'But I didn't go to your school,' Carol protested. She was the only one to go to the Grammar School.

'Yes well, we'll make an exception for you.'

Carol said yes, then spent the next few days worrying whether Jessica's father would be there. She had met Rob at the Saturday dance at the Village Hall when they were both sixteen, and they'd gone as a couple nearly every Saturday for two years. True, he hadn't been seen in the area for many years, but what if he was there?

June was anxious. 'There'll be Glenda Handy – she's a millionairess now. Everybody thought she was so sweet but she only ever made friends with people who she thought could be useful, or who had something she wanted.' It was insecurity. Forty years on and the differences would be showing – how you'd spent your life.

Two weeks later Carol stood in her mother's tiny bathroom, and peered into the ancient cabinet mirror to put on make-up. Saturday night at the Village Hall! Forty years slipped away. She dressed carefully, not in wide skirts and petticoats but in a black Aquascutum jacket, a grey silk blouse, black trousers and suede ankle boots – rather severe, but the effect was slimming, and smart.

The Hall appeared smaller. The immaculate gardens in which it once stood were now beaten-up grass and pot-holed car park. The imposing entrance steps had been covered with an ugly concrete ramp and iron railings, at the insistence of Health and Safety. Underneath the superficial changes it was the same – the sprung dance-floor, the stage with velvet curtains. The chattering crowd outside the Ladies was the same as ever.

A woman emerged from the crowd, walked up to Carol, put a hand on each of her shoulders and looked into her eyes. Clearly she was expecting some reaction – but what? Wrinkled face, short curly hair. Her familiarity made Carol uncomfortable. The eyes were brown and amused.

'Hello, you don't know me, do you?'

Carol looked hard. It was like looking at a magic eye picture. Out of the pattern of features emerged the face of Gloria Smith. Click – one minute a stranger, the next a childhood friend.

It became a game. Everywhere people were looking closely at each other, trying not to stare, looking for the friend in the stranger.

Patsy, June and Carol sat at a table near the stage. Across the floor on the edge of the dance-floor, she spotted Nigel, her boyfriend when she was thirteen. He was sitting with his wife and another couple.

'Go and say hello to him,' urged Patsy.

'No. I can't.'

'Why not? Go on.'

Nigel had been her first real boy-friend. For six months they'd had a sweet, innocent relationship. He'd married his next girl-friend, Beth, a girl from Carol's junior school class.

If you've reached fifty three and can't even say hello to someone you knew forty years ago, then it's really pathetic, she reasoned.

'Okay, if you come with me.'

They crossed the big open space of the dance floor and stood at Nigel's table. He looked surprised, but pleased. Beth was at the bar.

'Hello,' she said. 'It's Nigel, isn't it?' Of course it was. He hadn't changed a bit.

'Yes.'

'Well, you probably don't remember me. Carol Stone.'

'Yes, I do remember you. I recognised you the minute you arrived,' he said, and he blushed. Not just a little blush, but a great big one. No-one had ever blushed for her before. They talked, falling easily into familiarity, until Beth came back.

Chuck Berry, Buddy Holly, Elvis, Johnny Tillotson. She danced with her sisters and was sure she'd fall over and look a complete fool but no, she remembered the steps and began to enjoy the music. Paul didn't dance much, couldn't jive. She couldn't stop smiling.

At the bar she saw David Pitch, from the Youth Club. He'd gone to Art School. She began to talk to him, which she could never have done as a teenager paralysed by shyness, and asked him what he'd done after art school. He didn't know who she was, couldn't remember her at all. His face was the same, but wrinkled, the hair the same style but grey.

'Well,' he said, 'what would anyone do after an art course?'

'Teacher? Artist?'

'Nah – I joined the fire service – retired last year,' he laughed.

'The last job for heroes,' she said and he looked uncomfortable. Perhaps he thought she was taking the mickey, but she wasn't, just speaking the truth without considering how pretentious it would sound here.

Then there was Beryl Morgan, a year older and so sophisticated – she didn't remember Carol at all. 'I spent forty years wondering what happened to her, and she didn't even remember my existence,' thought Carol.

A whisper went round the hall. Glenda Handy, the fabulous millionairess, had arrived. She swept into the hall and women fluttered over to her, wanting to be recognised. Carol saw a short woman with straw-blonde hair and huge smoke-lensed specs. A black skirt and cream silky tunic concealed a ruinously fat figure tottering on elegant black heels. The face was rough, thickly made-up, falling in folds.

Fingers like sausages covered in diamond rings held a gold-banded cigarette, the chest wheezed into a cough when she laughed. She looked as though she'd spent the last forty years eating too much, drinking too much, and smoking too much. The chain of pubs she reputedly owned 'down south' was three. You can have a chain of three, thought Carol, one in the middle and one each side.

As she danced with Patsy the years rolled away. The music, the people and the place created the illusion of being fifteen –before she met Rob, before the troubles began. They danced and laughed. Patsy won the raffle. They danced some more. Life was carefree. There were no problems, only opportunities, new experiences, new people. Everything was in the future – to come.

Gloria showed her a photo of them both, taken when Carol was twelve, and she hardly recognised herself. In the loo she met a girl whose dad and granddad had been in the Pigeon Club – she still had the same big blue eyes and fine blonde curls, but now she was fifty one and about fourteen stone. The magic eye worked again and Dot Wright sprang out of her disguise as a fifty three-year-old – who didn't remember Carol at all. Jean gave her a lengthy account of who had died and what of – mostly cancer – which made them feel lucky to still be there.

She didn't see friends from the street where she'd lived when she was eight, but they may have been disguised as one of the enormously fat bristle-haired ladies sitting at the tables, pulling pale crimplene cardies over vast bosoms, chins tucked in, sipping little drinks, peering at passersby. She could hardly go and interview them all.

Handsome Ian Lang was still youthful, but inexplicably short. Len Evans, who filled her life with embarrassment when he asked her to dance at the Saturday afternoon Royal Dance Club when she was eight was the same but moustached and half-cut. He talked about his job at the junior school.

'Aye, I'm in charge of the school,' he said, sticking his chest out.

'Are you the headmaster?' Carol asked.

'No. I'm the caretaker,' he replied. 'I run the place.'

A blonde woman at the next table waved. 'Remember me?' she called.

Carol peered. Who the hell was it? 'I'm not sure....'

'It's Pat, the mobile hairdresser. I met you this morning when I permed your mum's hair.'

'Did going to a posh school do you any good?' asked Sheila Marshall.

'Not really. I'm a teacher now,' Carol replied.

'Well then, there you are,' said Sheila, enigmatically.

Behind this evening lay buckets of hair-dye, yards of Lycra, vats of moisturising cream, tons of mascara and lipstick, a cocktail of perfume, and enough extra weight to make two sides of a rugby team. Also laughter and memories and surprises.

As always at 11.40 the band played two slow numbers. This was the time when a boy would ask you for the last waltz and ask if he could walk you home. Carol had danced the last waltz with Rob many times. She sat with June and Patsy and watched the couples – some of them had been together for the past forty years. Miranda Church floated by with her husband, hair still waist length, but grey, face still unmade up but wrinkled. Much as she had enjoyed the evening, Carol was glad she had not spent her lifetime here. Paul would have hated this, though if he chose he could have charmed any of these women.

Nigel came over to say cheerio. It was pretty decent of Beth to let him, though not too much of a risk because if the pattern repeated itself she wouldn't see him again until they were both ninety three. Beth's first-born had been killed in a tragic accident. How, she wondered, could anyone survive the death of a two-year-old. She was lucky – she knew Jessica was alive and safe and happy, living a fulfilling life with her own children.

* * *

'They're building some new flats near the old church,' said Patsy. She'd come to visit mum and Carol.

Carol looked up from her newspaper. In front of her on the side table, on a crisp little tablecloth, was a cup of tea, a big fat wodge of orange cream sponge and a buttered scone. She leaned forward to reach the tea, and found the extra ten pounds she'd put on put it beyond reach.

'Oh, yes?'

'Nice ones. Do you want to go and see them?'

'When?' she said round a mouthful of delectable cake.

'This afternoon. The showflat is open.'

'With what in mind?'

'Just for interest - you never know – might suit you. Just look at the way they're furnished and that.'

'Shall we take me mam?' Her Yorkshire accent was reasserting itself.

'No - leave her here –she's going to chapel this afternoon anyway. We'll go on our own.'

The show flat was splendid, furnished in golds, burnt orange and cream. Rather sophisiticated for Rossingley. The galley kitchen had steel grey cupboards and floor, black granite surface, white tiles, and under cupboard lighting. The fridge freezer and dishwasher were smart stainless steel. The whole subdued colour scheme focussed attention on a huge colourful bowl of oranges and apples, and a poster with rich tawny swirls of amber, honey, ochre, silver. Severe, but pleasant. Two bedrooms, two bathrooms, lots of storage space. No garden, balcony or terrace, but the kitchen window looked out over the meadows near the church.. A total contrast to the cosy cottage she'd left behind.

Carol thought of her garden, of the years of happily planning, working, weeding, pruning. Was Paul tidying away the summer's growth, cutting back the dead heads, mowing the lawn? Was he missing her?

She imagined him, watching telly, on his computer, listening to music, cooking, sleeping, all on his own, undisturbed by her absence.

'It's nice,' said Patsy. 'You could live here –you'd be near all of us, so you'd never be lonely. It's got a spare bedroom for when Matthew and Nessie visit. You've got a brother and brothers-in-law, lots of men, in case the telly goes wrong, or something needs mending. You can lock it up easily and go away to visit your friends. I'd like it – get away from cooking and cleaning for my lot.'

'Yes...I do like it.'

'You could decorate it how you like – you'd enjoy that. Choose everything you like, no need to consult anyone else.'

'Yes, I would enjoy that.'

'You can't live wi' me mam for ever.'

'No – no of course not.'

'You're like a different person since you've been here. More relaxed.

You even laugh at things. Not like when you arrived.'

'Really?' It was true.

'You never know, if you get a divorce, move here, you might meet someone else.'

She was right, of course – except that Carol didn't want to meet anyone else. This few weeks were in limbo – but they couldn't go on indefinitely. Matthew and Nessie were grown up, but they were still a family, the four of them. What if Paul met someone else? She couldn't bear the thought of him with another woman.

'I've got to go to the supermarket. Why don't you stay here and have another look round and think about it?'

Patsy left and the silence closed in around her. Carol hated silence. At home she would switch on the radio or television, anything to avoid being alone with her thoughts.

She watched through the double glazed window as Patsy climbed into her little BMW sports car, the sound barely audible as the door snapped shut and she drove away.

Across the meadows the medieval church where the whole family had celebrated marriages stood under a blue arching sky framed with dark conifers and gold flecked oaks. She could just make out a scattering of ancient mossy gravestones, a reminder of mortality. She opened the window and heard birdsong, and the breeze rustling in the trees.

She had phoned Paul two days before.

He didn't say he wanted her to come back, which would have been nice, or say he loved her, which would have been great, or that he missed her, which she'd hoped for. But he did say that it was her home, and if she wanted to come back, then that was fine.

At this point a lifetime of problems had reached a crisis and resolved themselves. Maybe the reunion had not been all she had imagined and hoped it would be. How could it? She had expected so much, built her life round the dream of happy families when she should have been dealing with the reality.

But there was a good side. She knew where Jessica was, that she was happy, with a family of her own, that her adoption was successful with loving parents. Her life had been safe and secure, better than it would have been if she'd been brought up as an illegitimate child in the village in the 60's. Her dad might have come to accept her baby – but he might not.

And there was the future. One day she might know her daughter better. Her dream of reunion might have reached a full stop, but it wasn't necessarily going to stay that way. Things changed, and nothing stayed the same forever.

Her dad – he was long gone. There was nothing to regret, except the absence of regret.

Matt and Van had left home; it was in the nature of things that they should. They were now independent, leading their own lives, safe and happy.

And her mother, whose life had been so hard. She knew without a doubt that her mother loved her, loved all of them, dearly. The adoption had been her way of trying to protect her beloved child from a fate which her own life experience had taught her would be disastrous. She knew no other way. It had been a mistake, but the intentions behind it were for the best.

Carol realised with a flash of insight that the course of her life revolved round one moment. When she had told her mother, in the darkness of the kitchen 'I'm pregnant' her mother could have said,

'Well, that's lovely. I've always wanted a grandchild. We'll have a wedding and celebrate.' But if you want to retain the moral high ground and retain your pride you can't have weaknesses yourself. So instead, she had turned it into a problem, a secret, and it had remained like that for three decades. And as Carol had come to realise this last few weeks – other people's opinions really did not matter. How could her mother imagine 'they' were thinking of her. Everyone had their own lives to live. They really did not care. And if you judged others kindly, you would expect them to do the same for you.

The sun disappeared behind a dark grey cloud, leaving a fluorescent bright edge defining the division between the blue sky and the thunderhead. The air cooled.

She was at a crossroads now. She had choices.

She could stay here, eat cake, put on weight, reacquire her Yorkshire accent, and be reabsorbed into the safe familiar world of her childhood. She would arrive back at the beginning, completing the circle.

She could go back to Paul, and hope that her absence, her need for a family, her new insight into the fact that it wasn't entirely his fault that their life together had been such a disaster could carry them forward into a new beginning. Their marriage was founded on a lie, when she hadn't told him about Jessica, and that had been unforgiveable. She couldn't have been easy to live with, carrying all the baggage which came with the adoption and secrecy. He wasn't perfect, but he was really a good person, and the father of her children – they had just been unable to deal with the problems they had created together.

Or she could take her life in her own hands, decide on what she wanted, seek out a challenge, a different life, in a distant place, with other people, and use her experience and new-found confidence to do all those things she could have done at eighteen, but didn't. Finding Jessica had started changes in her which were still reverberating through her life. The familiar cloud of sadness under which she had lived had lifted. She was not the same person. It was not too late to begin again.

'Yes,' she thought, her heart lifting and filling with warmth as the sun reappeared from behind the dark cloud, flooding the air with late September heat. 'I can begin again. It's my life. I can decide. I do not have to please anyone else. I can do whatever I want. And I bloody well will.'

Printed in the United Kingdom by
Lightning Source UK Ltd., Milton Keynes
141109UK00001B/202/P